‘You will feel b
have got out of
and had so
Matthison said.

‘You have no idea what will make me feel better!’

How could he stand there so calmly, talking about eating, when her life lay in ruins?

Because he did not care. He had brought her to this. He had betrayed her! Held her in his arms and kissed her, when all the time…

She lurched to her feet on a wave of anguish and fury. Her fists were already raised before she knew how badly she wanted to hit him. But she did not manage to land a single blow. He caught hold of her wrists, his reactions lightning-swift.

She flailed out at his imprisoning hands, kicking ineffectually at his booted legs. His eyes widened in horror, then narrowed with grim purpose as he lifted her off her feet.

Annie Burrows has been making up stories for her own amusement since she first went to school. As soon as she got the hang of using a pencil she began to write them down. Her love of books meant she had to do a degree in English literature. And her love of writing meant she could never take on a job where she didn't have time to jot down notes when inspiration for a new plot struck her. She still wants the heroines of her stories to wear beautiful floaty dresses and triumph over all that life can throw at them. But when she got married she discovered that finding a hero is an essential ingredient to arriving at 'happy ever after'.

Recent novels by Annie Burrows:

HIS CINDERELLA BRIDE
MY LADY INNOCENT
THE EARL'S UNTOUCHED BRIDE
CAPTAIN FAWLEY'S INNOCENT BRIDE
THE RAKE'S SECRET SON
(part of *Regency Candlelit Christmas* anthology)

Also available in eBook format in
Mills & Boon® Historical *Undone*:

NOTORIOUS LORD, COMPROMISED MISS

DEVILISH LORD, MYSTERIOUS MISS

Annie Burrows

All the characters in this book have no existence outside the imagination of the author, and have no relation whatsoever to anyone bearing the same name or names. They are not even distantly inspired by any individual known or unknown to the author, and all the incidents are pure invention.

First published in Great Britain 2009
Harlequin Mills & Boon Limited,
Eton House, 18-24 Paradise Road, Richmond, Surrey TW9 1SR

ISBN: 978 0 263 86807 4

Set in Times Roman 10½ on 12¾ pt
04-1109-75367

Harlequin Mills & Boon policy is to use papers that are natural, renewable and recyclable products and made from wood grown in sustainable forests. The logging and manufacturing process conform to the legal environmental regulations of the country of origin.

Printed and bound in Spain
by Litografia Rosés, S.A., Barcelona

Author Note

When I was a little girl I loved reading fairy stories. One of my favourites was *The Sleeping Beauty*. The prince had to hack his way through a thicket of thorns to get to the castle where Aurora lay, bound by the wicked witch's spells. He would have got cut and bruised, probably ending up with half a forest's worth of leaves stuck all over his clothes and in his hair. He must have been quite a sight to wake up to!

I always hoped that the first thing the Princess would do would be to bathe his wounds…

Lord Matthison is convinced he has to fight his way through a thicket of thorns to rescue his own lady love from the spell that seems to hold her in its grip. But is she the one who is bound by a spell, or is he the one who is really under a witch's curse?

For Peter and Ruth,
Steadfast Friends

Chapter One

Lord Matthison reached for the area railings to steady himself, blinking up at the façade of the house where Miss Winters lived.

With her ambitious mother.

And her ruthless father.

He had no idea how he'd fetched up on Curzon Street, at the house of the scheming jade who had stripped him of his last vestige of hope.

He was drunk, of course. He had been drinking steadily since just before midnight. Any man who'd had the week he'd just had would have done exactly the same—made for the nearest gin shop and called for a bottle. Though he had assiduously avoided taking the road that led to oblivion during the past seven years, when the cards had turned against him, and he'd gone down to the tune of five hundred guineas for the third night in a row, he'd had to accept it was over.

'Cora,' he moaned, as the pain of her loss struck him

with an intensity he had not felt since the first day she'd gone. Gin was so deceitful! It promised to relieve all woe, but all it had done was strip him of the ability to pretend he did not care. He'd assumed he would have found at least a measure of respite, before coming round in some gutter. Possibly even staggering back to his own lodgings. He'd never dreamed he would turn out to have such a hard head, he would still be on his feet by dawn. Or that those wayward feet would have brought him to the last place on earth he would willingly have gone.

'But I won't marry you!' he yelled, shaking his fist at the shuttered windows.

A milkmaid who was passing eyed him with suspicion, and gave him a wide berth. He scarcely noticed her as he straightened up with renewed resolve. What did he care if Miss Winters was ruined!

He had not lured her into her father's study, tousled her hair, and torn the bodice of her gown. No, she'd done all that herself. Then launched herself at him just as the door swung open, making it look as though they had been locked in a passionate embrace.

Not that she wanted to marry him so much now, he laughed mirthlessly. He'd soon wiped that triumphant smile from her face!

'So, you want to dance with the devil, do you?' he had mocked, seizing her by the upper arms when she would have broken free.

'You are hurting me,' she had protested, beginning to look a little uncertain.

'But that is the kind of man I am,' he had answered. 'Have you not heard the rumours? Damsels of a sensitive nature practically swoon with fright whenever I walk into a room. With good reason, wouldn't you say?'

The confusion in her eyes had made him wonder if she really did not know. It was just possible. Her family did not mix in the best circles. Her mother had no intimates privy to the type of gossip circulating about him. They might have managed to secure a house at a fashionable address, but Miss Winters was never going to receive vouchers for Almack's.

'Or were you fooled by the fact that I still get invited everywhere?' he had mused. 'That was naïve of you. But as you do not seem to understand the ways of the *ton*, I will explain. Some of them ignore my reputation, because of the vast amount of wealth I have accrued since I made my pact with the devil. They claim not to care how I came by it, because my birth is sufficiently exalted for them to turn a blind eye. But they would never let me near any of their daughters.

'And there are others who are fascinated by the aura of evil I carry with me. They get quite a thrill from telling people they've been daring enough to ask the man who murdered his fiancée to attend one of their insipid gatherings. Oh,' he'd said, when a look of horror had spread across her face. 'So you had not heard? That I had made a pact with the devil, or that I had been engaged, long ago? To the innocent and unsuspecting Miss Montague…'

Suddenly it had felt like a kind of blasphemy, to

speak *her* name aloud while he was holding another woman in his arms. He had flung the trembling Miss Winters from him, but kept between her and the door. He had not finished with her yet!

'They never found her body,' he relished informing her, 'so they could never bring me to trial. But, since it was my best friend, the man who had known me since childhood, who brought the accusation against me, I must have done it, must I not?'

Miss Winters had begun to rub at the spot on her arms where he'd been holding her, but he'd felt not one ounce of remorse. He deliberately discarded the ice-cold persona he had adopted to disguise his state of mind, expressing all the bitterness that he normally held in check, through his next words.

'Since the day she disappeared, I have had phenomenal luck at the tables. Is that not proof that I have stained my soul with the blood of a virgin? I often wonder,' he'd grated, 'why people still sit down to play cards with me, when they know I can't lose. Just as I wonder—' he had paced slowly towards her, his fury unchecked '—why you expected this little charade to have any effect upon me. You do not suppose a man whose soul is as black as mine, is going to send off a notice to the *Morning Post* just because someone saw me in a compromising position with a virgin, do you?'

He had thought that would have been an end to it. Last thing he'd seen of her, she'd fled from the room, sobbing, and flung herself into her mother's arms. His mouth twisted into a cynical sneer as he recalled what a short distance she'd had to go. Her mother had been hovering right outside the door.

Anyway, he shrugged, she had definitely changed her mind about wanting to marry him.

Her father, though, was made of sterner stuff.

'Now look here!' he'd blustered, storming into Lord Matthison's rooms late the next afternoon. 'You cannot go about compromising young girls, and then scaring them off with half-baked tales that sound as though they've come out of a Gothic novel!'

'Is that so?' he'd drawled, not even bothering to raise his eyes from the deck of cards he was shuffling from his left hand into his right.

'It most certainly is! As a gentleman, you owe it to my daughter to offer marriage!'

'Out of the question,' he'd replied, taking the pack in his right hand, splitting it in half, and dextrously folding it over on itself with supple, practised fingers. 'I am already betrothed.'

That assertion had not silenced Mr Winters for more than a couple of seconds. 'Ah. You are referring to the Montague girl!'

Lord Matthison had felt the shock of hearing the man speak her name in such an offhand way clear through to his bones. And when Mr Winters had gone on to say, 'She's dead, ain't she?' the cards had spluttered from his hand to land in a confused jumble on the table top.

He'd got up, stalked across the room and leaned his forearm against the window frame, staring sightlessly down into the bustling courtyard while he grappled with the urge to do his visitor some serious bodily harm.

'Yes,' he had finally managed to say, with lethal calm. For nobody knew better than he that Cora walked the spirit world. 'Technically, I suppose you could claim I am free to marry again. But since nobody has ever managed to discover her body, her family prefer to think of her as missing. And I, therefore, am still legally bound to her.' With bonds that went beyond the realm of mere legalities, far tighter than any mortal man could ever suspect.

A nasty smile had spread across Mr Winters's avaricious face. 'Then we will just have to, legally, unbind you, will we not? So you can have no more excuse to avoid making an honest woman of my daughter.'

Before he could express his opinion that nobody had the power to make his daughter honest, since duplicity was such an intrinsic part of her nature, Mr Winters had declared, 'I do not care what it costs, or how long it takes. I *will* have Miss Montague declared legally dead. And then, my lord, we shall have you!'

Three days ago, that had been. Three days since Mr. Winters had declared his intent to instigate the proceedings that would kill Cora Montague all over again.

But he did not know Robbie Montague. Good ol' Robbie, he grimaced, folding his arms across his chest and leaning back against the area railings.

Robbie would have no truck with Mr Winters's suggestion that it was time to let go of his sister by holding a memorial service and finally putting up a gravestone.

Robbie would never set him free to marry again, and fill Kingsmede with children that were not his sister's. If he could not see him hang, Robbie's only satisfaction would be to make sure he remained suspended in a legal limbo.

Mr Winters, he smirked, had quite a fight on his hands.

The amount of hawkers pushing their handcarts up to the big houses, and the shortening of the shadows on his side of the street told him that it was well past daybreak now. Of the fourth day. His smirk turned to a grimace of despair. For the three consecutive nights since Mr. Winters had declared war on Cora's memory, he'd lost heavily at the card tables.

Last night, he had finally accepted what that meant.

He had thrown down his losing hand, tossed what he owed onto the green baize tablecloth, and stumbled from the gaming hell into the street. To confront his own personal hell. He'd had to clutch at the door frame for a few seconds, his heart had been beating so fast, while he'd fought down a rising tide of horror.

Not that he cared one whit for the money he'd lost. It was no longer financial necessity that kept him going back to the tables, night after night, but need of an entirely different nature.

'Cora,' he'd moaned uselessly into the empty alley way. 'I couldn't help it!' But there had not even been an answering echo.

She was not there.

For the first time in seven years, he could not feel her presence, anywhere.

He'd damned Mrs Winters for conspiring with her daughter to compromise him. He'd damned Miss Winters for forcing her lips against his in that unholy parody of a kiss. And he'd damned Mr. Winters for daring to speak of Cora as though she was of no account. Between the three of them, they had managed to do what even death could not.

They had driven her away.

He had never told anybody that she haunted him. They would have thought he had gone crazy. Hell, he often wondered about his sanity himself!

But it had only been a few days after the last time he had touched her warm soft skin, that he had felt her spirit hovering close by.

At a race track, of all places.

He had gone there with Robbie's accusations and curses ringing in his ears. He had been stunned when Robbie had accused him of murdering his sister. 'If you can believe that of me, then you will want this back!' he had yelled, throwing what was left of the money Robbie had lent him to pay for the wedding at his chest. 'I thought you were my friend!'

The purse had fallen unheeded to the floor. 'You have enough friends in these parts, it seems,' Robbie had sneered. 'Nobody will say one word against ye. And without a body, that magistrate says he dare not put the only son of the local lord on trial.'

They had flung increasingly harsh words at each other, which had culminated in Robbie yelling, 'Curse you and your title! May you rot in hell with it!'

Hell, he'd mused. Yes, he had felt as though he was in hell. And like so many of the damned, he had set out on a path of deliberate self-destruction, staking all that was left of Cora's wedding fund on a horse that was certain to lose.

He'd eyed up the runners, and been drawn to one that was being soundly whipped by its infuriated jockey. It was frothing at the mouth, its eyes rolling as it went round and round in circles. The jockey had lashed at it some more. He still couldn't get it to the starting line.

That horse doesn't want to be here any more than you do, he could imagine his tender-hearted Cora saying. *Poor creature.*

And that was when he knew he had to lay her blood money on the horse she would have felt sorry for.

When had it romped home a length ahead of its nearest rival, he heard her delighted laughter. He would swear to it. And pictured her clapping her hands in glee.

In a daze, he'd gone back to the betting post, feeling like Judas at the thought of the cascade of silver that would soon be poured into his hands. In the next race, he'd backed the most broken-down nag he could see in a last-ditch attempt to purge away his overriding sense of guilt. He *had* to get rid of that money. Robbie had cursed it!

As the pack set off, he thought he felt Cora sigh as the sorry specimen he'd backed lumbered wearily along the track. Dammit if he hadn't wagered on the very horse she would have chosen again! This time, he had felt there was a certain inevitability about the outcome of the race. Two furlongs from the finish, a riderless horse ran across the field, causing the leaders to stumble, and creating a few moments of mayhem, during which Cora's favourite wheezed up on the outside, crossing the finishing line while the rest were still disentangling themselves from the pile-up.

Cora had cheered. He'd heard her. No question.

The noisy crowds of race-goers faded from his consciousness as his mind had gone back to the day he had finally managed to place his ring on her finger.

'Nothing will be able to part us now,' he had said with grim satisfaction. And then, anticipating their wedding vows, he'd added, *'Except death.'*

'Not even that,' she had breathed, gazing up at him with naked adoration in her eyes.

And that was the moment he'd realised that no matter what Robbie might think, Cora was still his. He had felt her lay her hand on his sleeve, and hold him back when he would have tossed even those winnings away on the favourite in the next race. *'Enough now,'* she had cautioned him. And tears had sprung to his eyes, because he had known, beyond the shadow of a doubt, that she loved him far too much to want to watch him blight his future with reckless gambling. And he had walked away.

From that day forward, he had done nothing without considering what she would have made of it. And the more he asked her opinion, the more often he had felt her hovering close by.

Robbie had stormed off back to Scotland, his parents

had washed their hands of him, neighbours regarded him with suspicion, and former acquaintances shunned him.

But Cora had stood by him.

There had been times when he had sunk into such despair that he considered following her into the after-life.

But he could see her shaking her head in reproof, and hear her declaring that suicide was a mortal sin. He did not care if it was a sin, if it could bring them together. But something told him that whatever part of the after-world she inhabited would exclude sinners of that sort.

And so, since he knew she did not want him to take that course, he'd just had to go on existing. He could not call it living. Cut off from his family and friends, he had begun to haunt the lowest gaming hells in London. They were the only places whose doors were still open to him.

But even there, she watched over him, giggling at the stunned faces of the men from whom he'd won cash, deeds to mines, and shares in canal companies.

And it was she who urged him, when he had just donned the first set of good quality, brand-new clothes he had ever owned, to walk into White's and face them all down. She had crowed with laughter when he had walked out, £20,000 the richer.

It had brought him a measure of satisfaction to pay off the mortgage on Kingsmede, when his father had died. And to pay off his inherited debts out of winnings he'd gleaned from the very men who had fleeced his shiftless parent. Since then, he had gradually been able to make all the improvements to his estate Cora had talked about when she had been there. His tenants might whisper about him, and the way he came by his money, but it did not stop them from being glad he was re-thatching their cottages, or draining low-lying fields to improve their harvests.

Not that he cared what they thought of him. He was not doing it for them, but to please her. Her opinion was the only one that mattered to him.

She was the only person he felt any connection with any more.

Even though she was dead.

If that made him crazy, then so be it.

If it was madness that drove him back to the card tables, so that he could hear her muttering about the drunkenness of his opponents as he ruthlessly stripped them of their money, or feel her breath fan his cheek as she blew on his dice for luck, then it beat the alternative! He had not cared that her unseen presence, walking at his side, acted like a barrier between him and the rest of the world.

She was still there.

Until Miss Winters had kissed him.

'Cora,' he moaned again, sagging against the railings in defeat.

A seller of kindling, pushing his cart before him, shot him a piercing look, before shaking his head and hurrying on.

He knew what he must look like. He was standing here, in the first light of day, crying out for a woman who had been dead for seven dark, hellishly lonely years. And he didn't care what anyone might think. If he only had the supernatural powers that people attributed to him, by Lucifer and all that was unholy, he would use them now! If he really knew of some incantation…

A line from somewhere sprang to mind. Something about three times three times three…

And even as he muttered what he could remember of what he dimly suspected was something from Shakespeare, a movement from the area steps of a house further down the street caught his eye. A short young woman, modishly yet soberly dressed, in a dark blue coat and poke bonnet, was climbing up on to the pavement. At first, he did not know why, out of all the people bustling about their business, this one insignificant female had attracted his attention. But then she turned to scan the traffic before venturing out into the road, and he caught a glimpse of her face.

And it felt as though something had sucked all the air from his lungs.

It was Cora.

'Bloody hell!' he swore, clutching the railings even harder as his knees threatened to give way beneath him. Somehow, with all that three-times-three business, and invoking unholy powers, he had managed to conjure up her shade! For the last seven years, he had heard her, caught her scent on the breeze, felt her presence, but never, ever had she allowed him so much as one brief glimpse of her…

'Bloody hell!' he swore again. While he had been standing there, completely stunned at having called up her spirit, or whatever the hell it was had just happened, she had disappeared round the corner. She had walked away from him as though he was of no account. As though she had somewhere far more important to be.

Uttering another curse, he set off in pursuit. It should have been easy to catch up with her. She did not have that much of a head start. But as he attempted to break into a run, the pavement undulated beneath his feet as though it had a life of its own, throwing him into the path of a furniture mender carrying a bunch of rushes. Lord Matthison had to grab on to the man's shoulders to steady himself before he could lurch off in the direction Cora had gone.

For a few terrible minutes, he thought he would never see her again. The streets were full of tradesmen making early deliveries to the houses of the wealthy now, and it was as if the crowds had swallowed her up. Panic brought him out in a cold sweat, until he caught a glimpse of that dark blue coat on the far side of Berkeley Square, and he plunged into the gardens after her.

She was half-way up Bruton Street before he sighted her again, gliding effortlessly through the throng. He bit back a curse as a rabbit, dangling from the pole of its vendor, struck him full in the face.

'Cora!' he yelled in desperation as the rabbit seller laid hands on him, angrily demanding something…recompense for the damage to his wares probably, but he paid no heed. 'Wait!' he cried, thrusting the man rudely aside. He could not let anything prevent him from discovering where Cora was going!

He saw her half-turn. Felt the moment she recognised him with the force of a punch to the gut. For there was no tenderness, no understanding in her eyes. On the contrary, she recoiled from him, and with a look of horror hitched up her skirts and began to run.

He tried to run too, but she just kept on getting further and further away from him. She could melt through the throng, because she was a wraith. But his own body was all too solid, so that he was obliged to swerve around, or shove people aside. But he kept his eyes fixed on her. Until the very moment she darted into one of the shops on Conduit Street, and slammed the door behind her.

He stumbled to a halt on the pavement opposite what turned out to be a modiste's. A very high-class modiste with the name 'Madame Pichot' picked out in gold leaf on a signboard above the door.

His heart was hammering in his chest, which was still heaving with shortened breath. What was he to do now? Barge into the shop, which probably wasn't even open to customers yet, and demand they let him speak to the ghost he'd just seen take refuge inside? They would call for the watch, and have him locked up. In an asylum for the insane, most like.

He bent over, his hands resting on his knees as he fought to get his breath back. And make some sense of what had just happened.

Why, for God's sake, had Cora fled from him, the

very moment she had finally deigned to let him see her? And what was the significance of bringing him here?

He straightened up, staring at the shop front as though it might provide him with some answer to this unholy muddle.

'Evening gowns a speciality', read a card prominently displayed in the window, underneath a sample of the fabulously intricate beadwork that had become all the rage amongst the fashionable this year.

And a cold thread of foreboding slithered down his spine.

The very night after Mr Winters had declared his intention to lay Cora's ghost to rest for good, the first night he'd had a run of such spectacularly bad hands even he could do nothing with them, he had partnered a woman wearing a dress that came from this modiste. He had laid the blame for their defeat at whist at the feet of the woman wearing the expensive gown, a French chit, who had as little grasp of the game as she had of the English language. But in his heart he had known she had nothing to do with his wins or losses.

All gamblers were superstitious, but he supposed he must be the most superstitious of the lot. Knowing Cora's influence to be the source of his success, he had taken great pains, from the first day he had sensed her presence, to avoid offending her. He never touched strong liquor, nor did he succumb to the lures cast out by women who were fascinated by his aura of dark menace. How could he have contemplated bedding anyone, even if any woman had ever stirred him on any level, knowing that Cora hovered not far away, watching his every move? Not that she would have watched for long. Her puritanical soul would have been so shocked, she would have fled, perhaps never to return.

He had been right to take care. Cora's love was so strong it had reached out to him from beyond the grave. But a love strong enough to cheat death was not a force to be trifled with.

Miss Winters had kissed him, her father had begun to search for lawyers cunning enough to lay her spirit in the grave for good, and Cora had turned her back on him. And getting blind drunk, and shouting curses up at Miss Winters's windows, had not done him any favours. That slamming door was a clear enough message that even he could read it.

She had put back the barrier that existed between the living and the dead. And she was on the other side.

He ran a shaky hand over his face, feeling sick to his stomach.

He had only survived the last seven years because she had been right there with him. More real to him than all the gibbering idiots who populated the hells he frequented.

Would she come back to him, he wondered frantically, if he proclaimed the truth about her? He would not care if they declared him insane, and locked him up. He could afford to pay for a nice, cosy cell. It would almost be a relief to stop pretending his life made any sense. To stop hiding the anguish that tortured him night and day. He could just lie in the dark, and rant and curse to his heart's content.

Mr Winters would surely abandon his ambition to have his daughter marry a peer, if that peer was a raving lunatic! And even Robbie would reap some benefit. It would appease his quest for justice, to see the man he believed had murdered his sister finally locked away.

If that was what it took to appease Cora, he decided, his jaw firming, then it would be a small price to pay!

'You wanter cross or not, mister?' a little voice piped up, jerking him out of his darkly disturbing thoughts.

'Cross?'

A ragged boy with a dirty broom was standing, palm outstretched, gazing up at him expectantly.

A crossing sweeper.

'No,' he replied. There was no point.

No point to anything, any more. He had offended Cora. Driven her away.

'Want me to see if I can get a message to her?' the lad persisted.

'Message?'

'To the red-haired piece you chased up the street.'

'You saw her?' Lord Matthison stared at the boy in shock. He had assumed he was the only one who had been able to see her. Especially after the way she had melted through the crowds as though she and they existed on different planes.

The boy leaned closer, and took an experimental sniff, his perplexed face creasing into a grin.

'Clearer than you, I reckon, by the smell of your breath. Had a heavy night, have yer?'

Lord Matthison grimaced as the lad's words sank in.

He had not taken a drink in seven years. Had been astounded by what a tolerance for gin he seemed to have, marvelling at the fact he was still on his feet. Well, he might be on his feet, but he was sure as hell not sober.

The woman was real. He had not called some spirit up out of the pit. Cora had not deliberately turned her back on him, run from him, and slammed the door in his face. He had just seen some servant girl climb up the area steps from the servants' entrance, and go about her legitimate business.

Which had nothing to do with him.

The fact that she had looked uncannily like Cora was mere coincidence. Or…had she even born that much of a resemblance to his late fiancée? He frowned. He had not been close enough to see her face clearly. It had been her build, and the way she walked, that had convinced him he was seeing a ghost.

His head began to ache.

Typical!

He was getting a hangover before he was even sober.

He pressed the heels of his hands over his eyes, digging his fingers into his scalp. There was no point in trying to make sense of any of this until he had sobered up.

'Is this your patch?' he asked the crossing sweeper, running his fingers through his hair.

'Yessir!' said the lad, rather too loudly for Lord Matthison's liking.

'Then find out whatever you can about the red-head,' he said, dipping into his pocket, and flipping the lad a coin, 'and I shall give you another of these.'

The boy's face lit up when he saw it was a crown piece. 'Right you are! When will you be coming back?'

'I shall not,' he replied with a grimace of distaste. He despised men who loitered on street corners, hoping to catch a glimpse of the hapless female that was currently the object of their prurient interest.

'You will report to my lodgings. What is your name?'

'Grit,' said the boy, causing Lord Matthison to look at him sharply. And then press his fingers to his throbbing temples. It was all of a piece. The boy he was employing to spy on Cora's ghost could not possibly have a sensible name like Tom, or Jack! Everything about this night bore all the hallmarks of a nightmare.

'I will tell my manservant, then, that if a short, dirty person answering to the name of Grit comes knocking, that he is to admit you. Or, if I am not there, to extract what information you have, and reward you with another coachwheel.'

'And who might you be?'

'Lord Matthison.'

He watched the light die from the boy's eyes. Saw him swallow. Saw him try to hide his consternation. But Grit was too young to quite manage to conceal the belief he had just agreed to serve the devil's minion. He kissed goodbye to the prospect of ever finding out anything about the red-head who had worked him up into such a state. The lad would never pluck up the courage to venture to his lodgings. Or if he did, his conscience was bound to hold him in check. Even a dirt-poor guttersnipe would think twice about selling information about a defenceless female to a man of Lord Matthison's reputation.

'In the meantime, perhaps you could find me a cab,' he drawled, eyeing the shop across the street one last time. And then, because he got a perverse kind of pleasure from playing up to the worst of what people expected of him, he added, 'I dislike being abroad in daylight.'

Chapter Two

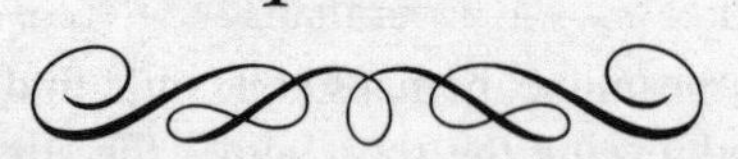

Mary dashed across the main shop, through the velvet curtains that divided it from the working areas, and pounded up the three flights of stairs that led to the workroom. The one place where she had learned to feel secure.

She had no idea why the way that man had emerged from the shadows on the other side of Curzon Street, with his black clothes, black hair and forbidding expression, had shaken her so badly. Or why, for an instant, she had got the peculiar impression that the shadows themselves had thickened, solidified and spawned the living embodiment of her nightmares.

It *was* terrifying, though, to feel as if your nightmares had invaded your waking life. Particularly since those nightmares were so vague.

All she could remember when she woke up from one of them was that there had been something hovering behind her. Something she dared not turn and face.

Because she was sure that if she did, it would rear up and swallow her whole. And so she would curl up, trying to make herself disappear, so the Thing would not notice her. But she could always feel it coming nearer and nearer, its shadow growing bigger and bigger, until eventually, in sheer terror, she would leap up and try to run away.

In her dreams, she never managed to move one step. But her legs would always start to thrash around the bed.

'Wake up, Mary,' one of the other girls would complain, prodding her with their sharp elbows. 'You're having one of your dreams again.'

They would tell her to lie still, and she would, clutching the sheets to her chin, staring up at the ceiling, terrified to close her eyes lest the dream stalked her again.

She sighed, rubbing the heels of her hands against her eyes. Deep down she knew that shadows did not turn into men, and chase girls down the street.

Though it had not stopped her running from him.

Just as she fled from whatever it was that stalked her dreams.

'Mary!' The angry voice of her employer made every girl in the workroom jump to attention. The fact that Madame Pichot had left her office at this hour of the morning did not bode well for any of them.

'What is the matter with you now? You are as white as a sheet! You are not going to be ill again, are you?'

Mary could not blame her for looking so exasperated. She was nowhere near as robust as the other girls who sewed for Madame. Never had been.

'That doctor promised me that if you took regular walks, your constitution would improve,' Madame complained. 'I cannot afford for you to take to your bed at this time of year!' Although the workload had slackened off slightly, now that the presentations in the Queen's drawing rooms had mostly taken place, there were still enough orders coming in for Madame to keep her girls working from dawn till they dropped into bed from sheer exhaustion.

Madame Pichot stalked across the bare floor and laid her hand on Mary's forehead.

'I am n-not ill,' Mary stammered, as much alarmed now by Madame's censure, as by what had happened in the street. 'B-but there w-was a m-man…'

Madame Pichot rolled her eyes, raising her hands to the ceiling in one of her Gallic expressions of exasperation. 'The streets are always full of men. I am sure none of them would be interested in a little dab of nothing like you!' she snapped, tugging off Mary's gloves, and untying her bonnet ribbons.

'N-no, he was shouting,' Mary exclaimed, recalling that fact for the first time herself.

'There are a lot of men hawking their wares at this time of the morning,' Madame scoffed. 'He wasn't shouting at you.'

'But I think he was,' she murmured, trying to examine what had happened without letting the panic that had gripped her on the street from clouding her perception. 'He chased me!' Though why some man she had never seen before should suddenly take it into his head to pursue her, shouting angrily, she could not imagine. But she had definitely seen him roughly pushing a tradesman out of his way. With his vengeful, dark eyes fixed on *her*. And for one awful moment, it had felt as though the curtain that separated what was real, from what existed only in her head, had been ripped in two. She had not known where she was. Or who she was.

That had been the most frightening moment of all.

'Mary, really,' Madame said, tugging her to her feet, and undoing her coat buttons, while the other girls in the workroom began to snigger, 'just because you saw a man running in the street, does not mean he was chasing you. Who on earth would want to chase a scrawny little creature like you, when there are willing, pretty girls for sale on every street corner?'

It should have been reassuring to hear Madame repeat the very fact that had her so bewildered. Except that she *knew* he had been chasing her. Her.

'Now, Mary,' said Madame firmly, shoving her back down on her work stool, and thrusting her spectacles into her hands, 'I forbid you to have one of your turns. There is no time for it today. Not when you have the bodice for the Countess of Walton's new gown to finish. Whatever happened outside, you must put it out of your head. Do you hear me?'

'Yes, Madame.' In truth, there was nothing she wanted more than to put it out of her mind. She was really glad she had such a complicated piece of work to do today. For concentrating on making something utterly beautiful had always had the power to keep her demons at bay. Even when she had been a little girl…

With a startled cry, Mary dropped her glasses. It always gave her a jolt, when one of these little glimpses of a past that was mostly a complete blank flared across her consciousness without warning.

Hearing Madame's huff of disapproval, Mary dropped to her knees to grope for them. They would not have slid far along the rough planks of the workroom. She would find them in mere seconds, pick them up, and be quickly able to get on with her work.

Why, she thought in anguish, could her mind not be as nimble as her fingers? Whenever she tried to catch hold of one of these little slivers of light that flashed into her mind, it was just like trying to take hold of a candle flame. There was nothing of any substance to latch on to. Except pain.

Well, only an idiot would keep on putting their hand into a flame, once they had learned that it burned, she thought, hooking her glasses over her ears. Instantly, everything beyond a few feet from her went out of focus, isolating her on her stool, like a shipwrecked mariner, clinging to a lone rock shrouded by fog.

When she had been a little girl, she sighed, unable to silence the echo of that memory straight away. Hastily she picked up a needle, but not fast enough to blot out the feeling that when she had been a little girl…with her head dutifully bent over her needlework…

'Pay no mind to anything but your sampler,' she

heard a gentle voice telling her. And for a fleeting moment, it was not Madame standing over her, glowering, but a kindly, protective presence that she instinctively recognised as her mother.

'For the Lord's sake, keep your head down,' the voice...her mother...continued as she became aware there had been someone else with them. Looming over them. A man with a loud voice and hard fists...and fear rushed up to swamp her.

Past and present swirled and merged. The child in her bent over her sampler, to blot out the raised voices of the adults, the violence that hovered in the air. And the woman hitched her stool closer to her embroidery frame. She leant so close her nose was practically brushing the cream silk net so that every time she breathed in, her lungs were filled with the sweet, aromatic scent of brand new cloth. With fingers that shook, she threaded a string of tiny crystal droplets on to her bead needle. Then she took a second needle which she would use to couch down the tiny segments of beading. She bent all her powers of concentration on to the intricate work, deliberately pushing away the vague images of violence that had almost stepped fully formed, into the light, just as that dark man had done earlier.

She had become adept at pushing uncomfortable thoughts away since she had arrived in London, bruised, alone and scared. And soon, her world shrank until all she could feel was the texture of the luxurious fabric, all she could hear was the pluck of the needle piercing it, the hiss of the thread as she set each meticulously measured stitch.

Her breathing grew steadier. Her heart beat evenly again. All that was ugly and mean slithered back into the shadows, leaving Mary conscious only of the work that occupied her hands.

She sensed, rather than heard, Madame Pichot step away. They both knew that now Mary's mind had turned in a new direction, she would soon forget all about the alarming incident in Berkeley Square.

It had been a long time since Lord Matthison had played against the house. The owners of gambling hells, such as this one, had become reluctant to admit him, until he had restricted his play to private games, arranged for him with other gentlemen. Or men who called themselves gentlemen, he corrected himself as he glanced round the table at the flushed faces of Lord Sandiford, Mr Peters, and a young cub by the name of Carpenter who was looking distinctly green about the gills.

Peters fumbled with his cards, reached for a drink, then, seeing his glass was empty, called for a refill from a passing waiter.

Lord Matthison leaned back in his chair with a sneer. Taking yet another drink was not going to alter the fact that once Peters threw down his hand, he would have cleaned them all out.

His mockery turned inwards. Had he not discovered for himself how deceptive strong drink could be?

Thinking he had summoned up Cora's ghost, by muttering something about three times three indeed! As soon as he'd sobered up, he had realised that the vision he'd had of Cora had sprung like a genie from a bottle, formed from a heady mixture of gin fumes and wishful thinking.

He had not been able to bear the thought he might have lost her all over again, that was what it boiled down to. And so he had let the gin steer him down a path of self-delusion.

Just as brandy was steering Peters down the path of self-destruction, he reflected, as the man gulped down what the waiter had just poured.

The man would have done better to stick to coffee, as he had done, he mused, as Peters, with a defiant flourish, finally displayed his hand.

Then slumped back when he saw what Lord Matthison had been holding.

'One more hand,' he begged, as Lord Matthison reached for his winnings.

'You have nothing left to stake,' Lord Matthison replied coldly.

'I have a daughter,' the man interjected, his eyes fastened on the pile of coins, banknotes and hastily scrawled pledges Lord Matthison was sweeping into his capacious pockets.

Lord Matthison regarded him with contempt. 'Do you expect me to care?'

If Peters had a grain of worth in him, he would have been at home, managing his business, not wasting his substance in a gaming hell like this! He should have considered what it might mean to his daughter *before* he gambled it all away. It was no use appealing to him now.

His own father had been just the same. When gambling fever gripped him, he forgot all about his wife and son, the dependants who looked to him for their welfare. All that had mattered to him was the next turn of the card, the next roll of the dice.

'No, no!' the man gibbered. 'I am saying that I still have a daughter—' a nasty look spread across his face '—to stake. Just give me one last chance to win something back,' he begged.

'Out of the question,' he replied, despising the man who had just ruined himself.

'She's pretty. And still a virgin,' Peters gabbled, sweat breaking out on his florid face.

Lord Sandiford, who had gone down to the tune of four hundred guineas without batting an eyelid, sniggered. 'You are wasting your time there, old man. Better sell her outright to me. Lord Matthison has no use for women.'

'Not living ones,' he agreed, shooting a pointed look at the hell's newest hostess, who had been hovering by his shoulder all night. At one point, he had found her perfume so cloying that he had told her quite brusquely to move further off. She had pouted, and looked up at him from under half-closed lids, purring that she would await his pleasure later.

'What do you mean by that?' demanded Peters.

Everyone at the table fell silent. Very few people

had ever dared ask Lord Matthison whether there was any truth in the rumours circulating about him.

Mr Carpenter shot Lord Sandiford a look of disgust, which turned to loathing as his eyes swept past Lord Matthison, got up so quickly his chair overturned, and made hastily for the exit.

'The only woman I am interested in, Mr Peters,' Lord Matthison replied, choosing his words very carefully, 'is Miss Cora Montague.' He felt a ripple of shock go round the room as he finally spoke her name aloud in public. Several men at nearby tables twisted round in their seats, hoping to hear some new titbit about the scandal that had rocked society seven years earlier.

'In her case, I was willing to stake my very soul on just one throw of the dice,' he said enigmatically. 'And I lost it.' He got to his feet, wondering whether proclaiming his allegiance to her ghost in a hell-hole like this would be enough to entice her back to his side.

What had he got to lose?

'She has my soul, Mr Peters.' And then, considering the massive amount he had just won tonight, his breath quickened. Even though he had not felt her presence, his luck had definitely turned. 'Or perhaps,' he added, feeling as though a great weight had rolled from his shoulders, 'I have hers.'

The girl who had been trying to get his attention all night was standing by the door. The owner of the hell was holding her by the arm, and talking to her in an urgent undertone.

Lord Matthison pulled out a banknote and waved it under her nose.

'Still think you'd like to earn this?' he taunted her.

She shrank back, her face turning pale as the owner of the hell moved away, leaving her alone with him. Lord Matthison put the money back in his pocket.

'Clearly not,' he drawled. 'Very wise of you.'

It was a relief to get out into the street, and breathe air not tainted by cigar fumes and desperation. 'Did you see that, Cora?' he asked of the black-velvet shadows of the alleyway. 'Did you hear me tell them?'

But there was no reply. She did not come skipping to his side, to keep him company on the long walk home. Instead, he had a fleeting image of what that nameless daughter would feel like when Peters went home and told her he was going to sell her to Sandiford. Swiftly followed by the horrified look on the face of that woman he had mistaken for Cora two days before.

'It is not my fault Peters tried to sell his daughter to me,' he growled as he set off through the dark, damp streets. 'I only went to the tables to find you.'

But she had not been there. And so the money that was making his coat pockets bulge meant nothing to him. He had no use for it.

When he reached his rooms, he drew out all the banknotes that had formed part of the winning pot and thrust them into his manservant's hands.

'I ruined a man named Peters tonight,' he bit out. 'Take this money, and hand it over into the keeping of his daughter. Tell her she is not to let her father get hold of it. Or she will have me to answer to.'

'Sir.' Ephraims's eyebrows rose a fraction, but he went straight out, without asking any questions.

Until tonight, Lord Matthison had felt not one ounce of pity towards any of the men from whom he'd won money. To his knowledge, he had ruined three.

But tonight, he could not bear to keep one penny of that money. He had only gone to the tables to find Cora. Not to bring more misery to the child of a compulsive gambler.

He went to his room, and shrugged off his jacket, the coins spilling from his pockets and rattling across the boards.

'I did not want that money for myself, Cora,' he explained, sitting on a chair by the bed to tug off his boots. 'You know I don't need it. I've invested wisely these last few years.' Somehow that admission only made this evening's work seem worse.

'I have ensured the girl will be safe,' he protested, untying his neckcloth and letting it slither to the floor.

'Does that please you, Cora?' he addressed the shadowed corners of his room. But there was no answer.

With a groan of despair, he lay down on top of the bed, still fully clothed, and flung his arm over his eyes. If she was not going to come back, he did not know how he could bear to go on.

There was no satisfaction to be had in ruining one man, or bestowing largesse on another.

Not when she wasn't there to see it.

He needed *her*.

God, how he needed her!

He felt as though he had barely closed his eyes, when he was woken by the sound of somebody knocking on the door.

Persistently.

Ephraims must still be out, he thought, sitting up and running his fingers through his disordered hair. He would have to deal with whoever was visiting himself. Probably one of the men from whom he had taken promissory notes the night before, he decided as he padded barefoot to the outer door.

However, it was not a shamefaced gambler who stood on his doorstep, but the grubby street sweeper from the night of the vision on Curzon Street.

'Grit,' he observed, opening the door wider to admit the rather scared-looking boy. 'You had better come into my sitting room.'

'Her name is Mary,' the boy announced without preamble, the moment Lord Matthison sank wearily on to the sofa. He did not really want to hear anything the lad had to say. But he might as well let him earn his tip, since he had plucked up the courage to walk into the devil's lair.

'The red-head you was after. She come to Lunnon about six or so years ago as an apprentice, and has been working her way up. Well, not that she's indentured regular, like, on account of her being a charity case.'

Lord Matthison brushed aside the apparent coincidence of that female appearing on the scene about the time Cora had disappeared. Hundreds of working girls came up to London from the country every year.

'No one can match the stuff she turns out now,' Grit added, staring round Lord Matthison's study with apprehensive eyes, as though half-expecting to see a human skull perched on one of the shelves. 'The nobs fight to get a dress wot she's had a hand in.'

Cora had been exceptionally fond of sewing, he recalled. But then, so were lots of gently reared girls. It meant nothing. Nothing!

'If you want to meet her,' the boy said, after a slight pause, 'she'll be in the Flash of Lightning Friday night. Her friend, see, has an understanding with a jarvey wot drinks in there. And they mean to sneak out and meet him. 'Bout seven,' he finished, sticking out his hand hopefully.

'Go into my room,' said Lord Matthison, jerking his head in that direction, 'and you can pick up whatever you find on the floor.' There had been several crown pieces amongst the coinage he had won last night. Grit was welcome to them.

He sat forwards on the sofa, his head in his hands. Last night, he had thought he had got it all clear in his mind. The woman he had seen on Curzon Street could not have been Cora. He had just been drunk, and had imagined the likeness.

But now he was beginning to wonder all over again. Take the way Grit had described her as a red-head.

The woman he had chased had been wearing a poke bonnet that covered her hair completely. So how had he been so sure it was red?

As Cora's was red.

And what about the way the bleak chill that usually hung round him like a mantle had lifted the second he saw the early morning sun brush the curve of her cheek? The way his heart had raced. As though he was really alive, and not just a damned soul, trapped in a living body.

He was not going to find a moment's peace, he realised, until he had looked the seamstress in the face, and proved beyond a shadow of a doubt that she bore no more than a passing resemblance to Cora.

'Stop worrying, Mary,' Molly cajoled. 'Madame Pennypincher won't know nothing about it unless we tells her.'

'She'll know it shouldn't take us so long to make a delivery.'

Ever since Mary had come back from the Curzon Street errand with her nerves in shreds, Madame Pichot had sent Molly with her on her daily walks.

Molly had been cock-a-hoop at escaping their relentless drudgery, shamelessly making use of their daily excursions to arrange this clandestine meeting with Joe Higgis, who worked out of a hackney cab stand on the corner of Conduit Street.

Mary did not begrudge Molly her snatched moments of happiness, she just did not see how they would manage to get away with taking a detour to a gin shop in Covent Garden.

'All we have to do is think up a story and stick to it,' Molly persisted. 'We'll tell her the housekeeper asked us to take tea in the kitchen, or the lady had some query about the bill.'

'I don't...I can't...' Mary felt her face growing hot. The very thought of telling her employer a barefaced lie was making her insides churn.

Molly clicked her tongue and sighed. 'Just leave the talking to me, then, when we get back. You can keep yer mouth shut, can't yer?' She gripped Mary's arm quite hard. 'Ye understand it ain't right to snitch on yer friends, don't yer?'

'I would never snitch on you, Molly,' said Mary, meaning it.

When she had first come to work for Madame Pichot, she had existed in an almost constant state of sickening fear. London was so confusingly crowded, so nerve-jarringly noisy. She had found it hard to understand what Madame's other girls were saying at first, so peculiar did their accent sound, and so foreign the words they used. But Molly had always been patient with her, explaining her work slowly enough so she could understand, even putting a stop to the acts of petty spite some of the others had seemed to find hilarious.

'Anyhow, Madame ought to let us have an hour or two off, once in a while, and then we wouldn't have to sneak off on the sly!'

No, she would not say one word to Madame about where they had been.

She would not need to.

She looked round uneasily as Molly towed her into the overheated and evil-smelling den in which her Joe liked to take a heavy wet of an evening, with the other drivers who worked for the same firm as him. Madame would only have to breathe in as they walked past to know exactly where they had been.

Molly soon spotted her beau, who got his pals to make room for the two of them at the table where they were sitting. A slovenly-looking girl deposited two beakers on the sticky tabletop in front of them, and Joe flipped her a coin.

Molly dug Mary in the ribs.

'Say thank you to Joe for buying us both a draught of jacky, girl. Ever so generous of him, ain't it?' Molly beamed at him, and his eyes lit up. Sliding closer to her, he slid his arm round her waist, and gave her a squeeze. Molly giggled, turning pink with pleasure. Mary might as well not have existed for all the notice he took of her.

She reached for her beaker, and bent her eyes resolutely on the liquid it contained, feeling slightly nauseous. She could not understand what Mary saw in Joe Higgis. He had sloping shoulders and a thick neck. His fingernails were dirty, and, given the nature of his job, he probably smelt of horses. How could Molly let such a man paw at her like that, never mind encourage it?

Molly had explained that he made her laugh, and that in this miserable world, you didn't turn your nose up at a man who could make you laugh, no matter what.

For Molly's sake, and to avoid hurting Joe's feelings,

she supposed she ought to try to look as though she was grateful for the drink he had bought her. Besides, she thought, glancing about her nervously, if she appeared to be concentrating on her drink, she would not look so out of place as she felt.

Tentatively, she tasted it, and was surprised to find it had a lightly perfumed flavour. Gin was not unpleasant, she grudgingly admitted, taking another sip.

'Friend of Molly's, are yer?' asked the man beside her, who had been eyeing her speculatively ever since she had sat down.

Mary bit down a scathing retort. She had come in with Molly. She was sitting next to Molly. What else would she be, but a friend of Molly's?

'Now, none of your cheek, Fred!' Molly suddenly stirred herself to say. 'Nor none of you others, neither,' she addressed the other men who were sitting at their table. 'I won't have none of you taking advantage of Mary, just coz she's too simple to do it for herself. I'll darken the daylights of anyone who so much as lays a finger on her!' she declared belligerently.

Fred raised his hands in surrender. 'I was just being friendly,' he protested.

'Well, stop it!' snapped Molly. 'She don't like men. They make her…' She paused, considering her choice of words. Mary stared fixedly into the depths of her drink, torn between gratitude to Molly for defending her, and sickening dread at what she might be about to reveal.

'Jumpy! Yes,' Molly declared, 'that's what she is round men what don't mind their manners. So just watch it!'

Having settled the point to her satisfaction, Molly climbed on to Joe's lap, and took up where she had left off.

Mary felt like a coin that had been tossed in the air, unsure whether she was going to come down heads, humiliated at having her deficiencies broadcast, or tails, grateful for Molly's spirited defence. Though Molly had only spoken the truth. Men did make her jumpy. She had not wanted Fred to speak to her, and she certainly did not want to have to answer him. In fact, she wished she could just shrink down into her coat and disappear. To conceal her confusion, she took another, longer pull at her drink.

Once it had gone down, she found her initial surge of contrasting emotions had settled down into a sort of dull resentment.

Molly had just told all these people that she was simple, and she did not think she was, not really. It was true that when she first came to London she had been confused about a lot of things. But she had been ill. She had still been getting the headaches for months after Madame took her in.

But now she wondered if some of those headaches had been due to the fact she had slept so poorly back then. For one thing, the streets were so noisy, at all hours of the day and night, and for another, she was not used to sharing a bed…

Though how she was so sure of that, when so many other things that other people took for granted were complete mysteries to her… She sighed despondently.

Perhaps Madame and Molly and the others were right about her. Perhaps she was a simpleton.

In an effort to distract herself from the perplexing muddle of her thoughts, she applied herself to her gin. Gradually she felt the knot of anxiety that was normally lodged somewhere beneath her breastbone melt away. What did it matter, really, if there was something wrong with her mind? She had a good position, where the skills she did have were put to good use. And she had friends.

Joe's friends, too, she realised, raising her head to look about the table, were not such a bad bunch, for all that they were so repulsive looking. She felt a giggle rising up inside as it occurred to her that if she had to come into a dirty, smelly drinking den, she could not have better companions than a group of hackney-cab drivers. Experienced as they were with handling highly strung creatures for a living, they had taken Molly's words to heart, and acted on them. Oh, not overtly. But they were not speaking so loudly now as they had been doing before. They were not crowding her with their big, male bodies, and they seemed to be trying not to make any sudden movements, that might startle her.

It was…quite touching.

London, she mused, cradling her cup of gin to her chest, was turning out not to be such a dreadful place at all. It had taken her a long time, but she was slowly growing accustomed to it. The more she explored its alleys and byways, the more familiar it became, the fewer terrors it held.

She would be all right.

One day, she would…

'Why did you do it, Cora?' A man's harsh voice rudely interrupted her reverie.

She looked up to see a gentleman standing over her. *The* gentleman. The one who had chased her clear across Berkeley Square. Same dark clothes, same forbidding expression, same angry voice.

She sucked in a sharp breath, waiting to feel the onset of that fear that usually surged through her whenever she felt threatened by something unfamiliar.

It did not materialise.

She peered into her beaker, wondering if this was why so many women grew so fond of gin. It seemed to be making her uncharacteristically brave.

Or maybe, she pondered, it was knowing that this man was outnumbered by Joe's pals. That she was, in effect, surrounded by a burly, bewhiskered, badly dressed cohort of bodyguards.

And so she didn't tremble. She did not shrink away. She just sat there, calmly looking up at him.

His face grew darker.

'You have to make me understand it, Cora,' he grated. 'Why did you run away?'

Cora? Ah, so that was it! She must resemble…her. That was why he had chased her, shouting so angrily. He must have been waiting for…Cora…and been completely perplexed when she had taken fright and run away.

'You have mistaken me for someone else, I think, sir,' she said gently. For she could see that he was really upset, and had no wish to add to his distress.

Yet he looked at her as though she had slapped his face.

If he had been mistaken in her, it had been seven years ago, not seven days!

She had said she loved him so much she did not care if they had to live in a bothy, whatever that was. Yet one afternoon, when nobody was watching, she had sneaked out on him. Without warning. Without excuse. Without reason. And started a new life. Here in London. Not half a mile away from his own lodgings. He might have passed her in the street countless times and not known…

Sheer rage gripped him at the magnitude of her deception. His whole existence, for the past seven years, had been based on a tissue of lies. She had lied to him. Robbie had lied about him. He had been lying to himself.

'You are supposed to be dead,' he hissed between gritted teeth. That she wasn't made him feel like a complete fool. What kind of an idiot would harbour the maudlin, pathetic sentiment that a woman could ever be true, let alone from beyond the grave! Since the day she had…no, not died. Left him, was what she had done. Left him with an accusation of murder hanging over his head. But since that day, *he* might as well have been dead. For nothing had mattered any more.

But what irked him most was the fact that he had still wanted to carry on believing all that claptrap *after* he had seen her in Curzon Street. When he had sobered up, after a few fitful hours of sleep, he had been determined to deny the evidence of his own eyes, preferring to believe alcohol had fuddled his senses so much that he had imagined the resemblance, rather than let go of his insane delusion she was haunting him.

And if Grit had not been heartless enough to sell information to a man of his reputation, he would probably not be standing here now.

He had only come here to get confirmation that he had imagined the woman's resemblance to Cora.

He had never expected to find himself looking at Cora herself.

A slightly older, careworn version of Cora, but Cora none the less.

Her voice had changed. Her accent was now almost indistinguishable from that of the other girls who lived and worked in this area. But there was still an unmistakably soft Scottish burr underlying the sharper vowel sounds, and a cadence to her speech that proclaimed her origins. The rest of her had hardly altered at all. Same fair skin that would break out in freckles at the most fleeting exposure to sunlight, same delicate features that made her face look all eyes, same mannerisms. The way she held her cup, the way she tilted her head as she looked up at him, though those green eyes, that had once blazed at him with what he had believed was the sort of love poets wrote sonnets about, were cold now. Blank.

Empty.

The enormity of her betrayal, her sheer deceitfulness, struck him all over again. There was no consolation in knowing she was not dead after all! He slumped down on to the bench beside her, in the gap that had opened up when her co-worker had climbed into the hackney-cab driver's lap and sucked in a sharp pain. Why had he not seen how deceitful she was back then? Look at her now, calmly sipping her gin after colluding in a clandestine meeting between her co-worker and her fancy man. Abusing the comparative freedom of her trusted position without so much as a qualm! His upper lip curled into a sneer. This woman was not trustworthy! She had waltzed off with his heart and his ring…

His ring! How could he have forgotten that? That ring had been in his family for generations. It was the only item of jewellery his mother had managed to prevent his father from selling. It was extremely valuable. Far too valuable to waste on a deceitful, brazen… He grabbed her hand, determined to take it back.

Her ring finger was bare.

'You sold my ring!'

How had she managed that? He had put up a reward, which he had been ill able to afford at first, in the hope that if it turned up, it would lead back to her. The antique ring, a blood-red ruby surrounded by tiny pearls, was such an unusual piece that he had been sure he would have heard if it had come on to the market.

She had somehow outwitted him, even in that. She must have sold it and used the proceeds to fund her flight to London. He scoffed at his own naïvety in thinking the paltry reward he had put up would have tempted a fence to turn in his supplier!

'Why, Cora?' he asked her again. That was what he

simply could not comprehend. 'At least, tell me why you ran away.'

If she had changed her mind about wanting to marry him, why had she not just told him, broken off the engagement and gone home? There was no need to have gone to such lengths to disappear so completely.

Mary's heart went out to the poor gentleman who looked so bleakly baffled. For she knew exactly how he felt. At one point, her world had frequently seemed to make no sense at all. And that in turn left her feeling scared and lonely and confused.

And when she had felt like that, a few kind words, or a smile, had helped her get back on an even keel. Summoning up a smile that she hoped conveyed her sympathy for his state of mind, she gently explained, 'I really am not who you think I am, sir. My name is Mary.'

'How can you sit there and lie to me?' he snarled. 'To my face! You got on your horse and rode off without a backward glance…'

'A horse?' Mary's eyebrows rose in surprise. If this man thought she was capable of climbing right up on top of a horse, when she was far too timid to even bring herself to pat one—no matter how earnestly Joe promised it was quite safe—then that just proved how badly mistaken he was about her identity! The very prospect of touching one brought on waves of uncontrollable panic. Panic so strong she could smell it. The smell came flooding to her nostrils right now. She swallowed down hastily, but her heart was already pounding in her chest. And she could smell damp leaves, mixed in with the scent of horse and leather, and taste that horrid, metallic tang of blood…

'…leaving me to pick up the pieces! Now you will not even do me the courtesy of explaining your outrageous behaviour! You said you loved me…'

His face dark with rage, he suddenly seized Mary's shoulders, and kissed her hard on the mouth.

Mary was so surprised, she had no time to react. He had not looked in the least like a man who was about to kiss a woman.

But before she could do more than gasp, all hell broke loose.

With an inarticulate bellow of rage, Fred rose up, reached over her, seized the poor, deranged gentleman by the lapels of his very expensive coat, and hauled him to his feet.

His sudden action caused the bench on which they were all sitting to topple over, sending Mary flying backwards in a tangle of skirts. Joe, whose reactions were lightning fast, had managed to leap to his feet as the bench slid out from beneath him, but Molly had tumbled to the floor alongside Mary.

'Quick, this way!' Molly shrieked, grabbing her by the arm even as she herself started to scramble on all fours out of the reach of the flailing boots of the three men now struggling together where, just a moment before, they had been sitting quietly drinking their porter.

By the time they reached the door, everyone in the place seemed to have been sucked into the brawl. Glancing over her shoulder as Molly hustled her out, she saw one of the serving girls bringing her tray down on the head of a coal-heaver who had a bespectacled clerk in a bear hug, while one of Joe's pals accidentally elbowed Fred in the face as he drew back his fist to punch a man in naval uniform. But she could not make out the dark gentleman anywhere amidst the sea of struggling combatants.

'What a night!' Molly gasped as they made it to the safety of the street, her face alight with excitement.

'Are you not worried about Joe?'

From inside the gin shop Mary could hear the sounds of furniture breaking, and men cursing and yelling.

'Sounds like—' she broke off briefly at a tremendous crash of breaking glass '—he's having a smashing time.' Molly giggled as she straightened Mary's skewed bonnet. 'Did you see how fast he was?' she added, dancing on the spot, and throwing a few punches at imaginary opponents for good measure.

'I scarcely knew what was happening,' Mary admitted. 'It all happened so fast. One minute that man was kissing me, and then… Oh dear—' she paused, casting an anxious glance over her shoulder '—I hope they are not hurting him.'

'Well, strike me!' Molly looked at Mary as though she had never seen her before. 'Here was I thinking you'd be all of a quake, and all you can think of is whether Joe and the lads are hurting your beau!'

'He's not my beau! I just feel…sorry for him, that's all. He seemed to think I was someone he had known once, someone who said she loved him, but then left him. That must have been why he followed me the other day, I must look very like her.' Even sitting face to face with her, in the glaring light of the tavern's lanterns, he seemed convinced she was his lost love. It was so sad.

Molly tucked Mary's hand in the crook of her arm, and stepped out briskly, muttering, 'I done the right thing, then. I weren't sure,' she said a little louder, darting Mary a sidelong glance, 'but the thing is, Mary, girls like us don't have a lot of choice.'

'What do you mean? What have you done?'

'It's for your own good,' she replied, puzzling Mary still further. 'And it's not as if you're scared of him now, are you? Not like you was the other day?'

'No,' Mary confessed, shamefaced. 'I was just being silly that day. He startled me, that was all, leaping out of the shadows like that…'

'There, you see. It will be fine!'

'What will be fine? Molly,' Mary panted, 'do we have to walk this fast? Nobody is chasing us now.'

'Sorry,' said Molly, moderating her stride to accommodate Mary's. 'You know I've always watched out for you, haven't I?'

'Yes.'

'Well, that's what I'm doing now. When Grit came to ask me what he oughter do about the questions Lord Matthison was asking about you, I told him to tell the gentleman whatever he wanted to know. Coz I don't think he'll do you any harm, Mary. There's places what cater to gentlemen of that sort, and he don't go to them. Not that I've heard…'

'Molly, I don't understand what you are talking about!'

'No, I don't s'pose you do. Look,' she said earnestly, 'how long do you think Madame will keep you on, once your health goes completely? She puts up with you now, because the kind of beading you do is all the rage. But there'll be a new fashion next season. Or your eyesight might go. Or…or anything could happen! And then, out you'll go!'

Mary shook her head. 'Madame took a risk, taking me in and giving me a job. She's always been good to me.'

'I've worked for her a damn sight longer than you, girl, and I'm telling you, she's like an old spider, she is, sucking all the life out of us, and then throwing away the husks what ain't no good no more! Mary, she don't even pay you! You get your bed and board, while she's making her fortune out of what your clever fingers bring in. Do you know how much she charges the Earl of Walton for those gowns you embroider for his wife? And do you see a penny piece of it? No! Coz you're too simple to stand up for yourself. Well, I'm doing it for you! You've caught the eye of a real live lord, girl. One of the wealthiest in town.'

'Well, yes, but only because I look like someone he used to know.'

'Makes no difference why he wants you. It only matters that he *does* want you. Gents like him can be very generous, if you give them what they want. And when he tires of you, he won't just chuck you out on the street. Point of pride with men like him, to leave their ladybirds comfortably off.'

'L…ladybird?' Mary echoed in appalled disbelief.

'Oh, yes! I reckon he'll be making you an offer quite soon. And when he does, you take it! You hear? Play your cards right, and this could be the making of you.'

'The making of me?' Mary gasped. 'The ruining of me, you mean!'

'Lord, Mary, don't be any dafter than you have to be. You don't dislike him, do you?'

'It's not that. I do feel sorry for him, but…'

'Well, there you are. No harm in offering the poor man a spot of comfort, is there?'

No harm? She did not know where to begin to explain the sheer magnitude of the harm that would come to her if she sold her body to a man! She could never regard becoming a man's mistress as a step up in the world. It was all very well for Molly to describe it as a chance to gain the kind of financial security she could never hope for, not if she sewed for Madame for a hundred years, but as far as she was concerned, it would be the ultimate degradation!

But there was no point even trying to explain all that to Molly. She would just see her scruples as further proof of her stupidity.

She hunched her shoulders against her friend's well-meaning meddling, and walked back to the shop in Conduit Street feeling like the loneliest, most misunderstood girl in London.

Chapter Three

Mary was standing on the edge of a cliff. She could hear waves pounding the shore far below, but it was too dark to see them. It was too dark to see anything. One false move, and she might go tumbling down to her doom.

Her heart started to race. Her legs shook. And, just as she had somehow known it would, the ground beneath her feet crumbled away and she was falling, falling, her mouth open wide in a soundless scream…

She landed with a bump, in the bottom of a small boat, winded, but unharmed. The dark gentleman had been there, waiting to catch her. His arms broke her fall.

It was not dark down here in the boat with him. The sun was shining. She felt warm and secure lying in the dark gentleman's arms, being gently rocked as the waves lapped against the boat. She could hear gulls keening. She looked up into a vast, cloudless sky, the kind of sky you never saw in London, fettered as it was by rooftops rank with smoking chimneys.

He smiled down at her as she relaxed into his hold with a sigh.

'I know you want me to kiss you,' he said, and lowered his head...

With a jolt, Mary woke with the blankets twisted round her legs. The feeling of tranquillity dissipated under a sharp blast of shame. How could she be dreaming about kissing a man? *That* man! She could not seriously be considering Molly's suggestion she become his mistress!

Could she?

Sick with self-disgust, Mary pulled her nightgown out from under Molly's leg, and wriggled out of the bed she shared with her and Kitty, one of the other seamstresses who lived with them over the shop.

She pulled her wrapper round her shoulders, and padded barefoot up to the workroom. The sun was not yet up, so she lit one of the lamps Madame Pichot kept available when her girls had to work beyond the hours of natural daylight, and settled onto her stool by her embroidery frame.

She had intended to distract herself from the disturbing feelings the dream had unleashed, by getting on with some work. But her mind stayed stubbornly focussed on the dark gentleman, like a stray dog gnawing at a stolen bone.

She had woken just before his mouth had touched hers, but she already knew what it would feel like. Though in the dream he would not have kissed her as he had done in the gin shop, with frustrated anger. No, he would have kissed her tenderly, lovingly, exactly as she would want him to…

No! She did not want him to kiss her! She was not that sort of girl! She did not want to snuggle up to him, and put her arms round him, and…and…comfort him with her own kisses…why that would make her no better than a harlot!

She could not understand the person she had become in the Flash of Lightning. Before last night, she would have sworn that she feared and reviled men. All men. She had never wanted to receive the sort of lewd advances that other girls found flattering.

So why had she not felt the slightest inclination to jerk her hand out of his when he had grasped it? Why had she not wanted to struggle away from him when he had crushed her to his chest and kissed her?

She supposed she could argue that she would have been glad of anything that distracted her from sliding down into one of her panics. And she had certainly not been able to think about horses once he had swept her into his arms.

He had overwhelmed every one of her senses. His breath had been warm against her face, his hands strong and determined, yet they had not bruised her shoulders when he had pulled her against the hard wall of his chest, where her nostrils had filled with the scents of him. Expensive linen and fine milled soap and warm, clean man…

She sucked in a sharp, shocked breath. There she went again, savouring an experience that should by rights have scared her. Why had the feel of his arms closing round her felt like…she forced herself to admit it…like coming home? She rubbed at a dull, nagging ache that was thrumming at the base of her skull. It was ridiculous! He was a complete stranger to her.

A stranger who had managed to breach all her defences with one kiss!

One kiss, she sighed, and she could not stop thinking about him.

Oh, she pressed her palms against her flushed cheeks, she hoped she never saw him again!

If Molly was right, and he was about to make her a dishonourable offer, she did not rightly know how she would answer. She knew what she *ought* to answer. Of course she did. But would she be strong enough to say no? If he spoke to her again, kissed her again, this time gently, persuasively, as he had been about to kiss her in her dream, would she have the courage to stand firm in her beliefs?

Because, for one blissfully sinful moment, until Fred had come to her rescue, she had felt as though there was nowhere else she would rather be.

She, who had felt alone amongst strangers for as long as she could remember, had felt a connection with him that defied explanation.

Surely she had the moral strength to resist the temptation to go away with the first person who had ever made her feel as though she belonged somewhere?

No wonder, she sighed, so many women abandoned honest, hard toil, and took to a life of vice. If she could feel this torn after one fleeting encounter with a man she knew practically nothing about… She shivered. Perhaps her first instinctive reaction to his advent in her life had been the right one. To run far, far away to a place where he could never find her. Because he was dangerous. Dangerous to her.

'Heavens, girl, what's to do with you now?'

Mary started, discovering Madame Pichot hovering over her, her lips pursed with disapproval. She had not heard her come into the workroom. Not that that was so unusual in itself. She was often so immersed in her work that hours passed without her being conscious of anything else that went on in the room around her.

What was unusual was that Madame had caught her staring into space, her hands idle.

No wonder Madame looked displeased. Mary had not been herself since the day she had come running home in a panic from her errand to Curzon Street. Her nights were full of disturbing dreams of the dark man. And all day long her thoughts kept straying in his direction. She had to keep yanking them back to her work by force of will. She hung her head, embarrassed to have to acknowledge that for the first time ever, she was behind with her work.

Madame reached down, took hold of Mary's chin in her strong, capable fingers, and jerked her face up.

'Stars in your eyes,' she muttered angrily. 'You've come back from wherever Molly took you last night with stars in your eyes.' Her fingers squeezed more tightly as Mary squirmed guiltily. She had known Madame would see through Molly's excuses for taking so long over what should have been a straightforward errand. She had sent the girls straight up to their room without comment, and Molly seemed to think they had got away with it. But Madame's next words chilled Mary to the bone.

'Once the gentry start going back to their summer homes, I'm turning that girl off for last night's work.' She looked right through Mary as she voiced her thoughts aloud, treating her, as she had done from the first, as though she was a half-wit. Mary could understand how that attitude had originated. She had been in a terrible state on the day she had arrived. Almost beside herself after the rigours of the journey, and what had happened to her before setting out. For weeks, the slightest thing had triggered debilitating episodes of blind panic, which had meant she hardly got any work done.

The other workers had soon learned it was not safe to ask her questions about where she came from. Whenever she had tried to provide explanations, groping back into the unrelenting blackness where the knowledge should have been, she was overwhelmed by such a devastating sense of loss that it brought her actual, physical pain. So severe she could scarcely breathe through it. It was like…drowning.

Pretty soon, the girls stopped asking her. And Mary stopped trying to probe into that maelstrom of darkness and pain. It was a bit like coming to an uneasy truce with herself. She did not deliberately try to provoke her memory, and for the most part, it left her alone.

And Madame, discovering that when Mary was calm

she could do far more than merely sew a seam, that she was in fact far more highly skilled with her needle than any of her other workers, had begun to treat her like a pet dog. A dog that could perform amazing tricks, and was therefore worth cosseting, but not quite on a par with a real person.

'I can get another such as her for the crooking of my finger,' Madame continued relentlessly. 'Girls who can sew fall over themselves to work in an establishment such as mine, Mary, where they can get fair wages for an honest day's work.'

Most girls, yes, but not her. Madame had only agreed to take her on as a favour to the friend who had sent her to London. Mary had her board and food. She got nice clothes, which she made for herself during the winter months, when custom was slack. She had sturdy boots, and attractive bonnets and warm gloves, for Madame insisted her girls looked well turned out when they went to church.

But hard coin never came into her hands.

'I trusted you to go out and take your prescribed exercise, because I thought you were different from the other girls. That you were so scared of men that you would never idle away my time flirting with footmen in the houses I send you to, or loitering on the streets to see if you can catch the eye of some Bond Street buck. And then you come back here, reeking of the tavern, with stars in your eyes!'

She let go of Mary's chin then, as though she was disgusted by the prolonged physical contact.

'I thought all you needed to keep you happy was a piece of satin, and a dish of beads! The longer you worked for me, the calmer you seemed to become. Are you not happy working for me?'

Mary heard the threat implicit in Madame's question and went cold inside. What would become of her if Madame turned her off? She had no family, no friends outside this workroom. Nor did she possess the survival skills of Molly and her ilk.

Mary stared at her, aghast. She no longer looked like the patient benefactress who tolerated her deficiencies because she had a charitable nature, but like a hard-headed businesswoman who had risen to the top of her profession by sheer determination. With her slightly protuberant eyes, her dark, wispy hair coiled round her head in a plait, and the way she had held Mary's chin with fingers that felt like steel pincers, she could see exactly how Molly could liken her to a spider, grasping hold of a fly she had caught in her web. Molly and the other girls had always seen this side of her. Because they had their wits about them.

Now she, too, saw how precarious her position was. How totally dependant she was on this woman's good will.

'Please don't turn me off when the Season is over,' Mary pleaded. 'I promise I won't go into a tavern ever again! Indeed, I did not like it!'

Madame glared at her for a few seconds, before apparently coming to a decision.

'I cannot go on pampering you as I have done, if

this is how you repay me,' she said coldly. 'A daily walk, indeed! None of the other girls are granted such indulgence.'

None of the other girls worked quite so hard as she did, though, Mary surprised herself by thinking mutinously. They did not get so caught up in their task that they forgot to eat. They chattered, and got up to stretch and peer out of the window, or peek at the titled customers that came into the downstairs showrooms, while Mary kept her head down, and worked relentlessly, exhausting herself so that when she was finally permitted to leave her station, she hoped she would fall into bed and sleep dreamlessly.

'Well, I shall certainly not permit you to leave these premises again until I can be certain I can trust you not to go making assignations. And no more sitting about, mooning over whoever it was you dallied with last night either. No man ever brought a woman anything but trouble. You must forget him! Do I make myself plain?'

'Yes, Madame,' said Mary with heartfelt relief. She was not, apparently, going to lose her job, and her home along with it, for the foreseeable future. Nor was she going to be going outside where she might risk running into the disturbingly seductive dark gentleman, either. And by the time Madame's temper had cooled down, so would his ardour. People of his class, from her experience of the spoilt débutantes and titled ladies who came into the shop downstairs, did not possess a scrap of patience. They all wanted their whims satisfied quickly, or they grew petulant. And he was a lord, she recalled. Molly had mentioned his title. It was something like Harrison. Something with a lot of 's' s in it, anyway. And a lord would not hanker after one particular seamstress for very long, if she knew anything about it. By the time she next ventured out of doors, he would have tracked down someone else who reminded him of his lost lady, and forgotten all about her.

'Well, then, go and get some clothes on,' Madame snapped. 'And do not even think about getting any breakfast. You have wasted enough of my time today as it is!'

It was a fitting penance. Every time her stomach rumbled, Mary would remember how tempted she had been by the deceptive kisses of a stranger.

'Thank you, Madame,' Mary breathed, thankful the entire episode was over. She only hoped she would soon stop feeling guilty. It was not as if she had invited the man to accost her. No, he had rudely invaded, and taken up residence in her thoughts without the slightest bit of encouragement from her.

She would just have to turn her back on thoughts of him, just as she shut out the other shadows that tried to creep up and menace her hard-won sense of tranquillity.

That was all she really wanted.

To be at peace.

Lord Matthison winced as Ephraims applied a fresh piece of raw steak to his rapidly blackening eye. His knuckles were grazed, and it hurt to breathe too deeply, but by God, it had felt good to hit someone. Several someones. Seven years of holding back his grief, his anger and despair, had erupted last night in the Flash of Lightning, he realised.

But the satisfaction in inflicting as much pain upon everyone around him as he bore within himself had only brought temporary relief. By the time he had limped home, his mind had been in complete turmoil over the red-head.

One minute he was convinced she was Cora. Then his whole being would revolt at the very notion.

Because if that woman was Cora, then what the hell had been going on for the last seven years? He certainly had not imagined the extraordinary success her shade had brought him at the tables.

Unless…he sat forwards, clutching the steak to his eye as Ephraims gathered his bloodied shirt up from the floor. Supposing winning on those horses had just been a fluke. One of those lucky streaks that happen to gamblers from time to time. He had been barely twenty years old, half out of his mind with grief, spurned by his family and friends at a time when he needed them most. Had he just clung to the idea there was still one person who would not turn her back on him?

And his subsequent successes—could they have more to do with the fact that he never played but when he was stone-cold sober? And that he knew when to stop?

He shot to his feet, flinging the steak on to the dish on the table, dismissing it and Ephraims with a peremptory wave of his hand.

'Don't be angry with me, Cora,' he pleaded, terrified

lest she be offended by this lack of faith in her. 'I still believe in you. I do!'

He refused to believe that red-headed woman could possibly be Cora! Why, she'd had no idea who he was or what he was talking about. He paced across the room, running his fingers through his hair. Cora would never have forgotten him! They had been everything to each other! Besides, the woman he had mistaken for Cora had looked completely at home amongst the denizens of that gin shop. Whereas Cora had been shy. And opposed to strong drink. It was unthinkable that she could have changed so much!

And Cora had no reason to flee to London. Not one that made any sense.

He paced the room for several minutes, torturing himself with an imaginary lover, with whom she had eloped. Of an illicit pregnancy, which she dared not confess to her brother.

He went cold inside. Robbie's temper was formidable. She might have been afraid of what Robbie might do. But surely, he groaned, she could have confided in him?

He went to the washstand, where he bowed over the basin, and dashed a jug of cold water over his head. And was flooded with relief at the recollection that there had been no mention of a child of any sort in Grit's report.

Of course not.

Cora had not taken a lover. Or been pregnant. She had loved him!

The woman was not Cora, that was all there was to it!

But what if she was? a persistent little voice nagged at him.

'Dammit all to hell!' he growled, reaching for a towel and burying his face in it. If the woman he had seen in the gin shop was Cora, then she owed him an explanation for the suffering he had endured on her account! And if not…he tossed the soiled towel to the floor.

Well, he was not going to break faith with Cora. He might have kissed the woman, but that was only because he had been so sure, in that instant…

He was just going to have to establish, beyond a shadow of a doubt, that she was *not* Cora, that was all.

And the quickest way to do that, he suspected, would be to walk back into that gin shop, and start to make enquiries amongst the people she associated with.

But not straight away.

He deliberately waited the few days it took him to regain his sense of equilibrium before returning to the gin shop where he had caught her carousing with…no, not scum. The men she had been with were at least honest and hard working. He paused on the threshold of the Flash of Lightning, scanning the room until he spied the men she had been with the night he had seen her, held her, kissed her…

Muttering a curse, he stalked across the room to the very same table where he had committed that act of gross folly. And stood there, calmly letting the conversation dry up as the men, one by one, became aware of his presence.

The one who had been sitting next to Cora, the one who had been so eager to rush to her defence, rose slowly to his feet.

'Thought we'd seen you off for good on Friday,' he growled. 'You got no right coming back here.'

The other men around the table growled their agreement.

Rather than argue that he had a perfect right to enter any drinking den in London, or anywhere else he chose, Lord Matthison kept his expression neutral as he replied, 'I have returned to compensate the landlord for any breakages that occurred. And to offer my apologies for poaching on your territory,' he addressed Cora's defender directly. 'She bears such a remarkable resemblance to my late fiancée, that for a moment or two…' He tailed off, with a slight shrug of his shoulders. 'I hope you will believe me when I tell you I intended no insult to your…wife.'

He had no idea what connection the red-head had to these men. But he had seen them all leap to her defence from what they interpreted as his assault, as if she was one of their own. If he wanted to find out more about her, this was the place to start.

'Mary's not my wife!' Fred protested, turning red as a couple of the other men at the table sniggered. 'But nor could I just sit there and let someone grab her like that. No, not if he was a royal Duke I couldn't!'

'Scurvy thing to do,' said another of the group. 'Taking advantage of a simpleton in that way.'

'It was as well it was Fred as saw you trying to steal

a kiss,' said another, 'after what Molly threatened not five minutes before you walked in.' There was a moment's thoughtful silence, then the entire group burst out laughing.

'She'd have torn you limb from limb!' declared the one who had been cuddling Cora's female companion, wiping tears of laughter from his eyes. 'You couldn't have employed that right hook against her!'

Taking advantage of the relaxation in the atmosphere, Lord Matthison took a place at the table, and clicked his fingers for service. After he had ordered a round of drinks, Fred clapped him on the shoulder, admitting,

'If it hadn't been you, it'd uv bin someone else. There's nearly always a fight in here of a Friday night.'

'Usually a woman what starts it, too, one way or another,' bitterly asserted a man on the other side of the table whose fists, Lord Matthison recalled ruefully, had made such an indelible impression on his ribs.

When he told him as much, the man's scowl turned to a grin of pride. 'For a gent, you pack quite a punch yourself. Spar with Gentleman Jackson, I suppose?'

He allowed the conversation to dwell for some time on the merits of the science that could be learned at such establishments, compared to the tricks learned in less salubrious surroundings.

There was a slight lull when the serving girl brought their tray of drinks, and once they had all toasted his punishing right, he turned to the topic he had really come in to investigate.

'What did you mean when you referred to…Mary,' he forced himself to call her, though he was by no means certain it was her real name, 'as a simpleton?'

They had spoken of her that way several times, and attributed their defence of her largely to that cause.

'Just that,' replied the one who had reminded him his name was Joe. His jaw, Lord Matthison noted with grim pride, was still rather swollen. 'She ain't all there. My Molly looks out for her at work, but…' He raised his tankard, and took a long pull.

'And she don't like men,' pointed out Fred, sympathetically. 'No disrespect to you, sir, but she's jumpier than an unbroke filly round men she don't know well. Couldn't let you go a scaring of a poor maid like that.'

'Molly reckons,' said Joe, setting down his tankard and aligning the handle with great precision, 'she's been took advantage of, before she come to London.' There was a murmur of assent from the other men. 'Not that she's ever spoke of it. Says she don't remember much of anything before she fetched up in town. Molly said she was a lot worse back then even than she is now. Headaches, and sort of fits, and that.'

Lord Matthison went cold. The girl had no memory of the time before she came to London? Six years ago? Could that account for the blank look in her eyes?

'Always having the doctor out to her…'

'Ought to have the doctor out to some of them others, rather than turning them off when she's wore 'em out,' put in the bitter jarvey with the rib-crunching fists.

He took a long pull on his tankard, listening to their

diatribe on the lot of girls who worked for grim-faced old gorgons like Madame Pinchpenny, as they called her. The long hours spent hunched over their work that ruined their eyes, rotted their lungs and generally sapped their stamina by inches.

'And all so the gentry can dance the night away in their silken gowns,' muttered Fred with disgust. 'They don't care the girls what make their finery ain't treated no better than slaves.'

'It's that old besom she works for I blame,' Joe argued. 'She don't need to drive them quite so hard.'

If this woman was Cora, Lord Matthison reflected, even if she had done the very worst he had suspected of her, she had more than atoned for it. He felt his anger towards her dissipate. She might have put him through hell, but she had been enduring her own form of purgatory. He recalled her pinched face, pallid in the lantern light. She had always been dainty, but on Friday night she had looked as frail as thistledown. As though one more blast of misfortune could shatter her, scattering what was left to the four winds. And the emptiness in her eyes…

'You got no call to worry about her,' Fred put in, misinterpreting the troubled expression on Lord Matthison's face. 'She didn't seem too bothered by you kissing her.'

'Well, the gin probably helped,' Joe pointed out.

Was this what Cora had sunk to? Drowning her sorrows in gin, like so many other working class women?

No. He slammed his tankard down on the table. Her eyes had been blank. Not glazed. And she most definitely had not been drunk the morning he had chased her down Curzon Street. He should know. It was impossible to run that fast, or display such agility in dodging the crowds, with the senses dulled by alcohol.

No. Something else had put that blank look in her eyes. These men all firmly believed she had something wrong with her mind. Something that had its origins in an assault she had sustained before she came to London. An assault that had left her afraid of men.

He felt as though an iron hand had reached into his chest and squeezed his heart until it almost lost the ability to beat.

There were only a few facts regarding Cora's disappearance he knew for certain. She had gone out riding one afternoon, alone, and had never come back. The horse had returned to the stables in a state of terror, mud and leaves all over its foaming flanks. At first everyone had assumed she had met with an accident. It was only when they could find no trace of her after days of increasingly desperate searching that Robbie had turned on him. After that, instead of pooling their resources to widen the search, each had shut the other out.

He had often wondered if she had been attacked and robbed. But robbers would have left her lying in the forest where the crime took place, surely? That theory did not account for her turning up in London.

He began to feel a bit sick. If this woman was Cora, then she had vanished from his estate, only to turn up several weeks later in London, so shattered by whatever had happened to her that she had never recovered her memory of it.

He felt ashamed of himself for experiencing a glimmer of relief at the thought that somebody might have taken her, used her cruelly, then disposed of her. Because if that was the case, terrible though it was, it meant that she had not willingly left him.

She had been taken. But she had not *wanted* to go.

All he had been left with, after Cora had vanished, was the conviction she would not leave him. And now, if it turned out this woman was her…

He breathed in deeply, closing his eyes on a surge of emotion he was completely at a loss to name.

It had been so long since he'd permitted himself to feel anything much at all. For the last seven years only his rigid self-control had kept him functioning with any semblance of normality. But getting drunk, and raging at his fate, had been like setting the spade to ground frozen by winter's hard frost. Now, one emotion after another was beginning to break through the fractures.

Maybe he should have got drunk years ago. Mourned her. Let her go.

But he had not been ready to let her go.

His jaw hardened with determination. He was still not ready to let her go.

If there was any possibility, no matter how slight, that this poor, abused woman could be his Cora, then he would do his utmost to rescue her from this life of drudgery, and restore her to full health.

He would need to find a really good doctor. One

who had experience in treating ailments of the mind, as well as of the body.

He had half-risen from the table before he saw the flaw in his plan. How was he to get her to see such a man? He had no influence over her any more. As far as she knew, he was a stranger.

He could not see any responsible employer letting one of her staff go off with a strange man. Especially not when the girl in question was afraid of men.

There was little chance he might be able to earn her trust, either. He had already chased her, run her to earth in this drinking den, railed at her and kissed her. Any approach he made now was likely to terrify her. She might even do something as drastic as running away if he made his intentions known. He slumped down on the bench, a dark frown marring his features. It had taken him seven years to find her. He did not wish to scare her so badly he ended up spending another seven hunting her down.

There was only one person who might be able to help him to persuade her employer to give her over into his keeping.

Robbie.

Robbie would only have to take one look at her, to know who she was! If his own judgement was clouded by wishful thinking, he could trust Robbie, at least, to look at the situation more dispassionately. He would never permit an impostor to take Cora's place in his life.

He would write to him, and tell him that he had found her. That he needed to come to London as soon as he could. Madame Pichot would not be able to argue with both her brother, and her fiancé!

In the meantime, she was safe enough where she was, he supposed. Madame Pichot guarded all her girls, he gathered from Joe's acid comments about the difficulties involved in seeing his sweetheart.

A malicious smile came to his lips as he realised that at least he could instruct his lawyers to block any moves Mr Winters might make with regards to his quest to declare her dead.

Cora would never be dead to him. And whoever this red-head turned out to be, he was not going to allow anybody to say she was!

Chapter Four

Kitty pounded up the stairs, poked her head round the workshop door, and panted, 'Such a to-do, you'd best come quick!'

Kitty worked mainly in the showroom because not only was she attractive, but she was also quite well spoken. But she never forgot the needlewomen hidden up in the attics. She would always try to alert them when someone really famous came in. Or, if she could not find an opportunity to do that, she would study the celebrity carefully, and give them her usually highly disrespectful impersonation of them later, in their bedroom.

All but Mary immediately set their work aside, thrilled at having something to break up the monotony of their day.

'You too, Mary, this time,' Kitty darted back to insist. 'And hurry up, do, else we'll miss all the fireworks!'

After only the briefest hesitation, Mary toed off her

shoes, as all the other girls had already done, and tiptoed across the bare floor. For once, she admitted, she was glad of an excuse to get up and walk away from work that no longer had the power to completely absorb her.

The other girls were already crowded together on the top four treads by the time Mary reached the back stairs, those who had been swiftest pressing their faces up to the knotholes in the partition wall. Which meant the fireworks Kitty had promised them were going off in Madame's private office. The knotholes that allowed them to peep into the showroom were all much further down the staircase.

'Unless you take steps to put a halt to this outrageous affair,' Mary could hear a strident female voice complaining, 'I shall see your business ruined!'

'Please calm yourself,' Madame Pichot replied, in an even, soothing tone. 'I choose all my girls with great care, and watch them assiduously.'

Mary had no problem hearing Madame almost as clearly as she could hear the complaining woman. The partition wall was flimsy, its only function to prevent Madame's wealthy clients from the terrible misfortune of catching a glimpse of the conditions that prevailed beyond all the opulence of Madame's plush showroom.

'I can assure you,' Madame said haughtily, 'that neither Mary, nor any of my other girls, is having an affair with Lord Matthison.'

The girls all turned to stare at Mary in mingled shock and excitement. She shrugged her shoulders, palms spread wide to indicate she had no idea what was going on.

'Not yet, perhaps, but he certainly has plans for her! He is intent on making my daughter an object of ridicule!' the first voice wailed. 'First he wilfully compromised her, and now he is trying to wriggle out of marrying her by claiming to have discovered his long-lost fiancée.'

Ah! The woman must be complaining about the handsome dark gentleman who had kissed her in the Flash of Lightning. His name was not Harrison at all. But Matthison. Lord Matthison.

'...working of all things as a seamstress! When everyone knows she is dead!'

'You are supposed to be dead,' he had muttered, looking at her as though he had seen a ghost. Oh, the poor man! He must be so convinced she was that Cora person that he had gone to the complaining woman's house, and told her... No, but wait a minute, Mary frowned. Something about all this did not add up. The woman said he had compromised her daughter. She shook her head, baffled. They could not be talking about the same man. The man she had met was so besotted with the woman who had died, she was sure he would never...unless this woman's daughter looked like Cora too. That was why he had kissed *her*, after all.

'There is no question of Mary agreeing to any such thing.' Madame's tone was still quietly contemptuous, in stark contrast to the almost hysterical tirade of the other woman in her office.

'Girls of that sort will do anything for the kind of money Lord Matthison could give her!' the other woman protested. 'And even if she did not wish to go along with it, he is ruthless enough to compel her! He might kidnap her, and terrorise her into doing his bidding. He is evil, I tell you, evil!'

It crossed Mary's mind that it was mighty peculiar of the woman to insist Lord Matthison had to marry her daughter, if she really believed he was evil.

'And if that happens,' the unbalanced female almost shrieked, 'we will not be the only ones to suffer! I shall make sure you are ruined! What do you think will happen to your business once word leaks out that you supply girls for gentlemen with unusual appetites? For that is what I shall tell the world. Do you think you will still get earls and dukes bringing their wives here if they think it is just a front for a bawdyhouse? Do you think any half-decent sort of man will allow his daughters to be dressed in gowns made by…by harlots?'

'My girls are all completely respectable.' Madame sounded a little shaken. 'There has never been any whisper—'

'There will be more than whispers if Lord Matthison gets his hands on that Mary! There will be such scandal that your reputation will never recover!'

There was a slight pause, then Madame said, in a voice that had regained its composure, 'He will not. I shall make sure of it. You have my word. Now, if that will be all…?'

She heard the determined rustle of expensive clothing, footsteps, and a door latch being lifted.

So did the others, who scrambled swiftly on their

stockinged feet back up to the workroom. Only when they were back at their respective stations, with the door to the back stairs safely shut behind them, and their feet decently shod, did the whispering and nudging begin.

'Mary,' said Molly, through a mouthful of pins as she deftly tacked a length of silk chenille round the sleeves of a bronze-gold evening gown, 'you won't go doing anything daft, will you?'

'Daft?' echoed Mary, trailing her fingers distractedly through a dish of iridescent turquoise sequins.

'Yes, like running off with that Lord they was going on about,' Molly muttered.

'But,' objected Mary, 'on Friday night you were saying that if he made me an offer I ought to accept.'

'That was then, this is now!' she snapped. 'I thought then that if you could come to some arrangement, you could ask him for a big fat parting present, and you would be set up for life. I was going to suggest you ask him to set you up in a little shop so's I could come and help you run it…what?' She rounded on the others, who had begun to mutter behind her back. 'Don't say you wouldn't jump at the chance to get out of here if you could do it!' She turned back to her garment, jabbing a pin into its bodice with unnecessary force. 'Now it looks as though I shall have to marry Joe and raise a pack of tow-haired snot-nosed brats.'

'I thought you liked Joe,' protested Mary faintly.

'Liking has nothing to do with it. It is one thing coming to an understanding with a man, where you both get something out of it. Quite another being completely under his thumb…'

'That's right, Mary,' put in Josephine, a plump girl with a gap between her front teeth. 'Accepting *carte blanche* from a gentleman, and letting him set you up in style, is a far cry from being stolen out of your place and being held against your will by some depraved monster.'

'Like you would know anything about being kept in style,' sneered Lotty, a sallow-complexioned, slender girl with stooped shoulders. Lotty and Josephine were currently at odds. Any conversation that took place up here lately seemed to fuel their simmering resentment of one another.

Before the conversation could descend into yet another slanging match, Mary hastily interrupted. 'Lord Matthison will not kidnap me.'

'How would you know?' breathed Josephine in a thrilled tone. 'You heard what that woman downstairs said.'

'Well, for one thing, Madame will not let me outside any more, so I don't see how he could possibly do it. And for another, he, well, he just would not.'

When Lotty made a noise that exactly expressed the depth of her contempt for such a naïve comment, Mary exclaimed, 'He is not evil! Even that woman did not really think so, or she would not be so set on having him marry her daughter.' That did give the other girls pause, she could see. Emboldened, she went on, 'I think he is just confused. I mean—' she frowned, trying to find words to explain how she was certain he felt towards her '—I am quite sure that he really, truly believes I am his long-lost fiancée. He asked me why I had run away.'

'Ooh,' breathed Josephine, 'do you think you are really a runaway heiress?'

'Don't be daft!' snorted Molly. 'Why would an heiress want to run away? Especially if she was betrothed to someone as rich and good looking as that Lord Matthison. No one in their right mind would give up that kind of life, to work in a place like this!' She gestured round the spartan room with contempt. It had skylights, as well as floor-to-ceiling windows on the south-facing wall, to maximise the hours of daylight, during which Madame Pichot could keep the girls working without the expense of having to light the oil lamps. It meant the room was like a hothouse in summer, yet impossible to keep warm in winter.

It took Lotty only a few seconds to come up with the scathing rejoinder, 'But then, we all know our Mary ain't exactly *in* her right mind.'

Everyone, except Mary, began to snigger quietly. She went to her stool and sat down, her cheeks burning with humiliation. It was not as if she was that bad! Not nowadays! Yes, she still got confused and scared sometimes. But she could read and write. And once, when she had caught a glimpse of Madame's account books, she had been able to grasp the significance of all the neat little columns. And had she not learned to find her way about the labyrinthine courts and alleys of London?

Madame never worried that she might get lost when she sent her out on errands!

What she could not do, though, she accepted with mounting chagrin, was to come back with some really cutting remark that would put a stop to their mockery as effectively as scissors snipping off a loose thread. She was still desperately trying to come up with one, when she heard Madame's heavy footsteps on the stair. They all bent to their work with renewed concentration.

When Madame Pichot marched into the room a few seconds later, she went straight to Mary. Raking a look over her embroidery frame, she said, 'How long will it take you to finish this up?'

Mary looked down at the intricate tracery of roses in their varying stages of bloom, which were to decorate a pair of evening gloves. She had already worked the same design on to a spectacularly opulent evening gown, and the satin slippers that went with it.

'There are several hours work left still.'

'Then get to it!' Madame snapped. 'Molly, when it is time for the noon break, make sure Mary comes down to my office.' With that, she turned and swept out of the workroom.

'Phew!' Lotty whistled. 'You're for it, Mary. Marching orders.' She drew one finger across her neck in a gesture denoting her fate was sealed.

Mary made no reply. Her mind was in turmoil. She could not decide whether it would be better to eke out her work, in the hope that Madame would keep her on until it was finished, or whether shirking would make her more likely to lose her job altogether. A shaft of pure terror shivered through her, at the sudden realisation that any of the other girls in this room could have accomplished as much as she had done, this week, even on a design as complex as this one.

Worry had reduced her to such a state that by the time Molly pushed her from her stool, and nudged her towards the stairs, she had set scarcely one stitch that would not have to be unpicked and reworked.

'Take a seat, Mary,' said Madame, when Mary timidly entered her office. Madame pointed to a low stool beside a table that was set for a light lunch. Mary decided it was a good omen when she noted two thick slices of plum cake as well as an array of sandwiches. Surely, if Madame was about to turn her off, she would not be doing it over a beautifully prepared repast, served up on the second-best china? She took her place at table, feeling somewhat relieved.

'Now, Mary, I do not want you getting upset by what I have to say. I do not believe a word of it myself, but I have a business to run, and the welfare of the other girls under my employ to consider.' She cocked her head, examining Mary with pursed lips, muttering, 'Not that I suppose you will understand the half of it, but there...nobody will be able to say I did not do my best.'

With a resigned sigh, she poured tea into Mary's cup, adding a splash of milk, and, after an infinitesimal hesitation, half a teaspoon of sugar.

'Sadly, because of a complaint I received today, I am

going to have to send you away from London for a while.'

Leave London! Just when it had finally started to feel like home. And go somewhere else, where she would have to start all over again! Her heart began to pound hard. 'No, Madame, please—'

'It is for your own good,' Madame Pichot broke in. 'London is not safe for you any longer. I told you,' she repeated with exaggerated patience, as though to an imbecile, 'a woman came here this morning and lodged a complaint against you.'

Mary was finding it hard to breathe now. She clutched at the arms of the chair, as though clinging to something tangible could somehow prevent Madame from forcing her to leave.

'I have not done anything—' she began.

'I am sure you have not!' Madame Pichot interposed, with an imperious gesture of her hand. 'Nevertheless, I have to demonstrate that I have taken steps to clear my name. You do understand, don't you?'

Madame squeezed her eyes shut as though recoiling from the impossibility of what she had just said. 'Well, even if you do not, the fact is, just having you under my roof is enough to jeopardise everything I have worked so hard to build up here. So you cannot remain under my roof.'

Mary wondered whether it was worth reminding Madame that she would not even be under this particular roof, if it wasn't for her. When she had first come to work for Madame Pichot, her shop had been only moderately successful. Mary's malady had completely transformed the whole nature of her business. She needed to work like other people needed air to breathe. She accomplished whatever task Madame gave her with a fervour wholly alien to girls who were only there to earn their pay. It was not long before Mary began to turn out gowns that were works of art. Soon, anyone who was anyone simply had to have at least one gown from the previously obscure French dressmaker. Madame had begun to be more discriminating about the clients she took on, and moved into larger premises in the more fashionable Conduit Street.

Mary must have made some inarticulate sound, because Madame's eyes flew open, and she looked at her sharply. 'You need not be alarmed, girl. I am quite sure the whole ghastly business will blow itself out before the end of the Season, and then, well…' She shrugged in that expansive way that indicated anything might be possible.

'You mean, I can come back?'

'You have always been a good worker,' Madame replied, with a wry smile. 'Better than I expected when I took you on. Drink some tea, girl,' she said in a bracing tone, 'and stop looking as though you were facing the end of the world. I am only sending you to Bath.'

'Bath?'

'Yes, on the six o' clock mail. I have already purchased your ticket. Have you finished that piece of work yet? Because if you have not, I shall have to get one of the others to pack your overnight bag. And put the rest of your things into a trunk, which I shall send on by carrier.'

'Bath,' Mary repeated, in a daze.

'Yes, Bath. Not so fashionable as it once was, but still full of shops that cater to the wealthy patrons of the city. And plenty of work available for a girl with your skills with a needle. I still have contacts with several dressmakers in the town. While Molly is packing up your things, I shall be writing a letter for you to take with you.'

Bath. She was not simply being turned out on to the streets to fend for herself. She would have work, and presumably somewhere to live. But before she could gather her thoughts and form them into questions, Madame put an end to the interview.

The afternoon rushed past in a flurry of activity, during which she had no leisure to speak to anyone except in snatched, furtive asides. Madame seemed to be everywhere at once, getting a trunk and a small valise hauled out of storage, and thoroughly dusted down, sending Molly to separate her things into two piles, one to tide her over the first few days, and the rest for sending on later.

Joe winked at her solemnly as they got into the cab that was to take them to Cheapside, reminding her again of the threat Madame had made regarding Molly's position.

'You will need Molly more now, won't you?' she managed to pluck up the courage to say once they set out for the coaching inn. 'Since I am leaving. You will not turn her off now, will you?'

'Impudence!' Madame muttered, turning her head away sharply.

Mary knew there would be no point in arguing any more. From the grim set of Madame's mouth, she had already made up her mind. The further they got from Madame's shop, the more upset Mary became.

Her one, meagre consolation was that she had managed to scribble a note on a slip of tracing paper, and hide it in Molly's scissor sheath, warning her that Madame did not mean to keep her on once the Season ended. It might give her the chance to make plans, at least. Perhaps she would finally marry Joe.

It was not easy to clamber out of the cab with her overnight case in one hand, and the basket of provisions Kitty had made up for her, in the other. But Madame did not stop to offer her any assistance. She strode off down the passage that led to the Swan with Two Necks, forcing Mary to trot to catch up with her.

She paused for a moment when they entered the yard, stunned by the sheer volume of noise that reverberated round the enclosed space. Horses whinnied and snorted as grooms led them towards the line of coaches drawn up beneath an overhanging balcony. There was the regular thumping of bags being tossed into the boots of coaches, the occasional crash of another being dumped onto the cobbles. The owners of the goods thus casually handled protested, and were answered with a volley of derision from insolent ostlers. The whole place appeared to her like a scene of utter confusion. Scores of people seemed to be scurrying about, ducking into doorways, or emerging from them with bewildering rapidity.

Mary instinctively clutched her belongings tightly, as though they were her only safe anchor in this whirlpool of transient humanity.

'There is your coach,' Madame suddenly announced, plunging through the maelstrom towards one of the smaller vehicles, a black, rather dusty-looking coach with the royal coat of arms emblazoned on the doors. The lower half of its body, she saw when she got a bit closer, was not covered in dried mud as she had supposed, but painted a dull brown. Mailbags were already piled high on its roof, while various other items of luggage were still being lifted from the ground, and tossed into the forward boot.

A large man, swathed in a wide-skirted green coat with large brass buttons swaggered up to the coach, clambered on to the driving seat, settled himself with a regal air, and pulled out his pocket watch. The bustling around his particular vehicle increased in frenzy.

Mary's own heart picked up speed.

'Make haste,' said Madame Pichot, pushing her in the small of her back. 'I know you do not wish to leave, any more than I wish to part with you, but at least in Bath you will be safe from That Man.'

'Yes,' Mary replied, her eyes skittering over the flaking paint, which made the coat of arms look like a crumbly cheese, to the rather gloomy interior of the coach. She could just, barely, make out a double stripe of crimson through the mud that coated the worn carpet. 'Yes,' she repeated, bolstering herself with the thought that it was far better to have honest work, than to fall into the clutches of a man about whom she knew virtually nothing. Leaving London would at least deliver her from the temptation he had been posing. And she would get used to Bath. Same as she had got used to London. 'I want to be safe,' she declared, ducking her head as she got inside, and took the one remaining seat.

She placed her valise on the floor between her feet, and set the basket on her lap.

'Here,' said Madame, leaning in and holding out a coin. 'You will need this to tip the guard.'

Mary took the proffered half-crown from Madame's outstretched hand with a rush of heartfelt gratitude. Madame had not *had* to pay the extra for an inside seat. She need not have arranged for her to get work in Bath at all, come to that. She knew Madame was motivated more by practicality than true charity, and yet, over the years she had grown quite fond of the gruff, no-nonsense woman who had taken such a risk in employing her at all.

'I will miss you, Madame,' she admitted shyly. 'I hope I may come back soon.'

Madame reared back, two spots of colour staining her cheeks. But she did not have the chance to make any reply. Somebody slammed the door, the guard blew the horn, and the coach lurched forwards. Mary pressed her face to the window to wave farewell, and saw Madame standing with her fists clenched, her brows drawn down into a fierce scowl as she watched the coach depart.

The scowl put some heart back into Mary. Madame seemed really angry at having to do without her, even temporarily. She might have known Madame would not want to lose the worker who had achieved so much for her, at so little cost.

She patted her pocket, feeling the letter that Madame had given her rustle reassuringly. She still felt somewhat nervous to be leaving the only home she could remember, but it was not as if it would be for ever. Madame valued her enough to want her to return.

She couldn't help contrasting the way she felt now at leaving the noisy, bustling metropolis, from the day she had first come here. She kept her face glued to the window as the coach rattled through familiar streets, bidding them a silent farewell. She had been almost beside herself with fear, back then, the letter of introduction she'd had in her pocket then bringing her no reassurance whatsoever. It had been even worse when she had alighted. The citizens of London were all so busy. Far too busy to stop and give directions to a bedraggled little waif fresh from the country.

But she had made it to Madame's shop, she reminded herself, lifting her chin. Madame had taken her in, and encouraged her to focus on what she could achieve, rather than getting all worked up about things she had no control over. That was what she must do now.

She had no idea what her new employer would be like, or if she would find another friend like Molly to help her settle into her new surroundings. But she had survived a far bigger upheaval in her life once. And she was stronger, calmer and more confident now than she had been when she'd arrived.

The choked city streets gave way to suburbs that were completely alien to her far sooner than she would have believed possible. Jostling buildings petered out into hamlets interspersed with fields. She craned her neck to keep her eyes fixed on the pall of smoke that hung over the horizon where the town's chimneys still breathed, but eventually even that last link with the only home she had ever known was severed.

Only then did she sit back in her seat and glance timidly at the other occupants of the coach. When she had boarded, she had only taken note of three bundles of assorted clothing occupying three corners of the dingy interior. Now they resolved themselves into human form.

All three, she noted on a swallow of dismay, were men.

Quickly, before any of them noticed her furtive glances, she looked down at the basket on her lap, her heart thudding alarmingly. It would be hours and hours until they reached Bath. The coach travelled non-stop right through the night. Already the shadows of the trees and hedges they were rattling past were growing longer. Soon it would be completely dark, and she would be shut up in here with three strange men… She sniffed, suddenly recognising the sweet fruity smell of spirits that hung in the air. Three strange men who were very far from sober.

Her stomach lurched. And not only because of the pothole the coach had bounced over.

She gripped the handle of her basket tightly, keeping her attention focused on its contents. The men would take no notice of her, if she took no notice of them. Why should they? As Madame was always telling her, she was naught but a scrap of skin and bone, of no interest to any red-blooded male…

Except Lord Matthison, a defiant spark of pride contradicted Madame's scathing tones.

Ah, well, but he was only drawn to her because she looked a bit like someone he had once cared about, pointed out Madame's voice with crushing accuracy.

Mary sighed wistfully. She did not suppose she would ever look into those dark, haunted eyes again. Or feel that hard mouth seeking a response from her startled, untried lips.

And that was for the best, she decided, unpicking the knot of the muslin square in which her supper was tied. Far better to sigh over what might have been, than plunge headlong into a course of action that could only be ruinous.

The cloth parted, and she discovered it contained a chicken leg, a wedge of cheese, an apple and a couple of slices of the plum cake she'd had at lunch.

At least eating gave her something to take her mind off the fact that she was shut up in cramped quarters with three complete strangers.

By the time she had finished her supper, two of the other passengers were snoring loudly. With their bodies slumped into their respective corners, hats over their eyes, they had gone right back to resembling nothing so much as untidy heaps of laundry.

That would be the way to cope with them. To think

of them as sacks of laundry, rather than men. In fact, if she shut her eyes, not only would it blot them from her sight, but she might even be able to doze a little, too. After all, they all seemed to be managing it.

Men, though, she soon found out, were far less inhibited creatures than women, even when asleep. She had to retreat deeper and deeper into her corner as their lax limbs sprawled all over the place. They produced a lot more unpleasant smells, too, at far greater volume than she had believed the human body capable of emitting. And even if it had not been for the sprawling, and the snoring, and the belching—not to mention the other noxious effusions they all began to produce at regular intervals—Mary would not have been able to sleep for more than a few snatched moments at a time, because the guard blew his horn at every turnpike, loudly enough to rouse even the slender young gentleman next to her, who was the most obviously inebriated of them all.

Mary was the only passenger who got out every time the coach stopped for a change of horses. She welcomed the chance to breathe fresh air for a few minutes, and walked up and down to stretch out her cramped limbs.

By the time they pulled up in the yard of the White Hart, just before ten the next morning, she felt as though she had been through a wringer. She eyed the others with resentment as they unfolded themselves from their respective corners. Though they looked a little crumpled, every one of them managed to collect their luggage, and then disperse, flapping across the yard like washing torn from the line by a gusting wind.

She flopped down the steps, limp and shaky, and would have slithered onto the cobbles if the guard had not grabbed her by the arm, and held her upright until she steadied.

'Someone comin' to meet yer?' he asked gruffly.

Mary hoped he did not notice how badly she wanted him to remove his great meaty paw from her arm. He was only trying to be helpful.

Mustering up a wan smile, she shook her head, explaining, 'I only have to get as far as Orange Grove, though. I believe it is not far?'

He shrugged. 'You best ask the landlord.'

To her relief, he let go of her arm then, to point to one of the doors leading off the yard. 'Get something warm inside you while you're at it.'

'Thank you,' she said, nodding as though she planned to follow his sage advice to the letter. Then she reached into her pocket and handed over the half-crown Madame had provided for her to tip him.

It worked like a charm. With a grin and a nod, he pocketed the money and stumped off towards the posting offices.

Mary lingered on the premises only long enough to get directions from one of the many porters employed there. She did not have any money to buy refreshments, and was besides so weary that all she wanted was to reach her destination, find a horizontal surface that was not bouncing about, and sleep the clock round.

She took the road the porter had pointed out, and the right-hand junction that he said led down to Orange Grove. It came out in the middle of a thoroughfare, which ran as far as she could see in either direction. To begin with, Mary turned the wrong way. She had to retrace her steps before finding Number Eight.

Which was a wig-maker's.

Puzzled, Mary pulled the letter from her pocket and looked at the address again, in case she had remembered it wrong. But, no. In Madame's neat round hand, it clearly stated *Cleopatra's, 8 Orange Grove, Bath.*

Perhaps, in all the hurry, Madame had put down the wrong number. Perhaps Cleopatra's was at number eighteen, or eight and twenty. Mary walked all the way up one side of the street, then all the way down the other, but none of the shops bore the name she sought.

Completely perplexed, she made her way back to the wig-maker's. Perhaps this had been the correct address, but the modiste had moved on. If so, she only hoped the new shopkeeper knew where the former tenant had gone.

To her dismay, the rather forbidding gentleman who came to the counter informed her in extremely frosty accents, when she asked if he had recently taken over the business from a modiste, that his shop had belonged to his father before him, and to his father's father before that. She left hastily, feeling embarrassed at having offended him, and unsure what to do next.

There had been, she recalled, a milliner on the corner, towards the High Street. She might have heard of Cleopatra's.

The milliner had not, but when, in a burst of inspiration, Mary further enquired if there was anyone in Bath who might have a connection with Madame Pichot, her eyes lit up.

'The French *émigrée* who makes such exquisite gowns for the *ton*?' she breathed. 'I did not know she had ever set foot in Bath!'

Mary frowned. Mentioning feet had reminded her how badly her own were hurting. Her boots seemed to have shrunk during the night, and felt as though they were sawing through the knuckles of her toes. Her head was beginning to ache, too, as she grew more confused and tired.

Had Madame actually said she had worked in Bath? She shook her head, bewildered. That conversation had grown hazy. She could not remember *exactly* what she had said. Only that she had mentioned having connections here. She looked down at the letter, which was beginning to look rather the worse for wear, wondering exactly what the connection with this Cleopatra was.

'If it is a high-class modiste you are seeking,' put in the milliner kindly, on seeing Mary's strained face, 'you might do better looking on Milsom Street.'

'Thank you,' said Mary, grateful for any suggestion that might lead her to the elusive salon. And, though her legs felt as though they belonged to a newborn foal, she set out in the direction the kindly woman had pointed with renewed determination.

Milsom Street was full of shops, the pavements thronging with their smartly dressed customers. But none of them, she ascertained by walking all the way up one side, and right back down the other, bore the name of Cleopatra above the door. The only thing she could think of was to go into every one that had anything even remotely to do with fashion, or might conceivably employ workers with a talent for stitchery. None of them could help her. And, as it came on to rain, and her appearance grew increasingly bedraggled, they became less than polite in the way they expressed their inability to be of help.

Cleopatra's must be somewhere! Why could nobody tell her where it was? Or had she somehow muddled up the directions? 'Stop and think,' she muttered under her breath. She had to get out of the rain, and try to work out what to do!

Ducking into a doorway out of the worst of the rain, Mary pulled the rather dog-eared letter out of her pocket yet again, and looked at the direction, half expecting it to be completely different from what she remembered seeing the last time she had looked.

But it still said Number Eight, Orange Grove.

It went against all her principles, but she knew the only way to get any more information about the mysteriously elusive Cleopatra was to open the letter and read it herself. Setting her bags down on the step, out of the puddles, she tugged off her gloves, turned the letter over, and broke the wafer sealing the single sheet of paper closed.

And her eyes widened in sheer disbelief.

There was nothing written on it at all.

She was holding a blank piece of paper in her hand.

She went cold inside as she realised what this meant.

There was no job. Probably no such person as Cleopatra. She was all alone, in a strange town, without a penny to her name.

For some reason, what hurt her the most was the way Madame had smiled when she had given her money to tip the guard. He was probably tucked up in snug lodgings right now, his belly full of tavern fare paid for with her half-crown, while she…her stomach clenched, feeling completely hollow, yet full of ice at the same time.

And that was when she began to shake.

She had trusted Madame. Molly had warned her what the woman was like, and she had still trusted her. She had got into the coach and actually *thanked* her for sending her away.

A gust of wind blew rain into the doorway, sprinkling the sheet of paper at which she was still staring in blank horror. And a wave of desolation swamped her, black and sickeningly familiar. She knew she had been alone, and cold and wet and miserable before. Feeling betrayed and deceived…

At that very moment, a shadow fell across the doorway. Even before she lifted her head, she knew who would be standing there. For some reason, she just knew that Lord Matthison would materialise out of the driving rain and deepening shadows to embody her feelings of misery and betrayal. She lifted her head with a sense of inevitability, and held out the blank sheet of paper, where her future security should have been written.

'It is all your fault,' she said.

He took it from her, frowning when he turned it over, and saw what Madame Pichot had done to her.

Then he looked straight at her, his expression as blank as the piece of paper he held.

'Not all of it, Cora. But even so, I shall put it all to rights.'

She did not ask him what he meant. She knew why he had come. Had known the second he called her Cora.

He picked up her valise, and held out his arm.

There was nowhere to run, no other choice she could make.

Head bowed, she laid her hand on his sleeve, and set out into the rain beside him.

Chapter Five

Mary was lost too deep in the maze of her own thoughts to notice where he was taking her. Why had Madame done this to her? Why? How could she have deliberately stranded her in a strange place, with no money, when she knew how badly it would scare her!

She stumbled, as something inside her seemed to curl up, twisting painfully at the thought of how stupid she must have looked, thanking Madame for sending her to Bath, and saying how she would miss her! She clung a little tighter to Lord Matthison's arm as she imagined Madame chuckling all the way back to the shop. For the price of a ticket on the mail, and half a crown to tip the guard, she had persuaded Mary to leave London quietly, thus averting the scandal the complaining woman had threatened to unleash. By making it look as though she *had* provided generously for Mary, she had dealt with the prospect of having to preside over workers simmering with resentment, too. Not that there would be much any of them could do, but she knew that if they learned of her current plight, they would all be angry on her behalf. For she had become one of them. Against all her expectations, considering the way they had once intimidated her with their cocksure ways and coarse language, she had forged a place for herself in that workroom.

She pictured them, clustered on the stairs, listening to that final interview she'd had in Madame's office, with their eyes to the knotholes, taking in the significance of the plum cake and the second-best china. And a cold hand seemed to reach into her chest and squeeze. Could Madame have known they were watching? Was that why she had been so determined to spell out exactly why she was sending her away, even though she was convinced Mary would not understand the half of it?

It all made a horrible kind of sense. If Madame *had* known her workers were in the habit of spying on her, she had used that knowledge to her own advantage, rather than reprimanding them.

'As I expected,' she heard Lord Matthison saying, 'the journey down has exhausted my wife. I trust you have our room ready?'

Mary blinked in bewilderment at finding herself standing in the foyer of what she had to assume was a respectable hotel, judging from the elegance of its décor.

'Indeed,' a neatly dressed man she supposed must be the landlord replied. 'If you would come this way?'

Wife? She frowned. 'But…'

'Not now,' Lord Matthison bent to murmur in her ear.

'You may berate me as soundly as you please once we are in private, but not just yet, hmm?'

He slipped his arm round her waist, and with all the appearance of a solicitous husband supported her up the stairs and along the maze of corridors that led to their room.

Their room. As she crossed the threshold, she took note of the single large tester bed standing at one end of the rectangular room, along with a washstand and clothes press. At the other, set before a cheerfully blazing fire, stood a small table and two inviting wing-backed chairs. A far cry from the kind of opulence she guessed a man of Lord Matthison's means would be used to. But then, as he led her towards the seating area, she caught the landlord eyeing her dishevelled appearance, then flicking an assessing glance at the plain overcoat that completely concealed Lord Matthison's exquisite tailoring. To him, they probably looked like any moderately well-to-do couple, who could not afford a suite.

As the landlord made to leave, Lord Matthison turned towards him, and began issuing a series of requests. Mary scarcely took them in. The sight of the fire had reminded her how very cold and wet she was. She left his side, and kept on going till she stood right in front of it. Crouching down by the fender, she held out her hands to the flames. She was not wearing her gloves. That was right, she had taken them off to open the letter. The letter that was no letter at all, but a symbol of the most horrible cruelty, perpetrated by a mean-spirited woman on a stupid, gullible fool…

Shaking with the force of her indignation, Mary reached into her pocket where she had shoved the letter after Lord Matthison had handed it back to her.

Molly had been right all along! She ripped the page in half. All Madame cared about was profit! She ripped the pieces in half again. She'd had Kitty packing up a meal, and Molly packing her trunk. Rip. Which, she suddenly realised on a fresh wave of anger, the old miser had no intention of sending on. Rip. Indeed she could not, because she knew very well Mary had nowhere to go. The pieces were now so small that Mary was having a struggle to tear them again. Furious at her inability to even tear the letter to bits small enough to satisfy her, she flung them into the flames with a cry of utter vexation.

'That's better,' said a dark voice from behind her, making her jump. She had almost forgotten Lord Matthison was there, for a moment, so completely consumed was she by the dreadful sense of betrayal she had felt, as she had stumbled through the devious workings of Madame's mind.

Lord Matthison thanked God he had employed Grit to keep an eye on the comings and goings at Madame Pichot's emporium. The lad had been bright enough to recognise the significance of the French woman taking Mary off in a cab, laden with luggage rather than carrying the neatly wrapped parcels that one might expect to see coming out of a dressmaker's shop.

He had known he had no chance of catching up with the night mail, but the amount of money he'd disbursed at the White Hart had soon bought him the information he needed. After securing a room at the Pelican he had made for Orange Grove, all fired up to enquire at every shop until he had located Cora. In the event, he had not needed to. She had been wandering up and down, in a bewildered state, alternately looking at the letter she held in her hand, and examining the numbers over shop doors. He had not intended to approach her today. The things he had learned from the jarveys had made him wary of frightening her. He just needed to find out where she was going to live before returning to his own hotel where he could work out what to do next.

As the day had worn on, he had witnessed her descent into exhaustion and despair. And eventually realised he could not leave her alone to deal with whatever it was that had so shocked her about the letter she had been clutching like a talisman.

He had crossed the street, all thoughts of remaining concealed from her erased by the conviction he had to help her. He had experienced a flare of triumph when he had perceived that she had no option but to accept his immediate protection.

But that triumph had been short-lived. The moment she had laid her hand on his sleeve in a gesture of weary defeat had been like suffering a blow to his heart. He had thought she looked fragile when he had discovered her in the Flash of Lightning. But it was only a foretaste of how she looked now. He'd had to half-carry her up the stairs, and the dazed look in her eyes had made him wonder if she was on the verge of a complete collapse.

So it was a relief to see a resurgence of some spirit, to see her rip up that damnable sheet of paper, and utter that cry of protest against all that life had flung at her. To know that this latest ordeal had not been the breaking of her after all.

'You will feel better still, once you have got out of your wet clothing, and had something to eat,' he said.

'You have no idea what will make me feel better!'

How could he stand there, so calmly, talking about eating, when her life lay in ruins?

Because he did not care. He had brought her to this. He had betrayed her! Held her in his arms, and kissed her, when all the time…

She lurched to her feet on a wave of anguish and fury. Her fists were already raised before she knew how badly she wanted to hit him. But she did not manage to land a single blow. He caught hold of her wrists, his reactions lightning swift.

She flailed out at his imprisoning hands, kicking ineffectually at his booted legs. His eyes widened in horror, then narrowed with grim purpose as he lifted her bodily off her feet and began to drag her across the room.

Her anger flipped to wild, ungovernable panic at the realisation that she could do nothing to prevent him forcing her on to the bed. She began to twist in his hold, clawing at him like a cat.

It took her a full five minutes before she realised that, far from flinging her on to the bed and ravishing her, he was merely restraining her in one of the armchairs.

She stopped trying to escape him, and looked up into his face. She was wrecked from the exertions of struggling against a being so much stronger than herself, but he was not even breathing hard. He looked completely in control of himself. While she had just behaved like some kind of…a wild woman!

Oh, it was all true, what they said about her! She was not right in the head! How could she have attacked the poor man like that! *He* was not the one who had betrayed her, and robbed her of the future she had worked so hard for so many years to secure. It was Madame Pichot who had done all that.

With a whimper of shame, she let her head fall forwards, on to his breast. And as her breathing slowed, and her heart quieted, the odour of singed wool permeated her senses.

And she felt even worse. When she had leapt to her feet, she had been careless of her proximity to the fire. Lord Matthison had only been pulling her away from the flames.

'I…I'm s-sorry,' she gulped.

His hands eased the pressure they had been exerting on her shoulders.

'Can I let you go now? Will you stay in that chair, and do nothing that might put yourself in danger?'

She nodded, too ashamed of her loss of control to muster up an adequate apology for having so badly misjudged his intentions.

It was only when he pulled away, and went to sit on the chair on the other side of the hearth that she could tell how shaken he was, too. His face was white, and his hands, as they curled round the arms of the chair, were trembling. It must be frightening, she expected, to have a crazy woman leap on you!

'You *do* need to get out of your wet clothes, though, Cora,' he repeated.

'My name is Mary,' she reminded him defiantly as she began to fumble at the buttons of her coat. That episode had stripped her of what little remained of her dignity. She had to claw it back somehow! And reminding herself that *he* was just as capable of leaping to the wrong conclusions about a person was a start.

'Whatever you call yourself,' he said so patiently it roused a strong desire to throw her sodden, singed coat at him, 'you need to accept the fact that I have no wish to see you hurt yourself. Nor,' he went on more firmly, 'will I let anyone else hurt you. I just want to look after you now. Protect you.'

Her fingers stilled on the strings of her bonnet. Protect her! Offering a woman protection was just another way of saying he wanted to make her his mistress, she knew that much, however simple everybody thought her.

But surely, if he really believed she was his lost love, he would not be offering her that kind of relationship? She eyed him with renewed suspicion. Had he known all along she was not the dead woman who had taken his heart to the grave? Was he not the tortured soul she had thought him at all?

She heaved a sigh as she lifted the bonnet from her

head. She was clearly no judge of character. Look at how wrong she had been about Madame Pichot.

The complaining woman from the showroom had accused him of trying to evade doing his duty to her daughter. Claiming Mary was his long-lost fiancée would get him off the hook all right…but not, she frowned as she leaned down to place her bonnet in the hearth to dry, if he only planned to make her his mistress! Many married men still kept mistresses.

And she had said he was evil. Kitty had said there were whispers he was in league with the devil. That all his luck at the gaming tables stemmed from a horrible murder he had committed of a young woman who he'd lured to his estate. Learning about that was what had made Molly change her mind about the advisability of Mary embarking on a relationship with him. It did seem odd, she thought, darting him a sideways glance, the way he had materialised out of the rain just when she was at her most vulnerable. How had he known she was in Bath? Let alone arriving the very minute she had discovered she was completely and utterly destitute?

A shiver racked her whole body, and instinctively she wrapped her arms about her waist.

'I don't care how much you pay me,' she said as firmly as she dared, 'I won't pretend to be somebody I am not, just so that you can get out of marrying someone you should never have asked in the first place if you do not love her.'

'What?' Lord Matthison sat bolt upright, staring at her as though she had just sprouted two heads.

But before either of them could say another word, a hotel waiter had knocked and entered, bearing a tray of coffee and sandwiches. While he was setting it down on the table, they sat eyeing each other, like two prizefighters getting their breath back between rounds.

'Will that be all, sir?'

'Not quite,' Lord Matthison bit out. 'Would you be so good as to take my wife's coat and bonnet, and dry them? And her boots, too, if you would not mind waiting for a moment.'

And then he was on his knees at her feet, deftly unlacing her boots, sliding them off, and handing them over to the wooden-faced waiter.

'Madam's things will be dried, brushed and returned first thing in the morning,' the man assured them, almost managing to conceal his disgust at the state of Mary's clothing. It wasn't until he had left the room with her coat draped over his arm, her boots dangling from his fingers, that it hit her that she was now trapped in this room overnight, with a man who was so determined to make her his mistress, he had pursued her all the way to Bath. She had just been so glad to see the back of those wretchedly uncomfortable boots she had not paused to think what the consequences of handing them over would be.

It would be useless to apply to any of the hotel staff for aid, now. She had walked into this establishment leaning on her would-be seducer's arm. They would not believe her excuse that she had been too dazed by the enormity of Madame's cruelty to know what she had been doing.

Besides, if she did attempt to escape him, where would she go? What could she do? She knew of nobody who might help her find work. Not just here in Bath. Not anywhere.

While she sat in gloomy contemplation of her utter stupidity in playing right into his hands, Lord Matthison calmly began pouring the coffee and making a selection from the plate of sandwiches, which he then handed to her.

The fragrant aroma of coffee made her nostrils twitch, and the daintily cut sandwiches set her mouth watering. She promptly decided that whatever was going to happen next, there was no point in trying to deal with it on an empty stomach.

And so it was that the chambermaid who came in not five minutes later with a can of hot water, found them sitting by the fire, facing each other, sipping coffee and tucking into their sandwiches like any unremarkable, staid married couple.

She felt her last chance of explaining to a member of the hotel staff that she was being kidnapped, or seduced, or at the very least, being forced into a situation that was completely repugnant to her, slip away while Lord Matthison ordered the disposing of the hot water, basin and towels.

And then he was kneeling at her feet again, a towel slung over his shoulder.

'Do not make a fuss about this,' he said sternly. 'Just remove your stockings so I can tend to your feet.'

The idea of a lord washing the feet of a seamstress was so shocking that Mary just sat there gaping at him.

'If you do not remove them,' he warned her, 'I shall be obliged to do it for you.'

'W-why?' she said stupidly. Why would he want to wash her feet?

'They are bleeding. Did you not know?'

She looked down, and saw that he was right. Her toes were numb with cold, but there was no mistaking the bloodstains on her stockings from where the boots had rubbed her feet raw. It would be silly to fight him over an issue like this, she decided, putting her half-eaten sandwich down. Besides, they had already established that when it came to a contest of brute strength, he must always be the victor.

As she reached up under her skirts to untie her garters, Lord Matthison turned away, bringing the basin of warm water closer to her chair, so that she could put her bared feet straight into it.

It seemed a remarkably considerate thing for an evil seducer and murderer of women to do. It would have been more in character for him to leer lasciviously as she peeled off her stockings. She studied the top of his bent head as he lathered his hands.

'I beg your pardon,' he murmured when she winced as he gently began to soap the raw skin.

His strong hands were incredibly gentle as he lifted her feet on to the towel he had spread over his thigh, and patted them dry. She felt tears spring to her eyes at the tenderness of his ministrations. It was all a far cry from how she might have expected him to treat her.

Could a man in league with the devil be capable of acting with such kindness?

'How, then?' she murmured as she wondered how he had managed to appear like a genie from a lamp at the most opportune moment. 'I mean,' she explained at his puzzled frown, 'how did you find me?'

'I followed you, as soon as I heard your employer had put you on the night mail, of course.'

'How did you hear I had got on the night mail?'

'I had been having you watched.'

She shuddered at the thought that someone had been watching her movements without her suspecting a thing. It was almost as horrible as thinking he had been able to locate her by supernatural means. Her revulsion must have shown on her face, because he said,

'I have had you watched from the day I found you. You didn't think I would let you slip through my fingers again, did you? After all I have been through these last seven years?'

'People don't behave like this,' she said, wondering what on earth possessed him to act in such a way. And then she closed her eyes, on a wave of giddiness. Everything she had believed about everyone she knew had been turned upside down so many times this day! 'This is like…a nightmare…'

'The nightmare is over, now,' he insisted. 'I have told you, I will look after you now. You have nothing to fear. I won't let you fall into the hands of unscrupulous people like that seamstress who treated you little better than a slave.'

She opened her eyes, saw the determined set of his jaw, and realised it was pointless getting upset with him.

It was not his fault she looked like the woman he had loved and lost. Not his fault Madame had vented her spite by pitching her into the worst possible scenario she could have invented. In fact, if anything, she felt sorry for him. For a moment, she had a crazy urge to reach out and put her arms round him. To tell him that she understood he believed he was doing the right thing, and did not hold it against him.

Instead, she ran her hand shakily round to the nape of her neck, closing her eyes against the need burning from his. He might say she had nothing to fear from him, but wealthy men did not pursue poor girls for any other reason than to amuse themselves for a while in bed. She might feel sorry for him, she might accept he sincerely believed he was coming to her rescue, but that did not mean she was going to abandon all her principles!

Even as she wondered how on earth she could find the words to explain all that was going on in her mind, when she was not sure she fully understood herself, he rose to his knees, placing one hand on each of the arms of her chair.

'Cora,' he grated, in a voice so full of pain and longing it touched her at the deepest level, 'wake up and love me again.'

She knew the second before he did it that he was going to kiss her. Or at least, kiss the image of Cora that she represented.

She had not the heart to repulse him, after that heartfelt plea. So she made no move to stop him.

Just before his mouth brushed against hers, she tensed, expecting to feel the dismay and revulsion that normally overcame her when a man got too close. But it did not materialise. Instead she felt a very strong wish that she could somehow take away his pain. A single tear slipped from behind her tightly closed eyelids as she put her arms round him, and began, very inexpertly, to kiss him back.

Her heart speeded up. She had dreamed of him kissing her like this, night after night.

Oh, how she wished she *was* the woman he had loved so much he was incapable of letting her go.

But she was not.

Her eyes flew open in dismay.

'No,' she said, her hands sliding from behind his neck, to push against his shoulders. 'This is all wrong. I am not *her*.'

'You are!' he insisted, the anguish in his eyes bringing fresh tears to her own. 'I did not believe it myself at first,' he said. 'I thought you were a ghost. And then, when I had sobered up, that you were just a woman who resembled Cora somewhat. That was why I came to find you. To prove to myself that it was a trick of the light, or...' He ran his fingers through his hair, leaving the damp locks ridged and furrowed. 'But then you spoke. And I touched you. Cora…' He seized her hands and began squeezing them repeatedly, as though assuring himself she was still there. 'No woman has ever been able to stir my blood the way you do. It is as though I've come back to life, after seven long years of wishing I was dead!'

She blinked at him, a shock running right through her. For she knew exactly what he meant. When he held her in his arms, and kissed her, it was as though she had come to life, too. She knew no other man could have this effect on her.

It *was* as though they belonged together.

But it could not be…

Seeing her tiny shake of the head, he groaned, and buried his face in her neck, clutching her to him so tightly it was a wonder she could still breathe.

'I'm sorry,' she murmured, stroking his hair. 'So sorry.'

She wished she did not have to hurt him. If only she was the kind of girl, like Molly perhaps, who would not mind pretending to be who he wanted her to be.

It seemed to take a long time before he stopped shaking. But even then, she could not bring herself to let him go. Holding him was a harmless enough way of comforting him. If only there was some other way she could help ease his suffering, without sacrificing her principles.

And perhaps there was.

'If,' she began hesitantly, 'I really was Cora, would you be treating me like this?'

'What?' he reared back, looking thunderstruck.

'She was a proper lady, was she not?' She must have been if she had been betrothed to this lord. 'You would not have taken her into a hotel, and kissed her and held her like this. You would have cared about protecting her reputation.'

She could see him take her argument on board, struggle with it briefly, then toss it ruthlessly aside.

'I am not letting you out of my sight again. Who knows where you might vanish off to if I once let down my guard!' He leapt to his feet, paced away, then rounded on her, fists clenched at his sides. 'And it is not as if you have any reputation left for me, or any other man to ruin is it? Not any more!'

Mary wondered why she did not feel in the least bit scared by this blatant display of masculine outrage.

But then it hit her that it was because it was not aimed at her, but at Cora.

And that it was Cora who had to answer his objections, if Mary was to stay safe.

'Are you saying you no longer care about my reputation?' she challenged him.

'No, I am not, damn you!' he snarled. 'It is your physical safety, your well-being that matter to me, not some damn stupid convention that would have us lying apart in separate beds all night. Cora, I need to hold you, to know I have you back! Do you think I would sleep a wink if you were in another room, when I have already spent the last seven years wondering where you are? Don't ask me to leave you.'

No, she sighed, she could not ask that of him. Not

when it would be such a cruel thing to do. She had already experienced far too much of cruelty for one day.

'Very well,' she sighed, though she knew she was going to regret it. 'I will not ask you to leave. But,' she said, lifting her chin in a gesture of defiance that was probably futile, 'I will not share your bed.'

'Not until we are married,' he agreed, a look of profound relief on his face.

'Married? I cannot marry you!'

'But of course we are going to be married. What do you think I meant when I said I would not let you out of my sight?' He looked wounded. 'Cora, you cannot think that because I said you had no reputation now that I could possibly be offering you anything less than marriage?' He looked as though she had struck him. 'I see that you did. What have I done to make you think that of me?'

Nothing, she realised. She had been troubled by the rumours others whispered about him, but she had never quite been able to believe them completely. Somehow she had always known that Lord Matthison was not evil. He was hurt, and angry and confused. That was what made him act in a way that seemed reprehensible to others. But she ought to have known better.

'It is nothing you have done,' she said in a contrite voice. 'It is who you are. Men of your class *never* offer marriage to girls of mine.'

He spun back to her, his face clearing.

'Of course. You still don't believe you are my Cora, do you?'

He returned to the chair opposite hers, and sat forwards, his hands clasped between his knees, looking intently at her.

'Very well, if you are not Cora, then who are you?'

Her heart leapt. 'Are you ready to hear the truth at last?'

And then it plunged. If she made him believe it, what then? The only thing that gave her any hold over him was his belief she was a lady. Once he accepted she was just a poor seamstress, she would have no means to prevent him doing exactly what she feared the most.

'Yes. Tell me…' He paused, then said with deliberation, 'Mary, where do you come from? Who were your parents?'

It was the first time he had addressed her by her real name. The truth was going to come out, now, no matter what the outcome.

She looked into the black depths of his eyes, and felt the shadows creeping closer. 'The truth,' she managed on a strangled whisper. She wished now she had not challenged him to seek the truth. Whenever she had tried to examine what lurked buried in the depths of her mind, all she had ever discovered was that it was dark and horrible and painful.

Uttering a little whimper, she began to massage the back of her neck, where the muscles had gone rigid with stress.

'I don't know!' she finally managed to admit. 'I don't know who my parents were. Though, sometimes, I think I remember my mother.'

Because he had asked it of her, she delved inwards, towards the vague image of the kindly, calming presence that had urged her to keep her mind on her sampler. 'She taught me to sew.'

'That is good,' Lord Matthison murmured. 'Is there any more?'

He reached across the space between them and laid his hand over the one with which she was clutching at the arm of the chair. 'What of your father?'

There was that menacing figure beyond her mother. The one she had never quite dared to try to examine. The one her mother had been so determined to shield her from. The one with the loud voice and the hard fists.

'He used to hit me!' Now she knew why it was second nature for her to sit quietly at her needlework, striving to become invisible to anyone else that might be in the room. 'He was always angry. Nothing I did was ever good enough.'

And then, before she could prevent it, a horrible image flashed into her mind. Of a woman lying on the floor, curled up on her side, with a man crouching over her, pounding her with his fists.

'Cora, Cora, what is it, where have you gone?'

She blinked, coming back to the present to find Lord Matthison holding both her hands between his, his dark eyes full of concern.

'He used to beat her, too…' She shivered. The image was so stark, so terrifying, the sense of loss and horror so deeply imbedded in her psyche that she suddenly knew why she flinched from the prospect of reclaiming any of her memories. 'I think he might have killed her.'

She had to block out this shattering revelation from her past! She had to turn her mind away from the horror. But she had no work to occupy her hands. No soothing, repetitive activity to calm her troubled mind. She got to her feet, in agitation, her breath coming in thin, reedy gasps.

In an instant, Lord Matthison was on his feet beside her. He hauled her into his arms, and began to rock her, crooning soft, soothing nonsense into her ears. And because there was nothing else she could use to block out those images, she concentrated completely on him. On the feel of his hands, running up and down her back. The sound of his voice, telling her over and over again that she was safe. The scent of his skin where her nose butted up against his neck. And the violent images gradually faded away, her breathing slowed, and the panic receded. She was not *there* any more. She was standing in a hotel room in Bath, with the fire crackling cheerfully in the grate, and the coffee cooling in the cups on the table. In Lord Matthison's arms.

'Your father could not have killed your mother,' he said, when at last she stopped spasmodically clutching at his jacket sleeves. 'He was a man of the cloth.'

The man who had been crouching over her mother had been wearing the clothes of a cleric.

She shook her head, vehemently pushing the disturbing image back into the shadows.

'Cora's father may have been a man of the cloth,' she

argued, pulling out of his arms and turning away. '*My* father was a drunken bully.'

It was one of those truths that slipped from her mouth without her knowing where it had come from. Yes, she sighed. She knew that was true. That was how she had been able to identify the sweet, fruity odour in the coach as spirits lingering on a man's breath. The other passengers must have spent some time in the taproom whilst waiting for the journey to start. It was the reason they had all slept so soundly, no matter how loud the guard blew the horn, or how deep the potholes that they bounced over.

Lord Matthison gently set her back on her chair, and went to his own, his face creased in perplexity.

'If you are not Cora Montague,' he said, shaken, 'then who the hell are you? Why do you look so much like her? And why did you only appear in London six years ago? Less than two months after she disappeared. With no clear memories of your past!'

'N-not clear memories, no,' she admitted. 'Just snatches, mostly.'

He sat forwards, his eyes narrowing. 'What do you mean, mostly? What have you not told me?'

'Well,' she admitted, feeling horribly guilty for not mentioning it before. 'I do remember the place where I lived before they sent me to work for Madame Pichot. A great house it was, in the country.'

'Where was it?' he demanded sharply. 'Tell me everything!'

'I...I can't!' she gasped, getting to her feet and pacing the floor in an agitated manner.

'Can't or won't?'

'Why are you torturing me like this?' she whirled on him. 'What do you hope to gain?'

He got to his feet too, and pulled her into his arms again, cradling her against his chest. In spite of her accusation that he was torturing her, she subsided into his embrace as though he was her only rock in a sea of uncertainty.

'You know what I want,' he groaned. 'I want you to be Cora! I want to find out what happened to you that day you went out riding and never came back. And how you ended up in London. But if—' he took her face in his hands and raised it so she had to gaze directly into his eyes '—if you turn out to be someone else…a girl perhaps who ran away from home after witnessing the brutal murder of her mother by her father…then I promise you, I will still take care of you. I swear, you have nothing to fear from me, whatever we find out.

'But don't you want to know the truth about yourself? I think,' he said, looking at her challengingly, 'we both need to unravel the mystery of your past, before either of us can begin to live freely again.'

'Y-you will take care of me?'

'Yes. It is not your fault you look like Cora. You have done nothing to merit losing your post and ending up in a town where you know nobody. If you are not Cora, then I swear, I will make amends for all of this.'

She knew he spoke the truth. Whoever she turned out to be, he would be responsible for her.

Just as Molly had said he would.

She pulled out of his arms, rubbing her hands up and down the sleeves of her dress. Now was the moment any sensible woman would negotiate terms. Tell him she wanted him to set her up in a shop when he was finished with her.

But, she realised on a shocked, indrawn breath, that was not what she wanted at all!

Somewhere during this long, confusing day, she had begun to wish she really could be his Cora. That she was fit to marry him, and could stay with him for ever! That was why she had allowed her memories to begin to tally with what he kept on telling her.

She sank down on to her chair.

'W-will you do something for me?' she asked in a tortured whisper.

'If I can.'

'W-will you treat me, as though I was…Cora, until we find out the truth?'

She did not think she could bear it if he treated her like a disposable commodity, not now she had caught a glimpse of how deeply this man could love.

'Nothing would please me more,' he said, his face relaxing into something approaching a smile.

It almost broke her heart. She was encouraging him to live out his fantasy, when she knew it would only be a matter of time before the truth blew it all to smithereens.

She was not the woman he loved.

It was one of those things she just knew.

Chapter Six

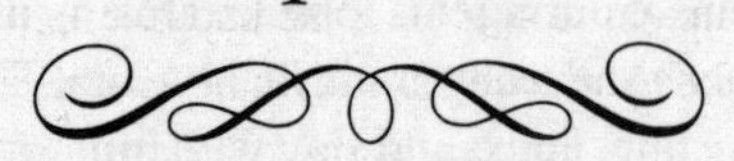

It was not as pleasant, having an enormous bed all to herself, as Mary had thought it would be.

She rolled over on to her side, tugging the blankets up round her ears as she went, wondering how it could be so hard to get to sleep when she was so exhausted. To think, when Lord Matthison had told her she could take this bed, while he made himself comfortable on a chair by the fire, she had felt nothing but relief! She had even mustered up a timid smile when he had pulled the velvet bed-hangings closed round her, assuring her that he would not intrude on her privacy. She had briefly imagined stretching out her aching limbs on the invitingly soft mattress and falling instantly into a blissfully deep and dreamless sleep.

As yet, she had not even managed to keep her eyes closed for more than a few seconds at a time.

It was too dark.

Almost as soon as Lord Matthison had drawn the

dusty brown curtains round her, she'd had to fumble her way to the edge of the bed and open them a chink. She had brought her overnight bag into her private cocoon, but dreaded groping for it in that thick darkness, and trying to locate her nightdress in its depths by sense of touch alone. It had been extremely awkward, wriggling out of her clothes, and into her nightdress whilst kneeling up on a surface that had the consistency of sponge cake. And when she'd finally succeeded, instead of relaxing back into the bank of pillows, she had kept on kneeling there, chewing on her lower lip, while she wondered what to do about her dress. She had felt how stiff the hem was as she'd tugged it over her head. What she really wanted to do was to rinse the mud out before settling for the night. She was sure, if she could hang it over one of the chair backs, before the fire, it would be almost dry by morning.

But that would mean venturing out into Lord Matthison's territory.

In her nightgown.

Swallowing down hard, Mary had draped her soiled dress over the footboard, telling herself that there were worse things than having to put on travel-stained clothing.

Far worse. She had experienced some of them today. When she remembered how desolate she had felt, standing in that doorway with that blank piece of paper in her hand, her insides clenched up and she had to wrap her arms about her stomach.

And it was not only what had really happened today that had left her feeling so raw. It was the glimpse of the past that Lord Matthison had goaded her into looking at. She could still see her father pounding his fists into her mother's curled-up body, every time she shut her eyes.

She sat bolt upright, her own fists clenched. She had always known that there was something so ugly in her past that her mind recoiled from remembering it! But worse, far worse, was the horrible, sickening certainty that there was more to come. She could sense it, lurking just out of sight, like a beast crouching in the shadows, lashing its tail as it prepared to pounce the moment she let her guard down…

Mary grabbed one of the pillows, and buried her face in it as she hugged it to her knees. If only she were back in London, with Molly on one side of her, and Kitty on the other. They would not have let her so much as roll over, never mind sit up and toss pillows about. But then, with the girls on either side of her, she would not be feeling so vulnerable. Even if they did not fully wake up, one of them would always reach out, and pat her sleepily, and tell her to pay no mind to her dreams. Without them to guard her, she gasped, blinking blindly into the inky blackness that surrounded her, she would never dare to go to sleep. With nobody to wake her, she might fall deeper and deeper into her nightmares until they swallowed her whole!

Her heart was beating so fast, her whole body shook with its force. She felt so utterly, completely defenceless, here in this town where nothing was familiar to her. In London, there was always noise, no matter what time of night it was. The rattle of carriage wheels passing in the street, the cries of the night watchmen, drunken revellers singing as they staggered home. Signs of life.

This place was as silent as the grave. She felt as though the very quietness of the hotel room was conspiring with its darkness to suffocate her in this velvet tomb.

And then she heard the creak of a chair as Lord Matthison shifted position. Some of the tension drained from her shoulders and she lay down, staring straight up where she knew there was a canopy over her head. If she fell asleep, and if she had a nightmare, he would hear her cry out. And he would wake her, wouldn't he? Before she went in too deep?

When the chair creaked again, Mary ruefully compared their positions. It didn't sound as if he could get comfortable. She should have taken the chair, and let him have the bed. She could have curled her smaller body up in a blanket, and watched the flames dancing in the grate. He could have stretched out here, in the kind of luxury he was used to. And at least one of them would have been able to get some sleep.

Instead, she lay rigid, listening to the sounds of his wakefulness, yearning for daybreak to put an end to their mutual discomfort.

She found it almost impossible to look him in the face the next morning. She was painfully aware that he had chased halfway across the country to rescue her, and rescue it had been—she shuddered to think what might have become of her if he had not been there. And far from expressing so much as a hint of gratitude, she had reacted with hostility and suspicion, and finally demanded he accord her the kind of respect he would show a woman of his own class.

'I will hire a post-chaise to convey us back to London,' he said, once they were seated at the table where a fresh-faced young waiter had set out a substantial breakfast.

'London?' she echoed, her curiosity roused enough to dart a timid glance at him. Immediately, she felt quite wretched to see the dark shadows that spending a sleepless night in a chair had put under his eyes.

'Yes, London,' he replied, cutting a slice from the succulent slab of sirloin that lay on his plate. 'That is the logical place to begin to hunt for clues to your true identity.'

Mary dejectedly bit into a roll she had mechanically slathered with butter and honey. He was not going to give this up. He was not going to rest until he had ferreted out the very deepest of her secrets.

'You say you worked in a big house before you went to Madame Pichot?'

She nodded, her mouth suddenly too dry to swallow, let alone form words.

'She must know something about your former employer. They must have given you a reference?'

Mary reached for her cup of chocolate and took a large gulp. Once Madame related the circumstances that had led to her being sent to London…

'She…Madame…might not be willing to tell us anything,' she said hopefully.

Lord Matthison looked at her sharply, and she hung her head. It was all he could do not to curse out loud. The dressmaker would *not* want to help them, that was what she meant.

He stabbed into his steak, savagely hacking off another slice and impaling it on his fork. Madame Pichot was a spiteful woman, to have served a girl she believed to be a simpleton such a cruel trick.

But it was his fault that she had turned on Cora at all.

He flung his fork, complete with the untasted morsel of rare steak, back on to the plate with a clatter. He had spent a large part of the night re-examining the events of the past few days, trying to come to terms with Cora's reactions to him. In particular, wondering why she assumed he had proposed marriage to another woman, when nothing was further from the truth. She could only have heard that there was any thought of an engagement from some member of the Winters family. Nobody else knew anything about it.

One of them must have gone to Madame Pichot and fed her a pack of lies. Probably breathing threats of scandal that could jeopardise the business.

He could curse them all for their cruelty towards a defenceless woman till the cows came home, but in the end, he had to accept that it was his own actions that had resulted in Cora losing her job and ending up on the streets, so lonely and scared she had accepted the protection of a man who was a virtual stranger to her.

No wonder she could not bear to look at him.

'She may not want to help us, but she will,' he said in a tone so implacable, his face going so hard that, for the very briefest moment, Mary felt a twinge of pity for her former employer. She could almost see why people believed this man was in league with the devil, when his eyes could burn with such malevolence.

Travelling in a post-chaise, Mary soon discovered, was an entirely different prospect from taking the mail coach. For one thing, the interior was too small to take more than two passengers. For another, they were not tied to anybody's schedule but their own. When they stopped to change horses and postilions, they could take a meal, or even a stroll if they felt so inclined.

The leisurely pace was less taxing, it was true, but it had the disadvantage that they would not reach London in one stage. And though Mary was in no hurry to face Madame Pichot, she still felt awkward about sharing a room with Lord Matthison. And she knew he would insist that they did.

Though, she mused, as they sat down to a light supper, set out in the private parlour he had obtained, she no longer worried he might not treat her with respect. He had been so attentive to her needs, getting ostlers to jump to attention, and landlords to scramble to serve them, with just one lancing look from his night-dark eyes. How she wished she was a real lady, and could always expect such consideration!

He was such a perfect gentleman, she sighed, wiping

her lips with a napkin, and laying it on the table beside her plate. He deserved to be with someone so much better than her.

'You can take the bed tonight,' she declared, the moment Lord Matthison closed the door to their bedchamber behind them. Marching across to the bed, she whisked off the quilt, helped herself to one of the pillows, and arranged them on the chesterfield that sagged on bowed legs under the window.

'And please, do not argue about this, my mind is made up,' she said when she saw a whole raft of objections flit across his face. 'I am so tired I could sleep anywhere. I can be quite comfortable on the couch, being so much smaller than you,' she pointed out.

With a weary shrug of his shoulder, Lord Matthison sat on the edge of the bed, tugged off his boots, then disappeared into the damasked folds of its hangings. To fall instantly asleep, she expected, curling up in the nest she had made for herself.

She did not think it would take her long to fall asleep tonight either. The shocks of the previous day had receded from the forefront of her mind. She had felt herself relaxing in Lord Matthison's company more and more as the day had progressed. He had been a perfect travelling companion, kind and attentive, and always treating her with the utmost propriety. She was really glad he would be staying in the room with her, though naturally, she would never admit as much to him!

Even so, when she closed her eyes, for a while she

had the peculiar impression that she was still bouncing along in the post-chaise. Her muscles had got so used to clenching and straining to compensate for the vehicle's lurching motion that it seemed to take them a while to accept they could all just let go.

But gradually, as exhaustion claimed her, her mind translated the bouncing movement of the coach that her body was still experiencing, into a dream of rocking, on a gentle swell, in a rowing boat, out on the open loch. She could hear seagulls keening as they wheeled overhead. And, of course, Lord Matthison was there. She felt his strong arms wrap her in a blanket of pure contentment. She nestled closer to him, laying her head on his chest, so that she could listen to the steady, reassuring thud of his heart as the waves lapped against the hull of their boat.

And woke with a jolt, to find herself curled up on the bed, cradled against Lord Matthison's chest.

He must have waited until she fell asleep, then carried her to the bed, intending to… She gulped. He had intended to swap places with her, of course! He must have succumbed to the temptation of holding her for a while, and fallen asleep again.

Well, it would not do.

Slowly, stealthily, so as not to disturb him, Mary tried to disentangle herself from the quilt in which she was wrapped like a swaddled baby.

'No…' he moaned, clutching her more tightly, and rolling over so that his leg now pinned hers down.

Without even opening his eyes.

Mary's heart melted. The poor man needed to keep her close. She knew just how he felt. Had she not missed the company of her bedmates the night before?

Did she really want to escape his hold badly enough to wake him? Where was the harm in staying exactly where she was? He was not going to do anything but hold her while he slept.

They would both get more rest, if she just closed her eyes again and shifted into a more comfortable position.

And she did feel warm and comfortable. And happier than she could ever remember feeling. The girls she slept with might have provided company, and warmth on a winter night, but they did not cling to her as though she was a rare treasure.

As though she mattered.

When she awoke in the morning, she was alone in the bed, with the curtains drawn closed. But she did not feel in the least lonely or scared, because she could hear Lord Matthison moving about the room. He splashed about at the washstand, and then she heard him huffing slightly as he dried himself, and then the rustle of fabric that told her he was putting on his clothes.

It felt peculiarly intimate, to hear him going about such everyday tasks, after spending the night held in his arms. When he approached the bed, and cleared his throat, before drawing back the hangings on one side, her whole body blushed with awareness. Every single one of her pores felt sensitive to his intense, dark gaze as he stood over her, for what felt like an eternity, while she drank in every detail of his appearance.

The look in her eyes reached right down into him, stirring feelings that he had thought were beyond recall.

She must be Cora! Surely, no other woman could affect him this way?

And yet, would the Cora he knew have been able to share a room with a man she barely knew? And wake up looking so calm?

This woman appeared to have a core of inner strength that Cora had lacked. Oh, there were times when she was unsure of herself. But then, she had no memory. Of course she experienced anxiety.

But despite that handicap, she had bravely forged a new life for herself in unfamiliar surroundings.

And look how she had stood up to him!

It must have been frightening to fall into the clutches of a devil like him. And the way he had behaved in Bath, falling to his knees and begging her to love him, must have convinced her he was as mad as a March hare.

Yet all she had done was hold him. Though she was clearly afraid, she had generously offered what comfort she could, when he had been at his lowest ebb. Without compromising her beliefs. She had stood firm on that point, insisting he treat her as though she was a lady.

She *was* a lady! Every inch of her. From the crown of those tangled curls, to the tips of her blistered toes. With as big a heart as Cora had ever had. Last night, seeing how weary he was, she had put his needs before her own, insisting he took the bed.

Until last night, Cora had been the only person who had ever seen what he needed, without having to be told. He did not want to lose that again.

He did not want to lose her.

If she was not Cora…

He recoiled from the alarming prospect.

'I shall wait for you in the parlour while you get dressed,' he said gruffly, breaking whatever spell it was that had rendered her powerless to do anything but gaze back at him with utter fascination. 'Will you be ready to breakfast in half an hour?'

Mary nodded, dimly aware of a vague sense of disquiet. It was not until she had finished her wash, and was stepping into her increasingly disreputable-looking gown, that she realised what had disturbed her. Lord Matthison might have phrased it as a request, but in effect, he had ordered her to bestir herself, and be downstairs within half an hour.

He had decided they were going back to London.

He had decided that they needed to unearth the secrets of her past that she would just as soon leave buried.

He had given her no say.

He had taken over her life.

And there was not a thing she could do about it.

By the time the post-chaise lurched to a halt before some buildings she recognised as being bachelor chambers in Albany, Mary was feeling more than a little resentful. He had promised to treat her exactly as he would have treated Cora, but she was certain he would never have brought *her* here.

He would have escorted her to a hotel…

The mere thought of being stuck in one of those rooms, all on her own, to lie all night in a great expanse of empty bed, with all those suffocating swathes of fabric round her, brought her out in a cold sweat. Thank heavens he *was* only paying lip service to the notion of treating her like a lady! She reached out and clung on to his arm as he steadily mounted the steps.

He looked down at her sharply.

'Don't be afraid,' he said gently. 'I will never hurt you. I just mean to see you settled in comfortably, before I go to deal with Madame Pichot—'

'No!' The prospect of being abandoned, the minute they had set foot in London, was almost as dreadful as the thought of being banished to a hotel.

'D-don't leave me on my own!'

She gazed up imploringly into his eyes, feeling profoundly relieved when she could not detect any hint of annoyance creeping into them. A man with a less even temper would be exceedingly put out by her contrariness. One minute she was complaining she did not wish to see Madame Pichot, the next she was refusing to let him go without her!

But he just laid his hand over her fingers where they curled into the material of his jacket like claws.

'I won't leave you alone,' he vowed. 'Never.'

For a moment or two, they stood there, gazes locked.

At what precise moment had Lord Matthison become indispensable to her peace of mind? During the journey, when he had demonstrated how kind he could be? Or during the night spent blissfully wrapped in his arms? However it had happened, she only knew that he had become a bulwark against life's alarms. She felt as though she would fall to pieces if she let him out of her sight for a minute.

And he just stood there, letting her search his eyes for as long as it took her to realise he understood, and even welcomed her dawning need of him.

'Come,' he said gently, 'let us go inside, and wash away the dust of travel. Would you care for something to eat before we go to beard the Gorgon in her den?'

She darted him an uncertain look as he led her inexorably up the stairs.

'Together,' he reassured her. 'Ephraims,' he said when a short stocky man with curly brown hair opened the door on which he had just knocked. 'We have a guest. She will be staying with us for the foreseeable future.'

While Lord Matthison issued a string of instructions, Mary surreptitiously took stock of the servant's reactions. She was pleased to note his swiftly concealed look of surprise when he had seen her clinging to his master's arm. And positively heartened by the way his eyes grew round when Lord Matthison instructed him to prepare the guest room for her use. It meant that he was not in the habit of bringing women up to these rooms. Whatever was happening between them was as extraordinary for him as it was for her.

'My name is Mary,' she told the servant over her shoulder, as Lord Matthison ushered her into a sitting room. She was glad he had not introduced her as Cora. It would feel like living a lie if he went round telling other people that was who she was, when she knew full well she was not.

She subsided into the chair he indicated he wished her to sit in, chewing on her lower lip. The truth was, she was only here at all because of his erroneous belief. But once they had visited Madame Pichot, and he found out who she was, and what she had done, all this concern would be snuffed out like a guttering candle.

She gazed up at him, her heart plunging at the thought that he would soon cease treating her as though she was a person that mattered.

'You have noted,' he said in a rather defensive manner, as soon as the servant had left the room, 'that I have ordered Ephraims to prepare the guest room for your use while we are staying here.' He paced across to the fireplace and turned to face her, running his fingers through his hair. 'I know I promised to treat you as though we had already established you really are Cora...and it is true that as you were, when I last saw you...seventeen, and untouched...' A look of anguish flitted across his face. He turned, staring into the empty grate for a while, and when he turned back to her it was like looking at a stranger. There was no trace of compassion in those world-weary eyes. She was, she realised, looking at the hardened gambler who had made his fortune ruining anyone who showed the slightest trace of weakness in his presence.

'Back then,' he drawled, 'yes, I admit it would have been outrageous for you to spend a night in a single gentleman's rooms. Or to travel with me, unchaperoned, as we have done. But things are different now. For the past seven years you have been out of society, living in a way that is bound to raise eyebrows...and I do not see that sticking to a set of restrictive regulations at this point will do anything to quell the gossip that will erupt once we marry.'

Mary plucked at the folds of her skirts. 'I dare say Cora would have objected to being brought here.' She scanned the room with inquisitive eyes, taking in the heavy, masculine furniture, gentlemen's magazines piled neatly on a side table, several decks of cards stacked on a felt-topped table under the window. 'But I do not.' She hung her head briefly, remembering her feeling of resentment that although he was paying lip service to the idea of treating her like a lady, he was not quite managing it.

'You—' she tried a tentative smile '—you are *trying* to treat me with respect. Far more respect than most gentlemen would accord a simple dressmaker.'

'But I am not quite treating you as though you were a lady born, though am I?' He grimaced. 'Dammit, this is so complicated. The sooner we have established who and what you are, the better!'

Though Mary could not agree with his statement, she kept that thought to herself. They barely spoke again while they shared the collection of cold cuts and bread and butter that Ephraims brought in. But his comment kept going round and round her mind while she freshened up in the room to which Ephraims later escorted her.

A room that Lord Matthison had promised was for her use alone. Now that he had her in his own territory, he did not seem to think it was necessary to keep such a close watch on her. And it was a nice room, she noted. It had carpeting on the floor beside the bed and by the washstand, lovely, leafy-green damasked hangings around the bed and at the window, and all the furniture was made of the same dark, heavy wood, with matching patterns inlaid in a lighter colour.

She wished she could stay here indefinitely. With Lord Matthison always close at hand to keep her feeling safe, and a servant to do all the cooking and cleaning, fetching and carrying. It would be lovely not to have to work until she dropped from exhaustion every night.

But once he discovered she was not Cora… She splashed her face with water, trying to wash away the creeping worries that kept on besetting her. He had promised he would look after her, no matter who she was, she reminded herself, patting her face dry on the softest towel she had ever held against her skin. She could trust him to keep his word. He was a gentleman.

She picked up a silver-backed hairbrush, and began to work it through her tangles, meditatively. Two weeks ago, she would have sworn she would never, ever, have considered becoming a man's mistress. But if that was the only way she could stay in his life…

And she did want to stay near him. She had never met anyone who made her feel like he did. So safe, and cherished. He even understood her confusion. He did not mock her, or pity her, or make her feel she lacked anything at all.

It was strange to think that a man others whispered was in league with the devil should rouse such feelings of trust in her, when she was apt to be scared of her own shadow. She tilted her head to one side, to work through the curls over her left ear.

Well, the rumours about him were quite ridiculous, that was why they did not bother her! For a start, he would not be so sure she was Cora, if he had done away with that woman all those years ago. And since his pact with the devil was supposed to have been sealed in that girl's blood, it was blatantly a piece of malicious gossip, made up by someone who… Angrily she set the brush down on the highly polished dressing table top. One of those people he had beaten at cards, she expected. And, no, she had no idea how he managed to be so amazingly successful at the gaming tables, when it was impossible to imagine him cheating. A man who was honourable enough to feel guilty for not keeping strictly to his promise to treat a dressmaker like a real lady, no, that was not a man who could cheat at cards! Or murder anyone. Or have any truck with anything unholy at all!

Most of the class who called themselves gentlemen would not have turned a hair at taking advantage of her in either of the inns they had stayed in. They would not have taken a chair, or just held her in their arms. Nor left her bed early, so that she should not even be troubled by the knowledge he had held her!

She was not sorry, she decided, lifting her chin defiantly, that he had taken over her life. The only thing she was sorry for was the hurt he would feel when he found out who she really was.

He would be so disappointed she was not the woman he had sought for so long. How would he feel about her then? What if he found it too painful to have her near, a constant reminder of all he had lost? She had no doubt he would set her up in a shop, if she asked him, but…

The prospect that he might send her away made her feel quite ill. She leapt to her feet, the brush dropping unheeded to the floor as she dashed back to the sitting room, suddenly fearful that he might have gone out without her.

He was leaning against the mantelpiece, his arms folded across his chest, his eyes fixed on the door.

Waiting for her.

She paused in the doorway, her heart beating wildly as she castigated herself for her lack of faith.

He had told her, over and over again, that he couldn't bear to let her out of his sight. And suddenly, for the first time, she knew he really meant it. That spike of panic that had just pierced her was the exact same feeling that had put that haunted look in his eyes, the one that had dissipated the moment she walked into the room.

For a moment or two she felt such an inexpressible sense of joy she scarcely knew how to contain it. But then he said, 'We should leave now. The sooner we get this visit to Madame Pichot over with, the better.'

And Mary's bubble burst. *She* was not really the

person that mattered to him. It was Cora who had this effect on him. She had to turn away, lest he detect the jealousy that ripped through her. If she ever came face to face with the woman who had reduced such an honourable man to this state of chronic need, she would be hard pressed not to slap her face.

He unfolded his arms, and came across to where she stood in the doorway, a frown still creasing his brows.

'We shall have to get you some new clothes,' he said, eyeing the sadly soiled garments she'd had to put back on.

He was looking magnificent, in a fresh suit of exquisitely tailored clothing. He might have dressed completely in black, but the cloth was of the finest quality, and cut by an expert hand, to set off his leanly muscular figure. The splendour of his tailoring made her more aware than ever of the discrepancy in their stations. With her mud-encrusted, crumpled dress, singed coat, and boots stiffened from their soaking, she knew she looked exactly like the penniless nobody she really was.

'I have my own things,' she heard herself say defiantly. 'I want to wear my own things.' She had slid far enough down the slippery slope of temptation where he was concerned. It was bad enough that he was demolishing her principles one by one. Once she started letting him buy her clothing, he would own her completely.

He raised one eyebrow.

'Molly packed them all up for me the day Madame sent me to Bath. She was going to send them…' She paused, shaking her head. 'The trunk must still be in one of the store rooms…unless she has already taken it to a dealer in second-hand clothes.' She bit down on her lower lip to stop the incipient tremor. She felt as though part of her identity had been packed away in that trunk. If she did not get her own things back, she would have to let Lord Matthison clothe her. And she would become entirely his creation.

'Then I shall make sure you get them,' he vowed, making her contrarily even more jealous of Cora. He would let Cora have her way about anything!

It felt strange to walk through the front door of Madame's shop on Lord Matthison's arm, as though she was a customer. It must have looked strange, too, because when Kitty saw them, her mouth gaped open in surprise. She backed through the blue velvet curtain to fetch Madame, as though she could not bear to tear her eyes away. And then she heard her pounding up the back stairs as Madame emerged from her office.

Her expression was decidedly frosty.

'I do not make gowns for anything but ladies,' she sneered, pointedly looking at the way Mary was clinging to Lord Matthison's arm.

'Then it is just as well we have no intention of purchasing anything from you,' replied Lord Matthison in equally chilling tones. 'Our business with you is of a personal nature, and I would be obliged if we could conduct it in private. I am quite sure you do not wish to run the risk of one of your clients coming in and hearing what a swindling, corrupt and downright cruel woman you are?'

Madame's eyes bulged, her cheeks turning red, but it was not long before she turned on her heel and stalked down the corridor that led to her office, at the back of the building.

As they walked along behind her, Mary's ears strained to hear the sound of her former workmates congregating on the stairs. The second they reached Madame's office, her eyes darted to the wall, where she knew the knotholes gave a view over everything that was about to happen. Then they swivelled back to Madame, who was taking her seat behind the desk. As Lord Matthison held one of the ladder-backed chairs for Mary, making sure she was seated, before taking a chair for himself, she could picture Lotty's eyes growing round. She knew how the girls would interpret this sign of chivalry towards her. They would assume she was his mistress already!

It was all she could do not to turn round, and mouth an explanation that it was not what it looked like.

'We have only come here for some information,' Lord Matthison began, when Madame sat glaring at him in brimming silence.

'And my trunk,' put in Mary, her hand reaching out to touch his sleeve anxiously.

This time, she did dart one look upwards, towards the spot where she knew the girls clustered.

'Ah, yes, the trunk,' Lord Matthison drawled, leaning back in his chair and crossing his legs. 'Which you had one of your other girls pack, under the delusion you would be sending it on to the carrier's.'

'I have not had time to do so,' Madame blustered. 'But of course, now that I know Mary is back in London, under your protection—' her voice took on a derisory tone '—I will arrange to have it sent to your address.'

'Will you?' he replied in a tone that indicated he did not believe her. Mary could almost feel the girls suck in shocked breaths at his thinly veiled accusation. 'I rather think Mary would prefer me to send my man to collect it in person.'

'Yes, I would,' she said. She no longer cared why Lord Matthison was humouring her over this matter, when she was sure he would rather dress her to suit his own tastes. Every pair of gloves, each change of stockings packed up in that trunk, represented hours of painstakingly earning her place in the world. She was proud of what she had achieved since coming to London. Whatever else anybody said about her, they all acknowledged her superior talent with a needle. And those skills had not just been the means by which she survived. No, they had launched Madame Pichot, and all her workers, into a new sphere. Mary had only to take one look at a client, to know what would suit them. While Madame did the cutting, it had often been Mary who made the initial sketches, though her greatest talent had been the intricate beadwork that required such intense concentration. Few girls could do that.

She felt as though her whole life, for the past seven years, was packed away in that trunk. She was not going to leave it behind! Nor could she bear to think of

Madame selling those gowns, when she had already profited so much from Mary's skills.

'And now,' Lord Matthison said, 'you will give me some information, if you please.'

'I do not know what you think I can tell you…'

'To begin with, you will tell me where Mary worked before she came to you.'

'I see no reason why I should do any such thing.'

'Be careful, Madame,' he said, his eyes narrowing in the way that had already sent shivers of apprehension down Mary's spine, 'that you do nothing to make me your enemy.'

'What more do you think you can do to me?' Madame replied, laying her hands flat on the desk, and rising to her feet. 'Stalking one of my girls, and leading her astray, and leaving me open to charges of keeping some sort of…of brothel? When I have worked my fingers to the bone since coming to this benighted country, raising myself out of the gutter with sheer hard work, to become one of the top modistes of the town?'

Her large, protuberant eyes were watering now, her whole body quivering.

Mary struggled with conflicting emotions. She could not help feeling some sympathy for her. Even though the woman had treated her so cruelly at the end, she thought she could understand what had driven her to do it. She must have been furious to lose Mary's particular skills. The fickle fashionables would turn to someone else once they knew they could no longer get the fabulously embroidered gowns that had recently become

Madame's trademark. Her clientele would dwindle. To keep up with her expenses, she would be obliged to accept commissions from people outside the *haut ton*. And then, once she lost her exclusivity, when it became clear that one could meet *anyone* in Madame's fitting rooms, the downward slide would accelerate.

'I do not think it is your fingers that have been worked to any extent,' Lord Matthison drawled. 'I rather think it is your unfortunate employees whose health has suffered in order to line your pockets. But, that point aside, let me remind you to choose your enemies carefully. There is bound to be gossip about this...' He waved his hand to encompass the three of them, sitting in the office. 'There will be no escaping it. The effect it has on your business, however, will largely depend on whose side you decide to take. And I should warn you that the Winters family are not highly thought of by people that matter. They have no background, no breeding. What money they have derives from trade,' he said with a curl to his lip that denoted exactly what members of the *ton* thought of vulgar mushrooms who pushed themselves in where they did not belong. 'Once Mary is my wife, nothing the Winters say about her, or her *friends*, will be considered anything more than spite.'

Madame's lips worked soundlessly as she weighed up her alternatives. Eventually, she said, 'You really intend to marry her?'

'I do.'

A nasty smile twitched at her lips. 'Then I shall be

only too delighted to tell you where she came from. It was a place called Oakham Hall, in the county of Surrey. She worked as a seamstress for Lady Sandiford. But they had to turn her off, because of her violent outbursts.'

The smile broadened, as her gloating eyes turned to Mary. 'Attacked and maimed a man, she did. The son of the house. Ah…' she sighed, as Lord Matthison leapt to his feet, his face twisted with rage. 'She didn't tell you about that unsavoury little episode, did she?'

Chapter Seven

Lord Matthison held out his arm for Mary to take. He opened the door for her, held back the curtain so they could pass through it into the showroom, and handed her into the waiting carriage with punctilious correctness.

But his face was white, and his eyes had taken on a murderous look.

Mary's heart was racing. Her stomach had been churning even before Madame had blurted out the truth she had hoped Lord Matthison would never hear. She could see he was barely containing his fury. She was not afraid he might do her any physical harm. But she dreaded what he would say once he got her alone. Now that he knew what she had done, he was bound to throw her out.

The bitter taste of betrayal rose in her throat. She choked back a sob.

His promises had meant nothing! Men never stuck to their word. They said whatever they thought would achieve the desired result, but there was no loyalty in them.

* * *

By the time they reached his chambers, her hurt had curdled into anger. It was his own fault if he was disappointed in her. She had repeatedly told him she was not what he thought she was.

'Don't you at least want to hear my side of it?' she said, as Ephraims took his master's hat, coat and gloves.

A spasm of something like disgust flitted across his set white features. He took her by the arm, and roughly dragged her into the sitting room, kicking the door shut behind them.

'Only,' he breathed, 'if you *want* to tell me about it. But you don't, do you? My God, I'm so sorry,' he groaned, taking her completely by surprise by hauling her into his arms and enveloping her in a hold so strong she could scarcely breathe. 'I should have left it all in the dark, not forced it into the light. That bastard Sandiford!' He let her go, but only to cup her face in his hands so that he could look into her eyes.

She blinked back at him in confusion.

'Y-you are not angry with me?'

'With you?' He looked stunned. 'For fighting off a brute like that? Of course not!'

She shook her head. 'Did you not hear what Madame said? How that I attacked him? Were you not listening?'

'I was listening to a spiteful woman trying to drive a wedge between us,' he bit back. 'But I know you, Cora. And I know Sandiford. So it is quite obvious what happened.'

'You do *not* know me!' she protested. If he had not

called her Cora, she might have taken comfort in his blind faith. But it was not faith in *her*. He was just so besotted with the memory of his fiancée that he could not see her getting involved in a scene so sordid, it had the power to make her feel ill to this very day.

She tore herself away from him, and faced him down, her fists clenched at her sides. How could he go on clinging to his delusion even when faced with the truth? She could stand it no longer.

'I did stab him!' she sobbed. 'Again and again and again! There was blood everywhere!'

The room seemed to go misty around the edges. Her lips went numb. Shakily, she reached for the nearest article of furniture, which happened to be a sofa, and dropped down on to it, covering her face with her hands.

She heard Lord Matthison cross to the sideboard, remove the stopper from a decanter, and pour something into a glass.

Then he was beside her, kneeling on the floor, pressing a glass into her hands. When he saw how badly she was shaking, he raised the glass to her lips, and poured the golden liquid between her chattering teeth. She spluttered a little as it burned its way down her throat. But once it hit her stomach, and she felt its warm tendrils snaking through her blood, she grasped the glass for herself, and took another gulp.

'You were only trying to defend yourself,' he said. 'You have no need to feel guilty about hurting him.'

'How do you know that?' she spat, raising her head to challenge him. The concern she saw in his eyes pierced her like a dagger. He only assumed she must have been the innocent victim rather than the instigator of the violence, because he thought she was that gentle, pure, nobly born Cora who could do no wrong!

Mutinously, she pried the brandy glass from him completely, and took another fortifying swig. 'Well, I *was* defending myself, as it happens,' she said sullenly, averting her face so she would not have to see the respect for Cora that blazed from his eyes.

'I know,' he said. 'Sandiford abducted you, did he not, and carried you off to Oakham Hall?'

'What? No!' cried Mary. 'I was working there as a seamstress!' It was not as satisfying to see him reel back, a look of confusion on his face, as she had thought it would be. 'He was not even there when I got taken on.'

'How did you come to be there, then?' he asked, looking completely perplexed.

'I…I don't recall, precisely,' she had to admit. 'There just is not anything much—' she tapped her temple with her forefinger '—before the big house…that is, Oakham Hall.' She drained what was left of the brandy, and set the empty glass on the floor at her feet. 'I can remember standing in the housekeeper's office, the day I got the job. And the lady who had taken me there saying they could only give me light work, because I had been ill. The housekeeper said they happened to be in need of a seamstress, and the other lady said I was a good needlewoman, and I can remember feeling very surprised. But I found all the tasks they set me very easy, so then I knew it was true. I *was* a good needlewoman.'

'You had been ill?' Lord Matthison levered himself off the floor, and sat on the sofa next to her, his hands clasped between his knees.

'I kept having these terrible headaches…' She ran her hand across the back of her neck, in a gesture that was becoming familiar to Lord Matthison. 'But I had been there for a *long* time before Lady Sandiford's son came home. He'd been away. I don't know where. And he…' She paled perceptibly. 'He kept coming up to the sewing room, to see the new girl, he said. That was me. And he would stand over me, and ask me how I was settling in. Did I like my work…?'

Her stomach contracted into a knot as she remembered his low voice, the foul stench of his breath as it gusted into her face. 'I could always smell liquor on his breath, no matter what time of day it was. And he would always stand just a bit too close. But I could not say anything. He was the son of my employer. Then he began to stroke my hair, and the kind of questions he asked frightened me. Even though I did not properly understand them, not back then.'

She paused for a moment, her pale lips pressed together tightly. Then she took a deep breath and plunged on, in a small voice. 'But I never asked him to stop. So I suppose it was my fault that he thought he could touch me.' She gestured towards her breasts, her cheeks colouring. Lord Matthison took Mary's hand as a single tear slid down her cheek.

'He squeezed very hard. It hurt me, and shocked me out of the state of servile acceptance that had made me cower before him. I jumped off my stool and backed away. He laughed, and made a grab for me. And I just acted without thinking. I still had the embroidery scissors in my hand, and when he reached for me, I…stabbed at his hands. And then everything happened so fast…' She hung her head, her shoulders hunching. 'He was howling, and there was blood everywhere…and people came running, and he grabbed me by the neck, and somehow we were on the floor and I was on top of him, and I kept on stabbing at his hands with the scissors to try to make him let go…and then two footmen were there, pulling me away, and he was screaming that I had gone mad and ought to be locked up…and they dragged me down to the wine cellar, which had the stoutest door in the house, but it was so dark in there—' she shivered '—when they shut the door, and so cold.' Tears were streaming down Mary's face now, as she recounted the horror of that time.

'I was so scared they would send me to prison. He was yelling about sending for the magistrate. I was sure nobody would believe a word I said in my defence. Why should they, when I did not know the first thing about myself? That was the most frightening thing of all. The awful space in my mind where there should have been…something! Anything! I did not even know my own name. When the lady who brought me there told the housekeeper my name was Mary, I felt dreadful. How could my own name come as a surprise to me?'

'Because it was not your name. It *is* not your name. You are Cora.'

'No, no! Have you not heard a word I have said?'

'Yes,' he said with infuriating calm. 'You have already told me more than you know,' he said, laying one arm gently about her shoulders while he pressed a handkerchief into her hands. 'But I still need to hear how you escaped from the wine cellar.'

'She let me out. The housekeeper,' said Mary, blowing her nose. 'I could barely see. It seemed so bright after being shut down there for so long. I felt as though the darkness had become a part of me,' she admitted, scrunching the handkerchief into a ball. 'It had seeped right inside me, and was eating away at me from the inside, until I had begun to fear there would be nothing left of me. I…I still have nightmares about it.'

And then, even though some traces of anger and resentment towards him remained, Mary found herself burying her face against Lord Matthison's shoulder.

'You are safe now,' he murmured against the crown of her head. 'I will never let anyone hurt you again.'

It was not his words that had her releasing her breath in a great juddering sigh. It was the solid warmth of his body, the strength of his arms as he held her tight. The scent of clean linen and the citrus tang that lingered on his skin from the soap he used. They were what drove the feelings of being cold and alone, locked up in the dark, from her mind.

'She…' She sat up jerkily. 'She did not believe his story either.' She reached up and laid her palm against his lean cheek. 'Just like you. She did not need to ask me anything. She said he had preyed on the young female servants for long enough and had only got what he deserved.'

Lord Matthison's stern face relaxed into something resembling a smile. 'She sounds like a sensible woman.'

'She wrapped me in a warm cloak and got one of the outdoor workers to put me on the stage for London, with a letter of introduction to Madame Pichot. Madame read the letter,' said Mary, completely skipping over the terrors she had suffered on that coach journey, 'and said she was willing to hide me if I promised to work hard and behave myself. She said she would feed and house me as a favour to her friend, and that if I was any good at my work, she would see about some wages, as well. She was very kind to me, back then,' put in Mary hastily, when Lord Matthison scowled at the mention of wages he knew very well had never materialised. 'She could see I was scared, and she sat me down with a cup of tea while Molly went and got me a clean dress. She said I wasn't to worry about that kind of thing happening as long as I worked for her, because she didn't allow no gentlemen to enter her premises and bother her girls.'

Mary looked up at him with an entreaty in her eyes. How she wanted him to understand!

Eventually, his face softened, and he nodded. 'You looked on that place as your sanctuary, did you not? And Madame Pichot as your saviour. You never really cared about the wages, did you?'

She shook her head, absurdly pleased that he had understood.

'My poor darling,' he said, when she had finished. 'You have endured so much.' He took a deep breath, and said resolutely, 'Though you may not like to hear me say so, I think it was a great pity that the housekeeper did not hand you over to the magistrate.'

When Mary reared back, anguished incomprehension on her face, he grasped hold of her hands tightly, saying, 'We would have had you home. You need never have gone to London and spent all these years wondering who you are!'

'I know who I am!' she insisted. 'I am Mary. A dressmaker!'

Lord Matthison's face set in obdurate lines. 'I can see that we will need to establish how you got from Kingsmede to Oakham Hall before you will believe it. The lady you mentioned, the one who spoke to the housekeeper for you, she must hold the key. What can you tell me about her?'

Mary snatched her hands back, and wrapped her arms round her waist.

'I can tell you nothing!'

'Then let me tell you a few things,' he replied sternly. 'It is less than thirty miles between Kingsmede and Oakham Hall. You were staying at Kingsmede with me. We were going to be married in the chapel on the estate. We were all busy with the arrangements. We were so happy.'

His eyes took on a faraway look that made Mary feel as though she had just disappeared.

'One afternoon,' he went on, oblivious to her growing

disquiet, 'you went out riding alone. Your horse came back to the stables riderless, with mud and leaves all over the saddle. At first we thought you must have taken a tumble in the woods. There had been a terrific thunderstorm. A bolt of lightning, or a loud thunderclap, could have spooked your horse. We were all in a panic. We did not even know in which direction you had ridden out. We searched until it got dark, and then went back for lanterns, and kept on looking. And when there was no trace of you anywhere…' His face suddenly closed up.

He got to his feet, and began to pace the room. 'Perhaps you *were* stunned in a fall, woke up wet, and confused, and made for shelter, somewhere. Probably with the lady who eventually took you to Oakham Hall. Though I must say—' he frowned '—it seems mighty peculiar of her not to have contacted us. After that first night, we organised search parties. There was not a house for miles around we did not visit. Everyone knew a young lady had vanished from my estate. Especially,' he added bitterly, 'once I was accused of your murder. After that, I admit, the area of inquiry narrowed considerably.' His face took on what she thought of as his devilish look. 'My coveys, ponds, haystacks, even the ice-house—they looked everywhere I might conceivably have concealed your body.'

'I'm sorry,' she said, feeling unaccountably guilty.

He shrugged one shoulder, turning to her with a grim smile. 'You have no need to be. It was clearly not your fault. But dammit,' he snarled, striding across the room to glare down at her, 'every time I get an answer to one piece of the puzzle, that answer only throws up another set of questions in its place. Who was that woman? Why were you under her care? And why did she take you to Oakham Hall, for God's sake, a place where nobody with an ounce of compassion would send a defenceless girl to work? Try to think, Cora.' He sat down and took her by the shoulders. 'Can you remember anything about the time you spent with that woman? Anything that might help us fill in the missing pieces?' He spread his arms wide in a gesture of desperation. 'Anything at all!'

Mary screwed her eyes tight shut, wrapping her arms even tighter round herself. It was useless to keep on protesting that she was not his Cora. The things he had just told her about what had happened back then, the staggering coincidences that had placed her so close to the scene of his tragedy, had helped her to see why he was more convinced than ever that she was that girl.

But she knew she could never have ridden a horse, like he said.

'I wish I could help you sir, I really do,' she forced herself to say. 'But whenever I try to reach back to those days, what comes to me, more strongly than the little snatches of things that happened, are feelings.' They were rising up now. 'Pain,' she moaned, rocking herself. 'And loss, and…' A great wave of utter desolation came crashing over her. 'I can't, oh, I can't go there,' she moaned.

'Hell,' he swore, immediately contrite. 'I should not

have pushed you this far.' He swept her into his arms, and rocked her as though she were a frightened child. 'Let it go, darling. Let it all go, and I will find the answers myself.' He smoothed her damp hair back from her tearstained face, saying, 'I can soon find Sandiford, and wring some answers out of him.'

'No! You must not! Please do not tell him where I am!' She clutched at the lapels of his coat. 'He will have me thrown in jail, or worse…'

His face hardened. 'Credit me with a little more sense than that! I have ways of getting information out of the man that will not involve revealing anything about your whereabouts.'

He got to his feet.

'You are going now?' Mary was aghast. 'Right this minute? But you said you would not leave me. You promised!'

A flicker of impatience crossed his face. 'You will not be alone. Ephraims will be here, to see to your every need. You have only to ring for him.' He indicated the bell-pull by the fireplace.

Mary felt herself shrivel inside. He said she meant a great deal to him, but the truth was that he was more interested in solving the riddle of his fiancée's disappearance than looking after her.

'And do not even think about coming with me,' he added sternly. 'You know the kind of man Sandiford is. I may need to trawl through quite a few places that cater to men of his tastes in order to find him.'

She promptly forgot her own grievances at the

thought he might be going into danger. 'You will be careful, won't you?' she said, rising to her feet and twisting the crumpled handkerchief between her fingers.

He reached out and stroked her cheek with one forefinger. 'I would descend to the lower reaches of hell to set you free,' he grated. And then, as abruptly as it had come, the look of tenderness in his eyes gave way to one of determination. 'You need not worry about my safety. The people who inhabit the kind of dens Sandiford frequents know all about me, and my so-called pact with the devil.' His face twisted in self-mockery. 'They would not dare cross me. But in the event somebody should be reckless enough to try anything, I am amply prepared. I fence regularly at an exclusive academy, and box at Gentleman Jackson's. In my trade—' he smiled cynically '—it pays to be able to take care of myself.'

'Please,' she said, plucking up every ounce of courage she possessed, 'do not go after Sandiford.'

His face shuttered. 'You must be tired after the rigours of the last few days. You must wish to retire to your room. Take a book.' He waved his hand towards an alcove whose shelves were crammed with an assortment of books and periodicals.

In spite of herself, she could not resist darting one covetous look at his impressive collection of reading materials. It felt like an age since she'd had the leisure to just sit and read.

He was perceptive enough to notice the longing that gripped her.

'You always did love to read,' he said.

'Cora loved reading, you mean,' she protested, tearing her eyes away from the treasure trove on his shelves.

'You know,' he said a touch irritably, 'if you really are just a humble dressmaker, from a lowly background, do you not wonder how come you can sense that you love reading novels? I doubt many working girls have the leisure to indulge in such a pursuit.'

Her shoulders hunched defensively. She had *never* had the leisure to read a book while she had been employed by Madame Pichot. So she did not know how she knew she loved reading. Just the same as she did not know from where her strict moral code came, the code which had put such a distance between her and the other girls she worked with.

'Perhaps my parents were well educated,' she said defiantly. 'Genteel but poor…'

'That is nearer the truth than you want to admit,' he said sardonically. Then, with obvious impatience, 'Why are you fighting me every step of the way? Can you not just be grateful to have the chance to indulge in an evening of leisure? Whoever you think you are?'

Then he turned and stalked from the room, leaving her stunned by his uncharacteristic outburst.

She went cold inside.

He was growing tired of her determination to maintain the identity she had fought so hard to establish. Was this only a foretaste of what she might expect if she did not begin to play along with his fantasy?

Could she really abandon her principles, though, and

play-act at being Cora, if that was the only way to avoid his displeasure?

She did not know how long she sat there, wrestling with the moral dilemma she faced. But eventually, she realised she was only working herself into a state of near panic by imagining increasingly unpleasant scenarios she might have to face. She would have to distract herself, or go mad.

Until now, she had relied on work to set her mind on a more productive path. But she was not going to find any materials for sewing in this bachelor residence! So she got to her feet, went to the bookshelves, and grabbed the first book that came to hand.

As soon as she flipped it open, the scent of good quality, printed paper reached out to her. After taking a couple of deep breaths, with her eyes half-closed, her nose a scant inch from the page, she ran her fingers over the slightly raised lettering on the title page. Feeling calmer already, she took the tale of *Rackrent Castle* to a chair by the fire, hoping that Maria Edgeworth would be able to take her mind off its own troubles, and send it to a happier place.

But the story was not powerful enough to completely absorb her. She found herself reading the same lines over and over again, or getting to the end of a page and having no idea how the story had progressed.

She could not help wondering where Lord Matthison was. Whether he had found Lord Sandiford, and if he had, what they were saying about her. And every time she heard footsteps on the stairwell, she tensed, wondering if it was him, returning.

But the only person to intrude on her lonely vigil was Ephraims, come to bank up the fire, he said, and to tidy up for the night. After snuffing most of the candles, and straightening everything in the room that was an inch out of place, he cleared his throat, and asked, 'Will you be wanting anything else tonight, miss? Only his lordship did intimate that you would be wishful of retiring early.' He glanced at the clock on the mantel. It showed close on midnight. 'Perhaps some hot chocolate?'

Feeling rather like a child being sent to bed, Mary trailed to the door which Ephraims leapt to open for her. She could as well read her book in her room as here.

She checked on the threshold. She had thought it lovely before, but since the last time she had been there, somebody had wrought a transformation in it. A vase of cream and gold roses now stood on the dressing table, which had been polished to a high gloss. She could smell the beeswax mingling with the sweet scent of the roses. Various other little touches told her that Ephraims had gone to some trouble to provide her with a feminine sanctuary in the midst of this distinctly masculine apartment. She would have to make sure she thanked him properly, in the morning.

Her trunk now stood at the foot of the bed, which had been made up with fresh linen. And a nightdress lay on top of a luxurious satin quilt.

She was glad to see the trunk, but less pleased to think Ephraims had been going through her things. She flung open the lid, bracing herself at the thought he might have unpacked for her. But all her things lay undisturbed, just as Molly had packed them.

She took a second look at the nightdress. It was not hers. She had never owned anything made of such fine silk. And a wrapper that matched it hung across the arm of the bedside chair. Lord Matthison must have bought them for her, just in case she did not have a spare in her trunk!

Nobody had ever bought her such a beautiful gift before. She sat back on her heels, her brow furrowing. To her knowledge, nobody had ever bought her *any* kind of gift before. She reached out, and ran her fingers reverently over the beautiful garment.

Then, trembling with anticipation, she undid her gown and pulled it off, went to the washstand and poured warm water from the pitcher into the basin. The quality of that nightgown demanded she wash before trying it on!

The soap, she discovered on working it into a lather, was not the same as the one she had used before. It was more finely milled, and smelled of roses.

Her favourite.

She froze, water dripping from her eyelashes and nose. It was uncanny, the way Lord Matthison seemed to know what she liked, without her having to tell him.

She reached for a towel and blotted her face dry, her pleasure in the room completely destroyed.

He was a clever man, Lord Matthison. He was employing every strategy he could come up with to convince her she might be his missing fiancée. And she was almost foolish enough to fall for them. Almost.

But she was not the only woman who loved the scent of roses. Nor the only one who craved the feel of silk against her skin. It did not mean Lord Matthison knew anything about her in particular!

She scowled down at the nightgown for several seconds before angrily sweeping it off the quilt, and thrusting it into one of the dressing-table drawers. In her trunk she had a perfectly adequate, clean nightgown of her own. She had made it herself from several roll ends of fine lawn. She had no need of his extravagant gifts.

She tugged it over her head, tied the ribbons into tight bows, right up to her neck, and clambered into bed, her breathing laboured.

Mary opened the book, at the page she thought she had been at before Ephraims had put an end to her vigil. The candle burned low, and began to gutter, but still she sat bolt upright in bed, clutching the book she could barely make out through the gloom, while her mind darted this way and that, like a wild bird trapped in a cage.

It was growing light when she heard the hall door slam shut. The book landed on the floor as she scrambled out of bed. It did not matter that she was still angry with him for trying to coerce her into going along with his fantasy; she had to know if he had found Lord Sandiford. And what the man had said. If he had been able to name the woman who had brought her to Oakham Hall, and whether she had any connection to Kings…wood? Kings Combe? She shook her head impatiently. It did not matter what the name of the place was where *Cora* had last been seen. It was *her* future that hung in the balance.

She went straight across the corridor, and knocked on the door that led into his bedroom. It never occurred to her that it was most improper to be running about barefoot, clad only in a flimsy nightgown, in the early hours of the morning. She was too worked up to think of anything but what Lord Matthison had discovered.

He was sitting on the bedside chair in a room that was the mirror image of hers, though somehow indefinably masculine. Ephraims was kneeling at his feet, removing his boots. Both men stared at her in equal surprise.

'What is it?' Lord Matthison snapped.

She faltered on hearing the less-than-welcoming tone of his voice.

Ephraims set the boots aside, while Lord Matthison got to his feet. The servant calmly helped his master off with his jacket.

Mary swallowed, her fingers clenching on the doorknob. Her eyes skittered away from the sight of Lord Matthison removing his clothes, only to come to rest on his shaving equipment, set out on the washstand.

'That will be all for tonight,' he said brusquely, drawing her mortified gaze back to where he stood, in his stockinged feet, by the dressing table. Only to realise, with relief, that it was Ephraims he had dismissed, not her.

She sidled into the room as Ephraims left it, her back pressed against the wall.

'Why are you here?' Lord Matthison said wearily as he unwound his neck cloth and dropped it to the floor. 'What do you want of me now?'

Mary fetched up with a bump against the edge of the wardrobe.

'I—I'm sorry,' she stammered, her eyes transfixed by the triangle of flesh that had just appeared where he had unfastened his shirt. There was a smattering of dark hair growing there. 'I…will l-leave you in peace,' she stuttered, edging her way back along the wall towards the door.

'The hell you will,' he snarled, crossing the room in two strides and seizing her by the wrist.

'I have had no peace for the last seven years! And you are not going to provide it by walking away from me after coming in here, practically naked, and making me think—' he swallowed '—making me hope—' He squeezed his eyes shut, muttered a low curse, then flung her from him abruptly. Turning away, he ran his fingers through his hair, and, keeping his back to her, he growled, 'Go, then! Just get out and leave me to burn in my own particular version of hell.'

'I—I d-don't want to,' she heard herself whisper. It was strange, but the minute she saw how hurt and angry he was, she remembered how very kind he had been to her whenever she had been similarly upset. He had not abandoned her to her fears. He had held her. Comforted her.

She closed the distance between them, and timidly laid one hand on his shoulder. He was standing with his back to her, his hands gripping the edge of the dressing table, his head bowed. He tensed when he felt her touch, but she sensed it was not with revulsion.

He wanted her to stay. Even though he had ordered her to leave.

He was being torn in two.

Just as she was being torn apart by her own conflicting emotions.

'It is not just your hell,' she said, stepping closer, sliding her arms about his waist, and laying her cheek against his rigid back. 'It is mine too. I am in it with you.'

He spun round then, and took hold of her wrists, holding her at arms' length.

'You don't burn for me, though, do you? Like I burn for you?'

She did not think he did burn for her, not really. It was the dead woman who held him in thrall.

'That was not what I meant,' she protested. 'You and I—' she frowned, trying to find the right words '—we are both out of step with the rest of the world. It is as though everyone else is indoors, in a ballroom lit by a million candles, and they are all dancing a complicated minuet. And we are outside, on the terrace, in the cold moonlight, waltzing to a tune only we can hear.'

Some of the anguish faded from his face. He took her into his arms, and held her tightly.

'I failed you tonight,' he admitted. 'The man could tell me nothing of any use. Oh, he talked.' A shudder ran through him, and Mary responded by wrapping her arms round his waist, and hugging him for all she was worth.

'He said a great many things I shall never repeat. Things that turned my stomach. God, that man is vile!'

'It does not matter,' she said, running her hands up and down his back, in an attempt to soothe him.

He buried his face in her hair, breathing her in as though his life depended on it. They stood like that, entwined in each other's arms, for several minutes.

When he eventually whispered, 'Let me kiss you,' she had no thought of denying him. She simply raised her face to his in mute surrender.

He groaned in heartfelt relief when she parted her lips to let him in.

Mary was only startled for a second or two by the ridge of hardening flesh that she could feel pressing into her stomach. She had learned a lot from the girls she had worked with in that stuffy little workroom. They had sometimes giggled about that part of a man's anatomy that ebbed and flowed with the tide of his lust. So she knew that it was the evidence of Lord Matthison's rising desire. Just as she knew that the molten sensation she was experiencing between her legs was her body making itself ready to accommodate him.

'I want you,' he moaned into her neck, before pressing such a heated kiss to her throat that it felt as if he was melting her bones. He nuzzled the neckline of her gown aside, his fingers working frantically at the ties so that he could bare her breasts.

She gasped at the thrill that shot through her when

his lips fastened round one pouting nipple, and began to suck. Now was the time to stop him, if she was determined she was not going to become his mistress.

'Stop me now,' he panted, echoing her thoughts, 'if you don't want me too. Or I shall not be able to stop.' He ground his hips against hers, his hands cupping her bottom to hold her in place.

'I don't,' she gasped, clinging to his shoulders, 'I don't want you to stop!' she cried, suddenly convinced that this was one thing the saintly Cora would never have granted him. She would never have deigned to come to a man's room, in her nightgown, and let him kiss her. Let him push her nightgown out of the way so he could feast on her breasts.

Before she had time to think better of it, Mary reached down and dextrously undid the buttons that held the fall of his breeches closed and delved inside. Molly had sometimes described the lengths she went to with Joe, in order to 'keep him on a leash'. Mary had never imagined she might be glad to have learned exactly what she needed to do to pleasure a man. But now all she felt was exultation as he gasped, and groaned, and strained against her hand. A fine sheen of sweat broke out on his brow as he grew harder still. She knew he was really, really close to release.

And she had brought him there!

She, Mary the simple-minded dressmaker, was able to give him something his idol never could. Because she was alive, and real, and…in love with him!

That was why the thought of him being angry with

her, of sending her away, had tormented her. Why she felt as though she would fall apart without him. She loved him.

She rained kisses over every part of him she could reach as he backed her towards the bed, feeling a sense of euphoria that she had roused him to such frantic urgency.

'I need you,' she cried as he swept her off her feet, and up on to the bed. It was as simple as that. He meant more to her than her pride, than her honour, than anything. 'I am yours!'

He reared back, tore off the remainder of his clothes, and came down on top of her.

Chapter Eight

There was a moment of searing pain.

'Cora,' he gasped.

Turning her pain to agony.

She had thought she could make him forget Cora. But even though it was *her* body spread-eagled, naked, beneath him, it was her rival he was making love to. He could not have wounded her more deeply if he had plunged a knife into her heart.

'My darling,' he murmured, stroking a tendril of hair from her damp brow. 'My love, I never meant to hurt you. I would rather die than hurt you. I just never imagined…' He shut his eyes briefly. 'Sandiford led me to believe that he…'

Her reticence to speak of what she could recall of her past had lent weight to Lord Sandiford's graphic description of the rape he had boasted of.

But it had all been a pack of lies!

God, how had she managed to remain pure, given the

circumstances to which she had been reduced? When he had seen her sitting in that gin shop, surrounded by jarveys, her eyes blank and weary, he had been ready to believe the worst. And ever since, he had been treating her accordingly. As a fallen woman.

Even though he had not held her to blame, at least, not for long, it had coloured all his actions. A man naturally thought of a woman with sexual experience, however gained, completely differently to the way he regarded a virgin.

But she had been a virgin. And rather than respecting her, he had just been so damned glad she was finally responding to him as he would wish, all he could think of was getting her to the bed before she could change her mind.

And now she was lying with her face averted, her eyes closed, her teeth clenched.

'I have heard that the first time can be painful,' he murmured, gently kissing her cheek. 'I should have prepared you better. I was impatient,' he admitted. 'But now that I am inside you, the pain will ease, I promise.'

It was the genuine remorse she could hear in his voice that got to her. With one final whimper of self-pity, Mary turned her face so that she could return his kiss.

'Yes, that's my brave girl,' he said, when she wound her arms around his neck. Though he instinctively wanted to bury himself deep inside her, he withdrew a little, and began to rotate his hips gently against hers. He wanted to give her pleasure, not just take his own.

It was not long before he could feel her tense inner muscles softening, her rigid body relaxing. He bent to suckle at her breasts, recalling how much she had enjoyed it when he'd done that before.

'I love you,' she whispered, sweeping her feet up and down the backs of his calves.

'I love you too,' he answered, initiating a series of gentle, rhythmic thrusts. Far from tensing up against his intrusion, she undulated beneath him, sinuous as a cat, even to making little mewing noises. He matched his thrusts to her gyrations, resisting the urge to plunge deeply until her own movements became demanding.

When he felt her come to a rippling climax, his sense of elation surpassed anything he had ever experienced before. His restraint shattered, he only had to thrust deep a few more times to bring about his own heady rush of pleasure.

'Cora,' he groaned, slamming into her one last time before collapsing on top of her, utterly spent.

Mary ran her arms up and down his back when she felt his hot tears scalding their way across her cheeks and neck.

It should have been her crying.

She knew she was not the first foolish, simple girl to let a handsome, wealthy man turn her head. But she guessed very few women would ever let a man use their body knowing full well he was in love with someone else.

She had nobody to blame but herself when he called out another woman's name at his moment of crisis. He had never tried to deceive her. On the contrary, he had done all he could to make her believe she was Cora, so that she could more easily cope with the role he wanted her to fill.

'What is it?' he said, once he had got his breath back. 'What is wrong?'

'Nothing.' She sighed despondently. 'What could possibly be wrong?'

He shifted so that he could look down into her face.

'I should not have done this,' he said ruefully. 'You trusted me, and I repaid you by taking your virginity.'

'I wanted you to take it,' she said, acknowledging to herself that this much, at least, was true. 'I wanted you to take me to bed,' she confessed, remembering how she had naïvely thought that, by doing so, she could defeat Cora. 'I want—' she blushed at the admission '—to be your mistress.'

One day he would come to his senses and realise she was not Cora. She would say something, or do something that would snap him back to reality where she was concerned. And then he would send her packing.

But until that day came, she would give herself to him completely. With her whole heart. No more qualms about the immorality of lying with a man to whom she was not married. She loved him. That was all there was to it.

'You will not be my mistress!' he protested. 'We will get married. Just as we should have done seven years ago.'

'I cannot be your wife.' She struggled out of his arms and sat up, pulling the sheets up to cover her breasts. 'I am just an ordinary girl, and you are a lord. If you won't have me as your mistress…' The thought of parting from him was so appalling she promptly burst into tears.

'I won't let you go,' he said, putting his arms round her and drawing her close. 'You are mine now you have given yourself to me. Are you not?'

She nodded into his chest, clinging to him as tightly as he held onto her.

'Then no more talk of parting. If I cannot convince you, once and for all, that you are Cora, then we will live together any way you please.'

They subsided back on to the pillows, wrapped in each other's arms. It was pointless to worry about how long their relationship might last. So far as she was concerned, he was the husband of her heart. Making love with him had been her way of showing him she would belong to him until the day she died. Only him. She would never love another man the way she loved him.

Lord Matthison stroked her hair soothingly until she fell asleep. Then lay there just watching her, his mind racing.

She needed him, this woman, in a way nobody had ever needed him before. She had nobody else, not even herself. What must it be like, to have no memories? To not know who you were, and where you came from?

He frowned. He had not understood what she meant earlier, about dancing to a different tune to the rest of the world, but he thought he could grasp it now. She was utterly alone. And he was an outsider because of what people believed about him. If only his parents had stood by him, everything might have been different. But their attitude had only served to give credence to Robbie's accusations. *'He must have done it,'* people had said, *'or his family would not have shown him the door.'*

Only *she* had demonstrated any faith in him. Though he could tell it went against all her principles, she had yielded her virginity to him. Even though she still thought she was Mary, and it would be impossible to marry him. A less scrupulous woman would have turned what she saw as his delusions to her own advantage. But not her. She just gave, and gave, and gave.

He wrapped his arms round her, and buried his face in her hair, a wave of possessiveness sweeping through him. He was not going to let her go, he vowed, no matter who she was!

When Mary woke, it was to find Lord Matthison, clad in a black velvet dressing gown, sitting on the bedside chair, studying her with brooding intensity.

Hastily, she reached for the covers, and drew them up to her neck, embarrassed to discover she had kicked them aside in her sleep.

He shook his head. 'I was enjoying watching you lying there, naked and flushed from our lovemaking. But you know—' he leant forward to tuck an errant curl behind her ear '—your instinctive modesty pleases me almost as much.'

He bent over and kissed her slowly, languorously on the lips. 'You are completely delightful.'

He got up abruptly, saying, 'But you must be

hungry.' He straightened up and went to the bell-pull by the fireplace. 'I shall have Ephraims bring our breakfast.'

When he saw her horrified gaze flick to the door, he said, 'Just draw the bed-hangings round you.'

She was grateful for his suggestion, but she still did not like to think of being naked, even behind the concealing curtains, with Ephraims in the room.

'My nightdress,' she said, pointing to where it lay on the floor. An understanding smile on his face, Lord Matthison picked it up, and had just handed it to her when Ephraims knocked on the door. With a squeak of alarm, Mary knelt up, desperately trying to pull the bed-hangings closed, whilst still clutching the blankets to her breasts with the other.

With a low chuckle, Lord Matthison shut them for her, before allowing Ephraims to enter. Gratefully, Mary scrambled into her crumpled nightgown, to emerge shyly only after the servant had deposited a breakfast tray on the console table by the door, and left again.

Lord Matthison was pouring her a cup of chocolate. 'How long will it take you to be ready to leave?' he enquired, handing her the brimming cup.

'L-leave?' Mary's heart came to a juddering halt in her chest. She had thought, after all he had said the night before, that he meant them to stay together. How had she got it so wrong?

'Don't look so appalled.' He frowned. 'You must surely realise I want to get you safe out of London as soon as I can. You have too many enemies here.' He broke open a roll, slathered it with butter and honey, as he explained, 'Madame Pichot has already demonstrated how spiteful she can be. Lord Sandiford, should he ever get wind of news that the girl who fought back, leaving his hands permanently scarred, is within his grasp...' He grimaced. 'And let us not forget the thwarted ambitions of Miss Winters. She has already attempted to destroy you once. I will be better able to protect you at Kingsmede.' He darted her an assessing glance, before adding, 'And of course, once we are there, we might be able to trace that woman. The one who took you to Oakham Hall.'

Mary laid her cup and saucer down on the bedside table and slumped down into the chair.

'We need to find her. Find some conclusive proof that you are Cora,' he persisted.

'Last night,' she remonstrated, 'you said we could live however I chose...'

'Once we have established your identity, yes! But dammit, I want to marry you!' he snapped. 'You should be able to take your rightful place at my side, not stay hidden away as though you have something to be ashamed of! And you told me that the only way you will agree to marry me is if I can prove to you that you are Cora,' he pointed out.

Mary shook her head from side to side, tears pricking her eyes.

'What are you so frightened of?' he asked when she began to tremble.

'That—' she gulped '—that once we find out who I

really am, you will send me away,' she finally managed to confess.

'No!' he bit out grimly. 'I shall never do that.' He came across to the chair, and knelt at her feet. With a visible effort, he softened the tone of his voice. 'I have already told you I will always take care of you. If, by some remote chance, we find out that you are not Cora, but some girl who is all alone in the world without family, or friends, it would be unthinkable to abandon you. You will need me all the more.'

He put his arms around her, and she leant forwards, resting her head on his shoulder with a sigh of relief.

'So, now you have nothing to fear, perhaps you can find it in yourself to tell me what you remember about that woman.'

Lord Matthison would never rest until he had solved the mystery of her identity. No matter how hard she wished he would. For in spite of his promises, she had a horrible, sick certainty that the minute they had established who she was, and where she had come from, it would all be over between them.

But all the fight had drained out of her. His will was far stronger than hers. He would keep on and on asking questions until she gave in and told him all she knew. She might as well get it over with.

'The first thing I remember,' she sighed, 'is waking up in a room that I have always believed was an attic. It smelled of dust and decay, and there was all sorts of old broken furniture stacked up in jumbled heaps. And no proper window. Just a skylight, at the far end, by the door.'

She felt his shoulder tense under her forehead. She knew he was thrilled that she was giving him more information, but she could not share his excitement. A pall of misery had descended over her.

'She only came in once or twice a day, with a jug of water, and a plate of what looked like the leftovers from someone else's meal. She thought me a great nuisance for being there. She never said, but I could tell. She would stand there, staring down at me as though she hated me.'

'What did she look like?' Lord Matthison broke in to ask. 'It sounds as if you were in a biggish house. Perhaps I know her.'

'She looked exactly how you would expect a female prison warder to look. Hard-faced, and hefty. Plain, serviceable clothing. Hard eyes. Hard hands…'

'You are doing well,' he said, running his hands up and down her back, and dropping a kiss onto her temple. 'Can you recall anything else?'

With his arms round her, the feelings that usually swamped her along with her memories had far less power.

And it struck her that when she had been bold enough to face him, in the Flash of Lightning, she had learned that he was just a man after all, and not some horrible phantom. She had realised that she had been silly to run from him that day in Curzon Street. She wondered if any of the things she shied from remembering were really as bad as she feared. Maybe, if she turned and faced those shadowy images that lurked in the hidden corners of her mind, they would all turn out to be equally harmless?

Had she not learned that things were hardly ever as bad as she feared? The girls who had so scared her, that first time she had walked into Madame's workrooms, for instance, with their rough, aggressive manners. They had become her friends.

Tentatively, she went back to the way she had felt that day, when she had woken in that attic. She had not known who she was, or where she was, and that had frightened her. But most of all, she had felt unbearably unhappy. So unhappy that she would lie there wishing she was dead, without understanding why. She could remember that it hardly seemed worth the trouble of eating, and keeping herself alive. She had only picked at what her warder brought because she had been afraid of what the woman would do if she came back and found the tray untouched.

'She used to come up to the attics at night, when she thought I was asleep. She would go to an old bureau that was half-buried under a mound of mouldering linen, open one of the drawers, reach her hand inside and press a hidden catch. I would hear the loud click, and then the sound of a panel dropping to the floor. And she would stoop, and pick up a ring.'

'A ring?' He disentangled himself from her, and held her by the shoulders, so that he could look straight into her eyes. 'What sort of a ring?'

'It was a big, heavy-looking thing. It looked very old, somehow. The setting…' She frowned, trying to picture it clearly. 'She would hold it up to the light, so that the flame flickered through the stone. It always gave me the shivers, because it would look as though it was bleeding.'

'A ruby,' he breathed. His hands had clenched so hard on her shoulders that it was almost painful. 'I think, I really believe, that it could have been your betrothal ring. It has been in the family for generations. It was the only item of her jewellery that my mother managed to keep hidden from my father. Our one and only family heirloom. He had sold or wagered everything else he could lay his hands on. When I told her we were to be married, she fetched it from wherever she had been hiding it, for me to give to you. Don't you see what this means?'

He got to his feet, running his fingers through his hair as he paced back and forth. 'You could have been set upon by robbers. She was probably the fence. In those circumstances, she would naturally have kept you concealed when we began searching the area. She would not want to give away her criminal connections…' He whirled to face her. 'Did you see anyone else while you were held in that house?'

A cold sensation slid down her spine. She had always had the conviction that the woman had no right to the ring. But she had been so weak, and that woman so strong and always angry, that she had never dared question her about it. Instead, she had told herself over and over again that it was nothing to do with her.

Something shimmied in the air, hovering just out of reach…

She shook her head. She had to stop this! She was

letting Lord Matthison influence the few things she did remember, now, because she wanted so desperately to be the woman he loved.

She focused on him as he kept on talking, and pacing the room. And as she watched the jerky movements that punctuated each sentence, the troubling sensation evened out, like ripples vanishing after a stone has dropped into a pond.

'Even if my surmise is correct about the motive for hiding you to begin with, it does not explain why she took you to Oakham Hall. Nor why the housekeeper was willing to take you on, just on this hefty woman's recommendation, when you were clearly hardly fit for any sort of work. And we cannot ask her. The one thing I did find out from Sandiford is that his former housekeeper died. He complained about how difficult he is finding it getting a replacement.' He paused, hands on his hips while he stared at her as though she was an intriguing puzzle. 'It almost sounds as if your gaoler was a person of some standing, locally. But your description does not fit anyone I know. Well, no matter,' he said, coming back to her, and sitting on the edge of the bed. 'We can circulate her description when we get down there.'

'Do we,' Mary said hesitantly, something inside her shrivelling at the prospect of searching for a woman she never wished to set eyes on again, 'do we really have to leave London? I know you say you are concerned for my safety here, but I would not want to take you away from your work.'

'My work?' He looked puzzled for a moment, then his face shuttered. 'You mean fleecing drunkards with more money than sense. I think you can safely say I shall not be sorry to leave all that behind.'

He looked at her, then at the wall behind her, then at his feet, then squared his shoulders.

'I have no need to earn a living that way. I have not needed to for some time. The only reason I kept going back to the tables…' His cheeks flushed a dull red. 'You are going to think I was quite mad.' He got up, stalked across to the table, and tore open a second bread roll.

'I had convinced myself that your ghost haunted me.' He jabbed his knife into the crock of butter. 'I attributed all my success at the tables to your benign influence. I went back, time and time again, just to feel you near me. How crazy is that?' He kept his back to her, as though spreading butter on to a roll required all his concentration. 'When I hate gambling.' He flung his knife onto the tray with a clatter.

His shoulders hunched as he braced his hands on the table top.

'I had a run of luck at the outset. The kind of winning streak real gamblers dream of. And then I began to tell myself you were guiding me, whenever I won. And if I did not win, I decided you were not in that particular hell, and went off to another one, searching till I found you.

'I despised the men who sat there, too drunk to know when they were throwing good money after bad, but all along I was far sicker than any of them.

'I was sleepwalking through some sort of…labyrinth of self-deception, making more money than I knew how to spend, when all the time…'

He straightened up slowly and turned to look at her, his face racked with guilt. 'You were within my reach all the time. Working yourself to the point of exhaustion for your food and lodging. If only I had kept on searching for you. If only I had…'

She got up and flung her arms round him, tugging his head down to the crook of her neck.

'Hush, don't,' she said. 'It is over now. Done with. I…' She steeled herself to be what he wanted, to say what he needed to hear in this moment. 'I am here now. And,' she continued, utterly sure that no woman could remain obdurate in the face of such sincere remorse, 'I do not blame you for any of it.' Whatever had happened to Cora, surely she would forgive him for carrying on living, the only way he knew how?

'I will make it up to you, Cora, I swear!' he vowed, tilting her face so he could kiss her. 'I want nothing so much as to leave London and its haunts of vice behind us, and make a fresh start. At Kingsmede.'

She returned his kiss with fervour, not really caring where he took her, so long as they stayed together.

'I suppose,' she said, reaching up to smooth the frown line from his brow, 'I would not like to run into Lord Sandiford on the street. And as for poor Miss Winters…I do not think it would be very kind of us to flaunt our affair in her face.'

'After what she would have done to you?' He looked incredulous.

'Well, she must have been heartbroken when she learned her engagement to you must come to an end…'

'Heartbroken? Not her! A more heartless creature it would be hard to find!'

'So why did you propose to her, then?'

'I did no such thing,' he growled. Then, seeing the sheer puzzlement on her face, he swept her into his arms and set her down on the bed. 'I can see,' he sighed, 'that I shall have to confess my stupidity in regard to Miss Winters, too.'

He went back to the console table, picked up the plate of buttered rolls, and pressed them into her hand. He took one, bit into it, then paced to the window, chewing.

'Mr Winters was a business acquaintance of mine. I have invested a good deal of the money I won at play in various enterprises. Usually, I carried out any business I had with Mr Winters in his offices, but occasionally he would invite me to his home. Along with other investors that might wish to have mutual dealings. His wife and daughter were sometimes present at certain parts of such gatherings. And—' he leaned his forearm against the window frame '—she impressed me, I have to admit. She was so different from the empty-headed society females who have been fluttering and cooing about me since it became known how successfully I had reversed my family's fortunes. She never attempted to flirt with me, but spoke to me in the same polite manner she addressed all her father's other guests.'

As he took another meditative bite out of his breakfast roll, Mary's heart sank.

'Did you find her pretty?' she found herself saying, though the thought of him admiring yet another female tore at her heart.

'Pretty?' He whirled round, an expression of complete bafflement on his face. 'What do her looks have to do with any of it? I have told you, she lulled me into a false sense of security, by behaving as though she had no interest in me whatsoever!'

The pain eased somewhat. Mary nibbled at her own breakfast roll as Lord Matthison resumed pacing.

'One night, I arrived at her home, to find her looking somewhat distressed. When I asked, as any gentleman would, if there was anything amiss, she…' He halted by the window, gazing down into the street as though whatever he could see out there had his full attention.

'She lured me into a room apart, on the pretext of saying she was in desperate need of advice she thought only I could give her. Of course, it was not advice she wanted from me at all. As soon as the door was shut, she flung herself at me…'

The disgust she could hear in his voice, the rigid set of his shoulders, paradoxically made Mary's own tension diminish.

'Naturally, our…clinch was witnessed. She had arranged it all down to the last detail.'

Mary's eyes strayed down the tense line of his spine, to where his legs protruded from the hem of his dressing gown. Bare legs. It had felt wonderful when she had stroked the soles of her feet over them.

'I wonder why she went to such lengths,' Mary

mused, her eyes riveted to his bare feet. It seemed strange to think of feet as objects of beauty, but Lord Matthison's were. 'She must have been quite desperate, don't you think? Or her family were. Do you think they compelled her to it?'

He whirled round to face her, an incredulous expression on his face.

'Oh, come now!' she said, licking honey from her fingers. 'You have a reputation for being dangerous. Fiendish even. I could never understand why Mrs Winters was so insistent that you marry her daughter, when she kept on emphasising how evil you were. They must be in some sort of financial difficulty.'

'Is it so impossible to believe she might have been in love with me?' he retorted.

'Do you think she was?'

He ran his fingers through his hair. 'Hell, no! If I have the measure of her father correctly, it was all about money and position. He wanted a title for his daughter, I suppose. But in the end, she was terrified of me. I made sure of it!'

'Really?' She drew her knees up to her chest, hugging them as she looked at him with her head cocked to one side. 'I cannot imagine being afraid of you.'

'You always saw the good in me when nobody else did,' he said. 'Even when…' A shadow flickered across his face. 'No, forget I said that. The circumstances at Kingsmede are completely different now, anyway, and…what are you laughing at?'

'You…you asked me to for…forget…' She giggled. 'When all you have wanted me to do up till now is to remember. I do wish you would make up your mind…'

It felt as though the sun had come out. This was his Cora, just as she used to be. Laughing at his absurdities. Making him feel life was not the serious business he believed, but a game they could play together. Chasing away his shadows with her sunny nature, her natural inclination to see the good in everyone, not just him.

The night before, when he had held her in his arms, and he smelled the scent of roses on her skin, it had been as though he was transported back in time. The years had rolled away and he was a boy full of optimism, honoured to be the first one to kiss her. The first to make love to her.

But this…this was a moment he would treasure till the day he died. She was sitting in his bed, her glorious hair tumbling round her pale shoulders, laughing again. A woman with less spirit would have forgotten how to laugh after all she had been through.

'You are happy,' he said, with satisfaction.

'Yes,' she said, smiling as she held out her hand to him. 'Because I am here with you.'

'Nothing else matters, does it?' he said. This moment was precious, yet he sensed the fragility of it. Like a newly blown soap bubble, anything that touched it might burst it.

He walked to the bed, untying the belt of his dressing gown.

'Have you finished with your breakfast?' he asked,

taking the plate from her and setting it on the bedside chair.

She said nothing, but the hunger in her eyes was all the answer he needed.

'Kingsmede will still be there tomorrow,' he growled, tumbling her down among the rumpled sheets.

'And the day after,' she agreed, twining her arms round his neck.

Chapter Nine

She had no idea how long they spent in that room. They kept the shutters closed, sleeping when they were sated with lovemaking, sending out for food when they were hungry.

But she knew their magical time out of time had come to an end when she awoke to the sound of Lord Matthison drawing the curtains. The pale grey light heralding the dawn of a new day had replaced the romantic glow of candles. One or two of them still smoked as though he had only just snuffed them. Her heart sank when she saw that he was fully dressed, with a determined look on his face.

'I have made the travel arrangements,' he said brusquely. 'Since you have not yet unpacked your trunk, we should be able to set out as soon as you have taken breakfast, and put some clothes on.'

When she made no attempt to stir from the bed, he frowned. 'I have spent long enough stumbling around in the dark. We need to return to Kingsmede.'

There was no point in arguing with him. When his mind was made up, she knew that nothing could sway him.

'I hope,' he said later, once he had handed her into the hired carriage, 'that you will not find life in the country too dull.'

He shot her an assessing glance. She had been so quiet this morning. And clearly unhappy about leaving London behind. Though she had not uttered one word of protest, she kept on looking out of the windows as they passed various landmarks, as though she was silently bidding them farewell.

'Many people find it somewhat flat, without all the amusements available in town.'

'Well, I did not see that side of life in London, did I? I spent sixteen hours out of every day shut up in an attic, sewing.'

He felt a rush of relief to have got a response from her, even if it was a rather negative one.

'So, it is not the prospect of boredom that has made you so waspish this morning.'

She turned to him in amazement. Surely he knew why she was upset? She would have been more than happy to have stayed in his room indefinitely. *He was the one who had grown bored. The one who needed more stimulation than she could provide.* The one who had opened the curtains, and let reality flood back into their lives.

'My mother,' he said when she made no contribution to the conversation, 'referred to Kingsmede as her prison. Though it was undoubtedly my father's profligacy that made it so. She never ceased complaining that she could not even afford to escape up to London for a change of scenery, while my father hardly ever set foot in the place. Not enough diversions for a man of his temperament in a rural backwater,' he finished drily, his tone suggesting he was quoting what the man himself had said. 'It will not be the same for us. Should you ever feel like a jaunt up to town, I shall take you. It is about time I purchased a carriage for my own use, rather than hiring one…'

'There is no need to purchase a carriage on my account,' she protested. 'I have no wish to return to London, and risk running into Lord Sandiford. No, no, I am sure I shall find plenty to occupy me at Kingsmede. After all, it will all be quite new to me. I expect it will take some time before the novelty of it all begins to wear thin.'

'The countryside is really very pleasant, in a quiet sort of way,' he said. 'Though not, of course, possessed of the rugged beauty of Scotland.'

'Scotland? Why do you mention Scotland?'

'It is where you grew up.'

Where Cora had grown up, she silently corrected him.

'However did you meet her, then?' she plucked up the courage to say after a few minutes. Her antipathy towards the woman who'd had such a devastating impact on this man's life was no match for the force of her curiosity. 'C-Cora, that is.'

'I was at school with your brother,' he replied tersely, his face closing up.

When, after some minutes, it became apparent he was not going to divulge any more, Mary turned to stare out of the window despondently. It was all very well for him to probe into her past, searching and interrogating until she was almost hysterical. But let her ask him one question about his background, and he wrapped his privacy round him like a cloak.

They must have travelled almost a full mile before she felt him reach for her hand.

'It is not always easy to talk about the past, is it?' he said with contrition. 'Not when it is painful.'

When she returned the pressure of his hand, signifying her understanding, he said, 'Now that we are together again, though, everything will come right.'

His misplaced optimism plunged Mary even deeper into the gloom that had dogged her from the moment she had first opened her eyes that morning.

'We were very close friends, your brother and I. We even spent our school holidays visiting each other's homes. I had always thought Kingsmede a completely joyless place to live before he burst into it like a whirlwind. My parents, you see,' he said, raising her hand to his lips and kissing it, 'had never been interested in anything I did. They were never proud of any of my achievements. But he interpreted their indifference as the most marvellous freedom.' He tucked her hand into the crook of his arm.

'That summer, we roamed the fields and woods from dawn 'til dusk, catching fish from our lakes and streams and cooking them over open fires, and generally living off the bounty of my neglected estate like a pair of poachers. Or gypsies, or bandits, or whatever else we decided to be on any given day. During the next long vacation, your mother insisted on returning the invitation, in spite of your brother's protests that he would rather come back to Kingsmede.

'That was when,' he said, turning in his seat, 'I met you for the first time. You were a shy little thing, with long braids, bony wrists and a freckled face.' He reached out and teased a few coppery tendrils from the braid she had pinned up beneath her hat, and wound them round his fingers.

Then, with a crooked smile, he went on, 'You stared in awe at your big brother's friend, then ducked out of sight, and kept well away from us for the duration of my visit. I could not even get you to speak to me at mealtimes. Not that conversation was encouraged at table.' He grimaced.

'I soon understood why your brother loved the ramshackle housekeeping that prevailed at Kingsmede. Your father was the very antithesis of mine. He ruled over you all with a rod of iron. And as for the sermons he preached…' He shut his eyes and shook his head. 'They did not have quite the effect—' he opened his eyes, and grinned at her ruefully '—on growing boys that he intended. We came out of the kirk on Sundays so utterly sure we were doomed to spend eternity burning in hell-fire that we just had to go out and find some consolation en route.'

He paused, as though choosing his next words carefully. 'There was more opportunity, of course, for sinning at Kingsmede.

'Things only really changed after your parents died,' he went on. 'Your brother could not leave you on your own, so I had no choice but to travel to Scotland when I wanted to visit. He warned me I would have to take things as I found them. But I did not care for that, nor the length of the journey. I knew I would be far happier in Auchentay, with my friend, and his sister, than on my own at Kingsmede.

'But during that last visit, he really was too preoccupied with winding up your late father's rather tangled affairs to spend much time with me. And so it was left to you to entertain me.'

He smiled at her, running his finger along the line of her jaw. 'Finally, there was nothing to prevent us spending as much time with each other as we wanted. We took full advantage of our freedom.' His heart turned over in his chest as he recalled that idyllic summer. The sun seemed to have shone every day. And she had never stopped smiling.

There was little left of that laughing, lovely young girl in the gaunt, troubled woman who sat beside him now. Irritably he pushed the unflattering comparison aside. There was not much of the young man he had been either. After she had disappeared, he had abandoned his own aspirations to attend university. Pretty soon, the only books he studied were books of form. The only human contact he had was with drunks and sharps and bookmakers. He had only slowly clawed his way back to some semblance of normality. But it remained a thin veneer, concealing his ravaged, embittered core.

The years, he sighed, had twisted and warped them both almost beyond recognition.

Robbie, too. He had taken to drink to blot out the horror of what he believed his young friend had done to his only sister.

He would be a fool to think that any of them would ever be quite the same again.

Though last night, she had been all he had dreamed of, with her hair tumbling round her shoulders like living flame, and her eyes alight with love. He had felt triumphant at winning this woman's heart.

Just as he had thought he had won Cora's once before. He had risked everything, back then, to hold onto her for ever. Yet she had still slipped through his fingers.

If he should lose her again…

When they reached Kingsmede, this fragile, tenuous relationship they were beginning to form would be put to the test. She would feel self-conscious, he knew, about continuing their love affair under the watchful eyes of his household staff.

'It will not be long until we stop for a change of horses,' he said gruffly. 'We may as well put up there for the night.'

She looked out of the window, baffled. 'It is scarce past noon,' she pointed out.

He returned her puzzled look with a scowl. He had woken this morning yearning to discover the truth about this woman's past, so that he could bind her to him for ever.

But now, all that seemed important was clinging to what they had right this minute. The truth could wait for a little while longer. He would be a fool to jeopardise what he had found with this woman who called herself Mary!

'It will be dark when we close the curtains,' he replied.

Her eyes widened. She blushed. But she did not voice any objections.

With a growl of satisfaction, Lord Matthison pulled her into his arms, and began his intended ravishment at her lips.

To Mary's disappointment, they spent only one night on the road. And Lord Matthison was particularly terse with his instructions to pack up and set off again. But only mid-way through the next afternoon, he grasped her hand, saying 'Not far now.' He leaned forward to point through the window. 'We are just entering Bamford, our nearest market town.'

It did not take them long to pass through the bustling, prosperous-looking town. Then the carriage slowed as the road out of it became quite steep. Just before they reached the top of the long incline, the coachman nudged the straining horses into a left turn on to a road that hugged the brow of the hill. Through Mary's window she could see acres of lush farmland rippling down into the valley below.

But then the carriage veered sharply to the right, and the vista of what promised to be a bountiful harvest disappeared as they entered a belt of woodland.

Soon they were passing through a pair of stone

pillars, on to a carriage drive completely overhung by a tangle of trees. They crowded the drive so thickly that once or twice branches scraped the sides of the carriage, sounding like the talons of unseen phantoms, trying in vain to impede their progress.

Mary shivered, telling herself that it was only because they had gone from bright sunlight into the greenish, mouldering gloom that she had conjured up such a macabre image. But she could not shake off the feeling of foreboding. It grew stronger with each yard they penetrated deeper into the woodland.

'Cold, love?'

She jumped as Lord Matthison patted her hand. She had almost forgotten he was there, so focused was she on watching as the shadows, like long, hostile fingers, insinuated their way into the carriage, inching their way ever nearer, as though they wanted to close round her throat, and choke the life from her.

'N-not cold,' she stuttered through chattering teeth. 'Sc-scared.'

Because the shadows were not only creeping into the carriage from the outside. They were seething up inside her, gathering such strength she was not sure how much longer she could hold them at bay. Perhaps she should not try to. Had she not worked out that things were never as bad as you imagined they could be? She had been afraid of Lord Matthison, that first time he had stepped out of the shadows. And yet, once she had faced him, she had learned there was nothing about him to frighten her at all.

'We will be out of it soon,' he said, slipping his arm round her shoulder when she turned a tense white face towards him. 'When we round the next bend we will be into the park, and you will be able to see the house.'

Her eyes grew wider, and though they were fixed on him, he felt as though it was not him she was seeing at all.

Nor was she. An image had taken possession of her mind. The image of an ivy-clad Elizabethan manor house, with barley-twist chimneys and dozens upon dozens of windows, the thousands of tiny diamond-shaped panes glittering in the low sunlight making the walls look as though they were studded with jewels.

'I sent word to have your old room prepared for you. The one you had when you were here before. I thought it would help you settle more quickly, and I also thought establishing you straight away as my fiancée would spare you at least some gossip…'

A panicky feeling swirled in Mary's stomach.

'You are going to make me sleep in *her* room?' She could see it. Vividly. There would be an ancient, canopied bed, giving a view over the park down to a lake. An intricately carved wardrobe, full of dresses, and shoes ranged up on the floor below…would he expect her to wear the dead woman's clothes, as well as sleep in her bed?

Her breath caught in her chest.

'I can't,' she gasped, tearing at the bonnet ribbons that felt as though they were choking her. 'Can't breathe…'

She clawed frantically at the top buttons of her coat, which had grown so tight it was like a vice squeezing her chest. The world began to spin. Through the haze that clouded the interior of the coach, she felt Lord Matthison reach past her, to pull the window down. She felt the cold air slap her cheek, and his voice saying, 'There, is that better?'

But as she leaned forwards, to gulp in the sunlight that had suddenly come streaming in, she saw something that stopped her breathing altogether.

It was a house. An old, ivy-covered house, with barley-twist chimneys, and diamond-paned windows…

'Cora, darling, breathe…' she could hear him saying, from far, far away. But she could no longer see him. He was not in the coach with her. It was another man. A younger man. And he was saying, 'Just look at what a grand place ye're to be mistress of. Did you ever see the like?'

And her heart was sinking. She did not want to be mistress of the place. That was not why she had come.

'Don't call me Cora,' she choked. 'I don't belong there.' She pointed at the Elizabethan manor. 'I never have, and I never will…'

And then she could no longer hold back the great wave of certainty that she had travelled this road before, feeling exactly as she did now. It surged up from deep, deep within, breaking over her and washing aside everything she had achieved in the last seven years, until she was reduced to a quivering, pathetic, young girl, whose heart was irretrievably broken.

'No!' she cried in desperation. 'I am not her. I am Mary!'

She could hear the wheels crunching over gravel. She

felt his hands on her, lifting her, pulling her somewhere she did not want to go. She could not fight the shadows, but she could fight him. And she did. With hands curved like claws.

'I won't, I won't be Cora!' She did not want to go back there. It hurt too much. 'I don't want to be her!' she screamed. 'I'm Mary!'

But it was too late. Mary was drowning in Cora's pain. And Lord Matthison captured her flailing hands between his own, and used them to pull her out of the comparative safety of the coach, and on to the shadowed portico of Kingsmede.

A door behind him swung open, and out from it barrelled a great giant of a man with an unruly thatch of red hair and eyes like shards of bloodshot ice.

'Put ma' sister down, you lying, cheatin' swine, so I can gi' ye the thrashing ye deserve!'

And everything she had kept submerged for seven long years broke free, drenching her in total awareness, and choking the very last gasp of air from her lungs.

She gave one strangled, agonised cry, and fell headlong into darkness.

Lord Matthison caught her as she fainted, and swept her up into his arms. He barged his way into the house, yelling 'Get some smelling salts!' to his housekeeper, who had trailed on to the portico in the Scotsman's wake, and 'Get out of my way, you damn fool,' to the giant who tried to block his path.

'What have ye done to her?' yelled Robbie as Lord Matthison carried her through to the morning room.

He could see the way Robbie's mind was working and it made his blood boil. He had dragged his terrified sister from the carriage, her clothing dishevelled, and then she had fainted dead away.

'For God's sake!' he snapped as he lowered her gently on to the *chaise longue*. 'If I meant to rape her, do you suppose I'd have invited you here to witness the crime?'

'Who can ever tell what is going on in that infernally twisted mind of yours?' He thrust his face aggressively close to Lord Matthison's.

The alcoholic fumes made his eyes water.

'Where have you been hiding the poor wee lassie all these years?'

'I have not been hiding her anywhere, you drunken fool,' he replied, pushing him aside, so that he could attend to Cora. She was so deathly pale. She lay so still he could not even be sure she was breathing. He leaned closer, meaning to see if he could find a pulse, when, with a roar of outrage, Robbie grabbed him by his collar and yanked him backwards.

'Keep your filthy, lecherous hands off her!'

'Don't be more of an ass than you can help,' Lord Matthison grated, desperately striving to keep a leash on his own temper. 'She needs—'

But Robbie was in no mood for talking. In the old days, the swing he took at Lord Matthison would undoubtedly have floored him. Had it connected with his jaw. But Lord Matthison managed to dodge it with ease. As he did the next wild swing, and the next, and the one after that. Seven years of drunkenness had taken their toll on his former friend. Robbie's size and aggression were now no match for the science he had spent seven years learning from Gentleman Jackson, and the cunning he had picked up on the streets.

But his inability to land more than the occasional glancing blow on his opponent was stoking Robbie's anger to the point of madness. With a roar he lunged forwards, arms outstretched as though meaning to trap Lord Matthison in a crushing bear hug. Had he succeeded, they would both have landed on the *chaise longue*, on top of Cora.

So Lord Matthison jabbed Robbie hard in the stomach, halting his headlong rush, then got his own shoulder into the larger man's chest, pitching him sideways, away from the vulnerable woman lying unconscious.

Robbie wrapped his arms round Lord Matthison as he toppled sideways. They both landed on the rug by the side of the sofa, kicking and gouging when neither could land a solid blow on the other's body, locked in a fight that had been seven years coming.

As Cora slowly surfaced from the depths of her faint, the first thing she heard was the all-too-familiar sound of her brother, grunting and cursing as he beat the living daylights out of somebody.

She felt extreme reluctance to take a look at his victim, yet somehow, her eyelids drifted open anyhow.

And there he was, rolling around on the floor with Kit Brereton, his best friend. She felt a moment's confusion. Not because they were fighting. There was nothing new in that. But surely Father would never allow them to scrap in the house…

But Father was dead. And Robbie was the head of the household now, so he…no, wait a minute. The ceiling above her head was ornately plastered. There was no ceiling anything like this anywhere in their house. It looked far more like Kit's house…

Kingsmede.

That was right…she had come to Kingsmede, to marry Kit, because…

For a few seconds, past and present swirled and shimmied around her, the eddies almost dragging her back under. But then the two men rolled against the sofa leg with such violence that, had she still been insensible, she would have been tipped on to the floor.

Not that either of them would have noticed. They were too engrossed in beating the tar out of each other. They seemed to have forgotten she was there.

Or, if it did cross either of their minds, they would just assume she would run away from this uninhibited display of masculine brutality. And wait for one of them to come to her, and inform her of the outcome.

Like they had last time.

Gripped by a cold fury, she sat up.

She was not a child any more, too timid to stand up and speak for herself! She would determine her own future! She was not any man's possession, to dispose of as though she had no opinion of her own!

When the fight rolled sufficiently far from the sofa

for her to leave it safely, she got shakily to her feet, and made for the vase of roses she had seen on a table under the window. She stood with it in her hands for a second or two, wondering which one of them deserved she smash it over his head the more.

In the end, since there was not a second vase with which she could dispense equal justice, she had to settle for merely dashing its contents over the pair of them.

'For heaven's sake!' she snapped when they both ceased hostilities long enough to stare up at her in incredulity. 'You are not schoolboys any longer!'

Lord Matthison disentangled himself first, shoving her brother roughly to one side as he rose to one knee. 'Cora,' he spluttered through the water that was dripping from his hair into his eyes. 'Are you all right?'

'Much you care!' she stormed. 'You…you hypocrite! And as for you…' She glared down at her brother. 'My God, Robbie, you've turned out just like Father. Using your fists first, and asking questions later.'

'That's no' fair!' he protested, brushing dank flower petals from his chest. 'You were out cold when the fight started. You cannot possibly know who threw the first punch!'

She reeled back from the smell that wafted to her on his breath. 'Exactly like Father,' she said. 'After all you said when he died, all the promises you made me, you've taken to drink…'

Robbie sat up, glowering at her. 'You don't know what I've been through these past seven years. No man could have stood it without a wee dram now and again.'

'You see?' She laughed. 'You are even making the same excuses he did. Nothing was ever his fault, was it? Someone else always drove him to it. Either Mother drove him to the edge of his patience with her constant ailments, or I was too much of a disappointment for any man to contend with, or you provoked him with your wildness…and the answer was always to punish us. And that's what you're doing, is it not? Punishing Christopher…for something that was not his fault!'

She sat down abruptly on the sofa as a whole new set of memories came flooding to the surface, set free, apparently, by simply alluding to them.

'You've remembered…' Lord Matthison grated, moving towards her, on his knees. Blood was streaming from a split lip, water dripped from his hair, yet his eyes were alight with what, only this morning, she would have said was love. 'Cora…'

'Yes, I've remembered,' she said in a voice so cold it halted him in its tracks.

She steeled herself against his look of baffled hurt. For no matter how convincing it looked, she knew it was all an act. She meant nothing to him. She never had.

Wrapping her arms round herself as the only barrier left against the pain, she groaned, 'I remember everything.'

Chapter Ten

'I apprehend you no longer require the smelling salts?' Mrs Paulding stood in the doorway, surveying the wreckage of the drawing room with distaste.

Lord Matthison scrambled to his feet, his brows drawn into a frown.

'As you see, Miss Montague has recovered from her faint—'

'And would now like to retire to her room,' Cora said firmly. Her heart was pounding, her whole body shaking with the effort of behaving correctly when what she really wanted to do was rage and scream and howl.

'I will come to your room once I have changed,' Lord Matthison said in an urgent undertone. 'We must speak…'

'It would be most improper to admit you to my room,' she replied frostily. 'In future, anything you have to say to me, you will have the goodness to say in public.'

His eyes widened. His face turned white, making

the streak of blood trickling from his lip look an even darker red.

As she turned to leave the room, he made to seize her arm.

'Oh, no, you don't,' growled Robbie, lurching to his feet, scattering water droplets and broken rose stems in all directions.

'Dammit all to hell!' cried Lord Matthison. 'You cannot think I mean her any harm?'

'I saw the way she looked at you. That's enough for me,' said Robbie, interposing his large body between Lord Matthison and his sister.

'Robbie,' Cora sighed, 'I do wish you would stay out of this.' He was itching for an excuse to take up the fight where she had obliged him to leave it off. Stepping to one side so that she could see Lord Matthison beyond her brother's belligerent bulk, she said, 'Please just do as I ask, Christopher, and leave me alone! I need time to…' She squeezed her eyes shut against another surge of self-awareness left her feeling dizzy. 'I need to think.'

A muscle twitched in his jaw. Without taking his eyes from her, he rapped out, 'Mrs Paulding, make sure Miss Montague reaches her room safely. And see she has everything she needs. She has journeyed far, and suffered a severe shock.'

The housekeeper obediently placed her arm around Cora's waist, and supported her from the room. Too grateful to be spared any further browbeating from either of the men in that room, Cora made no protest until the door was shut behind them. Only then did she halt, and turn to the grey-haired woman. More grey than she remembered, and more lines on her face, but then hadn't the years taken their toll on them all?

'You can drop the show of concern now there is nobody to see us. I know you have never liked me.'

'It is not my place,' Mrs Paulding replied, 'to express any sort of opinion regarding the young ladies his lordship chooses to bring into his home.'

Cora reeled away from her at the implication Lord Matthison was always bringing women here. And Mrs Paulding just kept walking, rigid-backed, towards the dark oak staircase. Cora made it to the foot of the stair and grasped hold of the newel post for support, her pain redoubled by a fresh wave of memories. She was almost as breathless as she had been in the coach, but now, she was having to deal with them completely on her own.

It had been seeing Mrs Paulding's back, turned to her after delivering a cruel aside, that had done it this time. She sucked in a deep breath, as she mounted the first step, deliberately avoiding looking back at the morning room, where Christopher and Robbie were still closeted together. Last time she had been in there, the woman lying on that sofa had not been her, but Christopher's mother. Christopher had kept a tight hold of her hand as he had made the introductions with his chin up, and more than a hint of defiance in his voice.

'Oh, Christopher,' Lady Matthison had wailed, pressing one hand to her bosom, which had heaved dramatically. 'Surely you cannot mean to make me so unhappy because of—' and she had waved her other hand in Cora's direction, lowering her voice to a tragic moan '—that Creature? I could have understood it if she was in the least bit pretty,' she had added, reaching for a scrap of lace with which to dab at her eyes. 'But when you know how desperately Kingsmede stands in need of an heiress...'

Cora opened her eyes, which she had inadvertently shut against the sting of the reception she had endured all those years ago. Mrs Paulding had reached the landing, and was staring down at her, bristling with impatience.

For a moment or two, past and present merged, and she was just a nervous girl on her first visit to her fiancé's family home. She had just been mortally wounded by her future mother-in-law's reaction to her, and there stood Mrs Paulding, bidden to take her to her room, staring at her with open derision on her face.

She had scarcely seen Kit's mother after that. Lady Matthison had made no attempt at extending any hospitality to the girl she saw as her son's great mistake, taking all her meals in her room. Kit and Robbie had shrugged off her attitude, telling Cora that mealtimes would be more congenial without her drooping over the table. But Cora had taken it to heart. Neither of his parents had approved of her. His mother had showed it by refusing to welcome her properly to Kingsmede, and his father by not even bothering to come home to meet his son's intended bride at all. And she could quite understand their attitude. Because she was not a worthy bride for a man of Kit's standing. He *should* have been marrying somebody pretty, or wealthy, or both. A woman who came from his world, who would know how to deal with servants who despised them.

No wonder, she gasped, she had felt so aware of the discrepancy between her station in life and Lord Matthison's this time round. It echoed exactly what she had felt before. When she had been his fiancée.

Slowly, her eyes came back into focus, drawn to the stony-faced housekeeper who still waited for her at the head of the stairs.

Last time Cora had been here, the woman had gone out of her way to make her as uncomfortable as she could. And Cora had never had the confidence to complain. Instead, she had begun to wonder, along with Mrs Paulding, why such a handsome young lord should have taken up with a plain, ill-educated minister's daughter? Long before the housekeeper had enlightened her as to what was really going on, she had begun to feel as though she had only dreamed he had asked her to marry him, and that one day she would wake up, and find herself back in Auchentay. Every day she had spent at Kingsmede had increased her fear that one wrong move on her part could bring everything crashing down around her ears.

Pressing her lips tightly together, Cora climbed the remaining stairs, her eyes fixed on Mrs Paulding's face.

'You still do not want me to marry Lord Matthison, do you?' she said, once she was on a level with the dour woman.

'You are not,' the woman replied with venom, 'and never have been, any good for his lordship. While you stayed away, Lord Matthison has prospered. He has looked after his tenants, improved his lands, and refurbished this house. You have not been back in his life for five minutes, and already there's brawling in the drawing room. That is my opinion, madam, and I shall stick by it.'

Certain things had not changed, then. Cora remembered the gleeful way Mrs Paulding had finally managed to convince her how little Kit really cared for her. Her eyes had flashed with malicious triumph as she had informed Cora that everyone knew the young master had only proposed to her because her bully of a brother had forced him to it. And went on to say that if she had any integrity, she would not hold him to an engagement that had already caused a breach between him and his parents.

She had lain awake all that night, weeping as she recalled the events that had led up to Kit's proposing to her.

He had taken her out on to the loch in the rowing boat. And he had finally kissed her. She had been yearning for him to kiss her for days and days.

No, longer. She had always admired Robbie's solemn-eyed friend, right from the first moment he had stepped into their home. He had fascinated her. He was so different from the men who lived in the village, and even from her irascible father, and brother. He had good manners. What her mother termed breeding.

But it was not that alone that drew the young Cora to him. It was the fact that he was always so calm, and controlled. He never spoke without considering for a moment or two, unlike Robbie and her father, who invariably said whatever was at the forefront of their mind. And occasionally lashed out with their fists without bothering to explain their thinking at all.

She lived for the times he came to visit, though she rarely plucked up the courage to speak to him.

Until that last summer. Robbie had been so busy, he had not been able to prevent her from spending every waking hour with the object of her adoration. It caused her almost as much pain as pleasure, finally being able to spend whole days with him, whilst wondering if he was only tolerating her company out of deference to his friend's difficult situation. Not that he ever made her aware of how he must have felt. His manners were far too polished.

'Come on,' he had said, with that smile she had always found completely irresistible for being so rare, 'I will teach you to row.' And they had climbed into the boat.

In order to show her how to handle the oars, he'd had to take hold of her hands as they sat side by side on the narrow bench. She had been able to feel his hip through the material of her skirts, pressing up against her own as they had each plied their own oar. She had felt as though she was in heaven. The laughter, the sunshine, their close proximity—it had all gone to her head. She blushed even now to think of how shameless she had been. A large wave had jostled the oar from her hands, and instead of lunging for it, she had clung to Kit for safety as the boat rocked alarmingly. He had put his arms round her, to steady her, and she had gazed up into his face with naked adoration in her eyes. She must have done, for he had said, 'You want me to kiss you.' She had nodded. He had obliged.

It had been, she swallowed, a moment of pure magic. Her first kiss.

But not his.

Even back then, she had sensed that a boy did not get that level of mastery without having practised on dozens of other female lips. Not that the knowledge had prevented her enthusiastic response. Pretty soon, they had tumbled to the bottom of the boat, meshed together from shoulder to hip, her skirts tangling round his legs as she twined herself round him.

And the sun had beat down on their writhing bodies while the waves lapped gently against the hull, rocking them. The gulls wheeled in the clear blue sky overhead, keening, but she had shut her ears to their warning cries. Her heart had been so full of exultation, she had vowed to treasure this moment for the rest of her life.

And when he had come to her, later that same day, and asked her to marry him, it had seemed too good to be true.

'You cannot mean that!' she had cried. 'You hardly know me!'

'I have visited your home many times,' he had replied seriously. 'I know you well.'

She had shaken her head, still too dazed by her good fortune to believe he could be in earnest.

'We are too young,' she had persisted. She had heard

him talking about going to university. Could he afford to do that, if he married her? Besides, his family would surely want him to marry a woman of his own class, a woman who had been brought up knowing how to run the kind of estate he would one day govern. 'I am not the kind of girl you should marry,' she had concluded sadly.

'But you want to marry me, though, don't you?' he had frowned. 'You would not have kissed me so enthusiastically this afternoon unless you were already thinking along those lines. You are not that sort of girl.'

She had opened her mouth to protest that she had not been capable of thinking of anything that afternoon. She had just been swept away by the yearnings of her heart, the insistent clamour of her body. But he had stopped her mouth with a kiss before she could explain anything. And had kept on kissing her until all power of rational thought deserted her. 'Say yes,' he kept murmuring between kisses. Until she was so hazed with passion she could scarcely remember what her objections had been.

She blinked away the mist that obscured her eyes, and the malevolent form of Mrs Paulding swam back into focus.

Mrs Paulding, who had shattered her dreams with her ruthless delivery of a piece of information that both Robbie and Kit had kept from her.

'Your brother was walking home along the headland overlooking the bay, and saw you frolicking in the boat with the young master,' she had hissed, barely a week after Cora's arrival at Kingsmede. 'He caught up with him in the boat-house, and set upon him. He did not stop hitting him until he had forced the poor lad to agree to propose to you!'

It had felt like the missing piece of the jigsaw, finally falling into place. She had wondered what they had been fighting about, down on the shore, when they should have been indoors, getting changed for dinner. But she had seen them wrestling dozens of times over the years, and had not thought there was any particular significance to that fight. Especially since they had eventually come in with their arms round each other's shoulders, grinning.

She had thought it peculiar, though, when Robbie had made himself scarce after supper, leaving her alone with Kit when his habit before had been to send her away, so that he and his friend could indulge in 'man talk'.

No wonder Kit had brushed aside her feeble objections to his proposal. He was, first and foremost, Robbie's friend. And wished to remain so. So much that he was even prepared to marry his gauche, unattractive little sister after being caught kissing her.

She had been completely wretched at Kingsmede after that, seeing everything from the moment of that fateful boating trip in a new light.

Kit had not wanted to make her his wife because he had fallen headlong in love with her! She had cringed to recall the numerous times she had poured out all that had been in her heart, and he had just smiled, and kissed her. She could no longer excuse his silence by telling herself he was not the kind of man who spoke about his feelings. The truth was that he simply did not have any deep feelings for her. But he was far too much the gentleman to tell her to her face that she had trapped him into a marriage he did not want. He had even managed to maintain a cheerful demeanour for the remainder of his stay at Auchentay.

When all the time, he must have wished he had never met her.

She had wanted to die.

Instead…

With a start, she came to herself, finding she was standing on the upper landing, gazing sightlessly at Mrs Paulding.

'You did all you could to make me leave,' she breathed.

Mrs Paulding gave her a considering look. 'You did the right thing.' She frowned. 'I thought you understood how unsuitable you were—and still are—to become mistress of Kingsmede. I cannot comprehend why you have changed your mind and returned.'

Cora felt a flash of surprise. Just now, in the hall, when that part of her memory had returned, it had seemed obvious that Mrs Paulding had been behind all that had happened that last day. Yet her words now showed she had no knowledge of it.

She turned and stalked along the corridor that led to Cora's room. Cora drifted behind her in a daze. How wrong she had been about everything. Everyone. Even Mrs Paulding. Though the woman had never made any secret of her animosity towards her, she was no criminal. Just a woman with strong convictions, and utter loyalty to the family she served.

Cora paused on the threshold of her room, assailed by yet more images from her past. The last time she had been here, the bed-hangings had been dusty, the curtains frayed and faded, and the bed linen so fragile that she had put her foot straight through the top sheet the first time she'd got in. She had been so scared of informing Mrs Paulding of the damage she had done, she had sat up half the night sewing it sides to middle. Only to have the housekeeper inform her scathingly the next morning, with the offending article draped over her forearm, that in the residence of persons of quality there were maids to attend to the linen.

Everything was fresh and new now. There was even a pretty rug beside the bed, thick and soft and luxurious for bare feet to step on to first thing in the morning. Not like the ragged old thing she had always been catching her heels in. And, as she stepped into the room in which she had suffered such agonies of self-doubt, she could not help noticing that everywhere smelled different too. The Kingsmede of old had smelled of dust and mildew. Now, the scent of beeswax and lavender hung in the air.

Mrs Paulding stood in the middle of the room, her hands clasped at her waist, her expression wavering between defiance and…apprehension.

It struck Cora that, this time around, she had far more power over events than she'd had before. If she really were to marry Lord Matthison, she could fire Mrs Paulding from her post.

Given the way she had treated her in the past, this

was clearly what the housekeeper expected. Cora frowned. Though she could not like the woman, she did not know if she had the heart to fire her. It would be hard for her to seek another post at her age. And utterly humiliating to ask for references from a woman she despised.

Suddenly the tension in the room became too much. She went to the armchair by the empty fireplace and sank into it wearily.

'Would you please get me some tea?'

'Tea?' the woman echoed. 'Or something stronger?' And then after an infinitesimal pause, 'His lordship did say you had suffered a shock.'

Cora might have been imagining the taunt, but she did not think so. Mrs Paulding was bracketing her with her brother, who no doubt had a decanter of something 'stronger' in his own room, to which he applied all too frequently, judging by the pungency of his breath.

Last time she had been here, she had put up with Mrs Paulding's attitude, because she felt the woman had only been following the line taken by Kit's parents, and because she did not have the experience to know what to do. But she was not a timid seventeen-year-old, with everything to lose should she put a foot wrong, any more.

'If you do not wish to continue working here, I shall quite understand,' she said coldly.

Mrs Paulding's mouth snapped shut. With one last defiant toss of her head she stalked to the door, leaving Cora to wonder whether she would be getting a tray of tea and cakes, as befitted a female guest, or a pint of gin, in keeping with the low opinion the woman held of her.

Uttering a groan, Cora lowered her head to her hands, almost wishing she could choose Robbie's road to oblivion. It had to be easier than wrestling with the maelstrom of thoughts and impressions that were whirling through her head. She felt dizzy with them. Sick.

How she wished Kit had never brought her here! She could have gone on being Mary, his mistress, and they could both have known some measure of happiness. Instead of which everything was coming unravelled.

From the moment they had driven into that dark, brooding forest that surrounded Kingsmede, she had been pitched back in time seven years. To the very day life as she had known it had come to an end.

She rubbed at the dull ache that was building from the nape of her neck. She had slowly been learning to let go of her fear of the unknown, that was the trouble. The very first time she had glimpsed Lord Matthison in the street, and she had sensed her shadowy past reaching out to grab her, she had acted out of instinct, and run from him. But she had not quite managed to outrun the persistent feelings he aroused. She had begun to daydream about him. The daydreams she had smothered by focusing on her work. And the dreams, that were now, she realised, based on things that had actually happened, she dealt with by waking herself up from them.

That was a trick she had developed, to save herself from the recurring nightmares about being locked in the cellar. And before that…in the attic room, where she had sensed danger hovering close by, she had wrapped herself round with a cloak of ignorance. It had been her only refuge against her gaoler. She had kept on hiding behind it, even when she no longer had any need to. Pushing away any stray thought that might threaten her hard-earned tranquillity. Because she had enough to contend with, just recovering from Lord Sandiford's attack, and learning to survive in the harsh conditions of Madame Pichot's sweatshop, without the added burden of the pain she would have brought with her from her former life.

Time and circumstances had given her material to shore up her defences against the truth, too. For she had fallen in love with a polite, shabbily dressed boy called Christopher Brereton. Kit, to her. He bore only a faint resemblance to the hard-eyed, wealthy gentleman who had accosted her so angrily. And she could truthfully tell herself she had never met anyone by the name of Lord Matthison before. Because she had not. The man who had borne that name seven years previously had been Kit's father. And from what he and Robbie had told her, she had always pictured him as an elderly, portly, carelessly dressed man with a complexion coarsened from drink and dissipation.

Without even knowing she was doing it, she had stubbornly resisted recognising him, cunningly shielding herself from risk of further pain.

She slapped the arm of her chair in vexation. It did not matter if she worked out how her mind had managed to protect itself from the prospect of unbearable hurt, her respite was well and truly over now.

A knock on the door, heralding the arrival of a maid with the tea things, could not have come at a more timely moment for Cora. Heartily relieved to have a diversion from the tortuous workings of her mind, she got up, and opened the door herself.

The young girl, standing on the other side, looked rather startled, but hastily recovered and bobbed a curtsy. The maid, who bore a tray stacked with pots, cups, cream and sugar bowls, was followed by a footman with a cake stand laden with cakes, sandwiches, slices of bread and butter, and pots of jewel-bright preserves. Behind him came a second maid with two cans of hot water, and a third with arms full of fluffy towels.

Cora could not help contrasting all this attention with the neglect she had suffered in this room before. Hot water! An unheard-of luxury in the Kingsmede she had known, but Cora could definitely see steam wisping from the can as the girl took it into the dressing room. She had never been able to wash in anything even approaching tepid before, and when she had been hungry, she, Robbie and Kit had occasionally raided the larder for ingredients that she had thrown together into something resembling a meal on the kitchen table.

Either Mrs Paulding had decided she wanted to keep her job after all, or Cora had allies amongst the lower staff, none of whom, she now noticed, had served under the previous Lord and Lady Matthison. By the way the maids and footman were all bowing and scraping, she guessed the latter. They all seemed extremely keen to ingratiate themselves with the woman they believed was about to become the new mistress of Kingsmede.

She frowned. Last time she had been here, everyone had believed she was about to become the new mistress of Kingsmede, too, but that had not prevented them from uniting against her behind Mrs Paulding's formidable antagonism.

The only person who had even *pretended* to be friendly had been Frances Farrell. The vicar's daughter.

She did not want to think about her. She really didn't, but she had rashly opened the floodgate in her mind, by the tiniest crack, and the force of what had built up behind it was too powerful to let her slam it back shut.

Tottering to the tea table by the window, she sank to the chair, and accepted a large slice of fruit-cake from the obsequious footman.

'Yes, that will be all,' she managed to say, once the footman had poured her tea exactly as she liked it. Part of her wanted to beg the servants to stay. With them to distract her, she could almost manage to ignore the latest pack of memories that had come baying round her like hounds scenting a fresh kill.

She had felt so lonely and friendless and insecure back then that she had welcomed the slightly older girl's overtures of friendship. Because Frances was Mrs Paulding's niece by marriage, she had been a frequent visitor to Kingsmede. In spite of her family connection, Cora had soon begun to look forward to her visits. Robbie had spoken about Frances before she had arrived, telling her she was a grand lass. And Frances had been such a good listener that Cora had opened her heart to her. She had confided her intention of impressing Mrs Paulding with her grasp of household economy. She had admitted she would not care if Christopher could not afford to dress her fashionably, or show her the entertainments London had to offer. She would be content to stay on his rundown estate all year round, if need be, so long as they were together. She had waxed lyrical about how she would be as good as any heiress for him, with her plans for economy and good housekeeping. And her boundless love.

She set her cup down in her saucer with a snap.

Stupid, stupid, stupid!

She could not believe how stupid she had been. How blind to what had been going on around her.

The moist fruit-cake turned to ashes in her mouth, which almost choked her as she forced herself to swallow the knowledge of her monumental idiocy.

Frances, just like her aunt, had eventually been only too pleased to enlighten the starry-eyed Cora about Christopher Brereton's nature.

'I am so sorry to have to be the one to tell you this,' Frances had said, laying her hand on Cora's forearm, 'but Christopher is playing you false. He has gone to meet the young lady in question this very morning.'

'He has gone out with Robbie!' she had protested.

'They have ridden over to Bamford to see the tailor about wedding clothes!'

Frances had shaken her head pityingly. 'I have no idea where your brother may be, but Christopher has gone to a certain woodman's hut in the western beech wood, where he always meets her. If you do not believe me, why don't you go there and see for yourself?'

She had flounced down to the stables in a blaze of outrage, determined to prove Frances wrong. The first blow had been to find Kit's horse in its stall. If he had gone to Bamford, he would have ridden there. She had gone cold inside. Why had he lied about going to Bamford? More by luck than judgement, she had managed to get the massive creature saddled, and scrambled on to its back with scant regard for the propriety of hitching her morning dress up round her hips.

And soon she'd had proof he had lied about everything. Through the grimy window of the tumbledown hut she had seen him holding a practically naked woman in his arms. She had stood there long enough to see him kiss the woman whose bared breasts were crushed against his waistcoat and then, at the thought she had let those lying lips loose against her own mouth, she had fallen to her knees and lost her breakfast.

Everything after that had taken on the quality of a nightmare. She had managed to remount the horse, just as the heavens had opened, and the creature had taken off on a course she had not cared to correct. She had no idea where she wanted to go anyway. Where *could* she go to escape from Kit's betrayal? Against a backdrop of flashing lightning, and the thunder of horse's hooves, she had felt her heart tearing apart in her breast.

Cora drew in a great, shuddering breath, and wrapped her arms about herself.

She was not a seventeen-year-old virgin any longer, with no experience of the base nature of men. She could appreciate now that, technically, Kit had never lied to her. For he had never once told her he loved her, or promised to be faithful. She had believed what she wanted to believe, without being offered one scrap of evidence.

She got to her feet, too sickened by her own culpability to stomach so much as the smell of food, and found herself wandering over to the wardrobe.

It was the one item of furniture in the room that looked exactly as she remembered it. It appeared frozen in time, with one of the hinges still slightly askew, and the carved oak-leaf panels peppered with woodworm.

Had he preserved it, she wondered on a swell of something like hope, for some sentimental reason? When they had talked about this room in the coach earlier, she had gained the impression he regarded it as a shrine to her memory. She had dreaded the thought he might want her to put on a dead woman's clothes…

But now, the thought that he might have kept all her things, preserving them, treasuring them…

With wildly beating heart, she tugged the door open.

It was empty.

Something inside her crystallized and froze solid.

Of course the wardrobe was empty.

Just as his black heart was empty!

The only reason, it came to her in a flash, that he had made such a show of clinging to her memory, was to get rid of poor Miss Winters!

But if he thought she was going to let him use her to break another poor young woman's heart, as he had broken hers…

'No!' she cried, slamming the door on the empty wardrobe and marching over to her trunk, which sat at the foot of the bed.

It was time to change her gown, and go downstairs, and set a few things straight.

Kneeling down, she flung open the lid, and plunged her hands into the jumble of goods she had amassed in her life as Mary. The mingled smells of hard work, cheap soap, and Molly's scent that wafted up as she rummaged for the gown she sought were vastly comforting.

Ah, there it was! Her Sunday best. A long-sleeved gown of bronze silk with a square neckline. Probably not the sort of thing ladies wore to dinner in the country, but she did not care. She was not a lady. And she had no intention of becoming one.

There was more of Mary in her now, than Cora. Not that Cora had been a lady either. In fact, Cora had not been very much of anything, she huffed as she pulled off her stained travelling gown. No wonder she had never regained the strength to resurface after having all her hopes so comprehensively trampled in the mud.

She had been, she frowned, tugging her fresh gown over her head, a timid child to start with who had been prevented by an overbearing father from developing any opinions of her own. Never mind expressing them! And then her mother had taught her how to become more or less invisible. There had only been a brief period where she had tried to unfurl her wings. That summer, after her parents had died, while Robbie was too busy to keep her caged. She had flown free with Kit, like a butterfly newly emerged from its chrysalis…until the day he had ripped her wings from her heart and she had spiralled downward into despair.

But Mary was made of sterner stuff. She lifted her chin and regarded her reflection squarely in the mirror. Mary had fought off the lecherous Lord Sandiford, preserving her virtue whilst leaving her mark on his vile, grasping hands. She had gone to London, got a job, excelled at it and then, when she had felt so inclined, had been bold enough to take a lover.

Cora would never have been capable of doing any of that!

Giving Cora's prim reflection one last derisive glance, Mary squared her shoulders and went downstairs.

Lord Matthison and Robbie were waiting for her in the antechamber that led to the dining room. Both got to their feet as she entered.

'I hope you will be in a fit state to travel in the morning, Robbie,' she said tartly, eyeing the almost empty glass dangling from his fingers. 'So that you can take me home to Auchentay.'

It was only as she took a comfortably upholstered chair, and accepted a glass of wine from the same footman who had brought her tea, that it occurred to her that Robbie might not live there any longer. That he might even have a wife, who would have something to say about a stray sister turning up uninvited on her doorstep.

But it was Lord Matthison who answered her, once he had dismissed the footman from the room.

'Your home is here with me now, in case you have forgotten.'

'There is no need to mock me, my lord,' she snapped back. 'I may have been suffering from some kind of…' She shook her head as she failed to find words to adequately describe what had been like a dam, holding back all those overwhelmingly painful memories. 'Some kind of blockade in my mind,' she eventually continued. 'But now that it has collapsed, I remember all too clearly the reasons why I should never have agreed to marry you in the first place!'

Lord Matthison got to his feet, his face ominously grim.

'Do you mean to tell me you ran out on me seven years ago?'

She had just taken a breath, to explain what had happened to her shortly after she had galloped away from the woodcutter's hut, when Lord Matthison flung his glass into the fireplace with such force that it exploded into a cloudburst of splinters.

'You faithless bitch!' He swore, turning away and striding to the far side of the room. When he turned round his face was contorted with rage. 'After all the protestations of love you made, you did not even have the decency to come to me and break off the engagement to my face!'

'No...' Of course she hadn't! She had not had the chance. 'You see...'

But he did not let her finish. Striding over to where Robbie sat slumped in his chair, following the argument through narrowed eyes, he said, 'For seven years you've let your brother mourn you. And as for me...hah!' He looked her brother straight in the eye as he said, 'For seven years I have had to bear the burden of having the man who was once my best friend believing I had killed you! Do you know he accused me to the magistrate, Cora, after you ran off? I could have hanged! Only that they could not find a body...'

'Of course not,' she began. Because she had not died. Only lost her memory.

And how she wished it had never come back! Bearing his indifference back then had all but destroyed her. Facing his contempt was tearing her apart all over again.

'No, because you were never dead. In spite of letting us all believe it! How little you care for anyone but yourself! Well, let me tell you something.' He strode back to her, leaning his hands on the arms of the chair, making her cringe back in her seat. 'I have no intention of letting you run out on me a second time. You are not going to crawl back to Scotland and evade your responsibilities towards me this time!'

'You...you cannot stop me,' she gasped, almost afraid of this man's unleashed anger. 'R-Robbie...' she pleaded.

'Don't think your brother will take you back into his home now. Not now I have bedded you!'

She heard Robbie gasp. She wanted to turn her head to see what he was thinking, but somehow she could not tear her eyes away from Kit's.

'You could be carrying my child,' he growled, his eyes raking down the front of her gown, coming to rest on the small mound of her belly.

Why, oh, why had he gone and told Robbie that? If only he had kept that quiet, she could have gone home to Scotland and lived a quiet, spinster existence, keeping house for her brother. But now Robbie would never rest until they were married. Look how adamant he had been that Kit should marry her, when all he had done was kiss her!

But how could he imagine she might contemplate any kind of relationship with him when he could accuse her of such dreadful things, with such implacable hatred for her burning from his eyes?

And then he dealt the death blow to any last, lingering hope they might be able to salvage anything from the current situation.

'You owe me seven years, Cora,' he snarled. 'Seven dark, blighted, hellish years…'

'I don't owe you anything!' she cried, finally finding the strength to close her eyes and turn her head aside. She owed him nothing if he could believe she had lied about how she felt about him back then. Or was capable of just walking away without one word of explanation.

And then she heard Robbie growl, 'You have to marry him, Cora. Nothing else for it now you've slept with him. A man's heir, you know…'

And she saw another door slamming in her face.

She might have known Robbie would side with Kit against her. Men did not care how miserable women were made by their decisions.

Beasts, the lot of them!

With a wild cry, she raised her arms, and pushed Lord Matthison hard in the chest, forcing him far enough back for her to get to her feet.

'I hate you both,' she panted, looking wildly from one to the other. For years, growing up, their friendship had excluded her, the little girl who did not have the freedom to escape the stultifying atmosphere at home. How she had envied them their education, their freedom to stay out of doors all day long, their freedom to choose each other for a companion! For a brief time, when she travelled with them for the first time to Kingsmede, she had thought they would include her. But they had not. They had both lied to her, and evaded her, and now they were siding together, to thwart her, and contain her, and control her.

She cried out again, an inarticulate sound that expressed all her rage and pain and betrayal. She did not need either of them! For the last seven years she had earned her own living, and she could jolly well do it all over again if necessary!

The door opened. 'Dinner is—'

The butler got no further than that, as Cora pushed

past him in her desperate need to get out of the room, and away from the two men who had so spectacularly betrayed her. Again.

Chapter Eleven

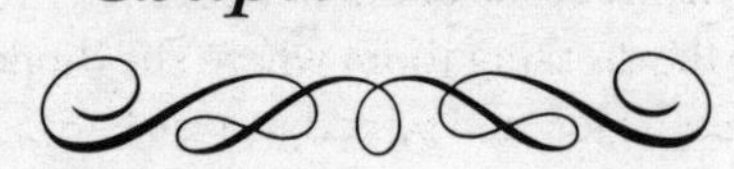

She was too distraught to hear the sound of footsteps pounding up the stairs after her. Not 'til she reached her room, and yanked open the door, did she become aware that Lord Matthison had chased after her.

But she was too quick for him. By the time he caught up with her, she had slammed the door, and locked it.

'Cora, let me in, damn you!' he yelled, pounding on the door.

'No!' she yelled back in defiance. 'Go back to London and marry Miss Winters! She can have your blasted money and your rotten title. I don't want any of it. I don't want you!'

And then her legs folded under her.

She had been desperately trying to hold herself together ever since her memory had returned. Now she had completely run out of will-power. She bowed her head, and yielded to the grief she had held in check for seven years, her only concession to dignity being to muffle the sound of her sobs by burying her face in the carpet.

When she eventually ran out of tears, she could not say she felt any better for having given way to her emotions. Her eyes were swollen, her head throbbed and every muscle in her body was shaking. Her hair had come down and hanks of it were plastered to her face and neck.

When she tried, she could not get to her feet. So she crawled to the dressing room where she dipped a wash-cloth in cold water, and wiped it over her face.

And then she sat down on the pile of towels on the stool, wondering what on earth she had been crying for.

This emotional storm had been sparked off by Kit's angry insistence that she marry him. Should that not have made her heart leap with joy? She had loved him for as long as she could remember. Even when her mind had not allowed her to recognise him, her heart had somehow known it belonged to him.

She eyed her reflection with some hostility. She rather suspected it had been Cora doing all the weeping. Mary had always been too determined to hang on to her self-control to let her emotions get the better of her. Yes, she turned more fully towards the mirror. But then Cora had just discovered the man she adored did not love her back.

That was what all the weeping had been about. She was having to deal with the pain her seventeen-year-old self had never had the chance to purge from her system. She had just remembered exactly how she had felt when she had seen that woman opening her bodice and offering Kit her bared breasts. When he had walked towards her with a smile, taken her in his arms and kissed her, she had felt as though he had plunged a dagger into her heart. For a few minutes, she had been out of her mind with grief…

And then she had gone down to dinner, the intervening years gone in the blink of an eye. She was still reeling with the sense of his betrayal, and instead of him giving her any sort of explanation, or even an apology, he had accused her of all sorts of crass behaviour. How dared he?

She straightened up with a sniff, anger restoring her backbone. Unable to find a handkerchief about her person, she inelegantly wiped her nose on her sleeve. Her gown needed laundering anyway, after rolling about on the floor in it.

Seven years, she reminded her reflection crossly. It had all happened seven years ago, not yesterday! Even though that was what it felt like.

She twisted the washcloth between her fingers, studying it, rather than the woebegone reflection that inhabited the mirror. It was all very confusing. One minute she felt like Cora, the heartbroken girl who had just discovered her idol had feet of clay. Then next, she was Mary, older, wiser…but no less in love with the same man.

She sighed, cupping her chin in her hands and regarding herself in the mirror with resignation. It made little difference which version of herself she felt like; both of them were hopelessly in love with a man who did not love her back. As the starry-eyed Cora, she had shut her eyes to reality, grasping at a fairy-tale ending where the prince married the peasant and they all lived happily ever after in his castle. She had not even noticed the wicked witch hovering in the background, casting her spells over the gullible young princess-to-be.

She shook off the fancy, returning to the knotty problem of why she recoiled from the prospect of marrying a man she had been in love with, one way or another, her whole life.

She could not entirely blame her reluctance on the idealistic, youthful, Cora part of her. Even Mary, who knew the value of financial security, respectability and freedom from drudgery had baulked at the prospect of marrying him. Mary, who had loved him so much she had tossed her scruples aside, had declared she would rather be his mistress.

Well, it would have been impossible for a seamstress to marry a wealthy Viscount. But now she knew she was Cora…why should she not marry him? Her father had been a gentleman, after all. And her mother from a perfectly respectable family. There was not such a vast gap between their ranks that a match was ineligible.

And she belonged to him. Even when her mind had refused to let her remember what had passed between them before, her heart had leapt at the very sight of him. For he held it in the palm of his hand, to cherish or crush as the whim took him.

She gasped.

That was it! She was afraid he would inflict untold misery upon her. She did not want to be enslaved by the love she bore for a man who could not return even a tenth of her feelings.

What, then, should she do?

As if in answer, her stomach growled. It was hardly surprising. She had eaten virtually nothing all day. She crossed to the bell-pull, and yanked on it to summon a maid. Dealing with her hunger was at least something practical she could see about. A self-deprecating smile came to her lips. Putting off thinking about unpleasant topics was something that Mary had always been extremely good at.

It was not long before she heard a tentative knocking on her bedroom door.

Her head spun a little as she rose to answer it, confirming that her decision to send for food had been a wise one. There was no sense in making herself ill, on top of everything else.

'Cora, are you all right? You look so pale.'

It was not a maid, standing in the doorway, but Lord Matthison.

'Don't lock the door again,' he pleaded, his hand shooting out to push the door wider. 'I will not come in, if that is what you want, but…' He thrust his fingers through already disordered hair. 'If anything should happen to you…'

To look at his haggard expression, anyone would think he really cared about her. But a little voice that she could not quite manage to silence pointed out that he had already been accused of murdering her once. He had spent seven years under that cloud. It would get even worse if any harm befell her now, whilst she was under his roof.

'I rang for a maid,' she said resentfully. 'I need something to eat.'

An expression of incredulity flashed across his face. Then he straightened up, his eyes hardening.

'Of course.' For the first time she noticed the girl who had brought her tea earlier, hovering further down the corridor. At a brusque gesture from Lord Matthison, the girl scuttled off on her errand.

'You cannot remain in your room indefinitely,' he said coldly. 'We have matters to discuss. Arrangements to make.'

'Yes.' She leaned against the doorframe, her arms folded round her waist. 'But not now. Not tonight. Please…' She could not bring herself to look him in the eye any longer. The coldness emanating from him in waves was already making her shiver. 'Please, just let me have tonight to myself,' she begged him. Just standing here talking to him was more than she felt able to cope with.

'We can discuss—' her broken heart, her unrequited love, the other women in his life '—matters tomorrow, if you are determined to proceed with the betrothal we entered into seven years ago.' She still could not quite understand his determination to marry her, when he could look at her so coldly. 'I suppose, technically, it still stands.'

Could it be as simple as that? He had made a pledge? And a man of honour did not withdraw, once he had given his word. She did look up at him then, but his eyes had narrowed, and he was looking at her as though she was a complete stranger.

She supposed she was in a way. She was certainly a stranger to herself. Part Cora, part Mary, and completely muddled.

'You came to my bed,' he grated, as though he now found it hard to believe.

How cruel of him to remind her how weak she had been! And yet, she realised miserably, if he were to put his arms round her this minute, and murmur a few soft words, she would cling to him, and beg him to come into her room, and stay with her all night. How she wanted him to hold her, as he had held her last night! Tenderly, as though she was precious!

'You could be carrying my child,' he said, growing noticeably angrier.

She flinched. Cora had only trapped him with a kiss. Mary had done it with a potential pregnancy. He had been gentleman enough to spare Cora any expression of resentment. Mary, the wanton, could expect no such consideration. She felt tears stinging her eyes again. She had survived waking in the shattered, blasted ruins of the life she had dreamed of as a girl. But she did not think she could bear hearing him systematically destroying the illusion that taking her to his bed had meant as much to him as it had to her.

'Please, Christopher, don't say another word! I cannot bear any more! If I am carrying your child…' Oh, how she wished he wanted her to be the mother of his children! 'But even if I am not…' She faltered. If she was not pregnant, she might be able to persuade him to let her go. A vision of a future without him in it stretched out like a wasteland before her. It would be unbearable! She shuddered. She could see herself going to her grave loving him, and him alone. It was hopeless. 'I could never marry anyone else.'

Unable to bear standing so close to him, yet feeling so far apart, she retreated into her room.

Lord Matthison stared balefully at the door she had shut in his face. Cora did not want him in her room. She did not want to marry him. The thought that she might be carrying his child had been so distressing it had brought her to the verge of tears.

But she could not marry anyone else now. By taking her to his bed, he had effectively ruined her!

God, how he wished he had not insisted on waking Cora! Mary had loved him unreservedly, giving him her whole heart along with her virginity. She had trusted him with her future, even though she believed she could only ever be his mistress.

But he, damn fool that he was, had wanted to be able to marry her. As Cora.

And now, without knowing quite how or why, he had lost them both.

The maid returned, and nervously cleared her throat. She could not get to the door while he was standing with his nose to it, glaring at it as though he could blast it to smithereens by force of will alone.

Muttering a curse, he stepped away. The girl darted him a wary glance, tapped timidly on the door, and scuttled inside with Cora's supper. She looked as though she thought her employer had lost his mind. She was probably right. It had been a long time since he had known anything remotely resembling sanity. Every time he had thought he'd begun to make sense out of the chaos Cora had left behind, a new twist in his path had made him re-assess where he really was. And always, always, she had been dancing just out of reach, like some elusive sprite.

From the very first, it had been that elusive quality about her that had tantalised him. The slender girl who had darted shy glances at him across the table when she thought her father was not looking. The prim, untouchable maiden who had taken on the burden of housekeeping for her exacting father after her mother's death. That ethereal, otherworldly quality she possessed had been what had made it so easy to think of her as a spirit, wandering the earth. Last night as he'd held her in his arms, he had thought he'd captured her at last, but today…

He stepped back from the door that separated them, a shaft of pain lancing through him.

She still eluded him. Even as Mary, there had been a part of her he could not reach. She could have been his mistress, but never his wife. He had thought he would get what he wanted once she knew she was Cora. Instead, she had gone and slammed the door in his face. And turned his world upside down all over again.

Had she ever really loved him?

If she had, surely seeing him again would have restored her memory? But no, it had been coming back to Kingsmede, and hearing her brother's voice, that had freed her mind from the chains that bound it.

He found himself halfway down the stairs, his hand clenching the banister, breathing hard. Why had she told him she loved him if she had not meant it? Why, he thumped the banister with his clenched fist, had she felt the need to make such a colossal fool of him?

She had made him believe she welcomed his kisses. That day he had taken her rowing and she had wound up in his arms, and he had finally thrown caution to the winds…she had responded with an eagerness he thought matched his own! He had really believed they could overcome all the barriers he had feared might keep them apart. Her youth, his rank, their complete lack of funds.

That, he decided grimly, that was the moment he had lost his mind. He had been crazy to have thought they could make it work.

Crazy.

'Christopher!'

He lifted his head at the sound of Robbie calling his name, to find he was standing in the middle of the hall, so completely lost in thought he had forgotten why he had gone down the stairs at all, never mind which room he had been heading for.

Robbie was standing in the open doorway to the library.

'What you said to Cora,' he growled. 'Before dinner. It did na' make sense to me.' He shook his shaggy head. 'I've been thinking about it all evening. You accused her of leaving you.' He scowled, shaking his finger at him.

'But when you wrote me, ye said she had lost her memory and did nae know who she was when you found her. Which is it? For I canna see how both can hold true.'

He stood back, inviting Lord Matthison to join him in the library. 'I think it is high time we had a long talk, and worked out just what the hell has been going on.'

Cora groaned and rolled over in bed.

She would have sworn she had not slept a wink all night, but sunlight was streaming through a chink in the curtains, and last time she had opened her eyes the room had been completely dark.

Her throat was raw, her tongue felt too big for her mouth, and her head ached all the way down to her knees. In fact, she felt so dreadful, she might just as well have drunk the contents of the decanter that had come up on her supper tray the night before.

Oh, no, no! She shook her head, flinging back the covers and setting her feet on the luxuriously soft rug. One thing she had decided during the long hours of the night was that she would never succumb to the false comfort alcohol offered.

There were those who let the circumstances of life crush them. The streets and alleys of London were littered with them. Both men and women who gave up hope, and turned to drink, or worse. She had heard of women who would let their babies starve while they spent their last pennies on gin. But there were others, afflicted with like circumstances, who just gritted their teeth, and got on with it. Mary had been on the verge of collapse when she had found herself in London, with no memory of her past, terrified by her colleagues within doors, and the bustling, noisy, threatening crowds without. But she had gritted her teeth, performed every task that was set before her, and doggedly refused to let her mind dwell on those nameless fears that seemed to lurk round every corner.

Or had that been Cora?

Both of them, all of her, she no longer knew how to describe herself, but one thing she had learned about herself through all this, she nodded, tugging hard on the bell-pull: she was a survivor.

The person she was now was stronger than the naïve, dreamy Cora, or the self-effacing Mary. Nothing had managed to destroy her so far, and she was not going to succumb to the kind of self-pity that might do so now!

She was no longer a silly child who had never set foot outside her village. She was not going to throw away her entire future happiness because the man she loved had committed an indiscretion.

Two, if you counted the passionate affair he had begun with her, when he was still not quite sure who she was.

And at least she could be sure she ranked higher in his esteem than poor Miss Winters.

He was quite determined not to marry Miss Winters, no matter what stratagems she might employ to snare him.

And equally determined he *would* marry her. For whatever reason.

And she was going to accept him.

Cora had been devastated by witnessing her fiancé kissing a half-naked woman. But Mary had learned a lot about the nature of men from listening to her work mates talking about their lives. A man could see nothing wrong with marrying one woman, and keeping another as a mistress. They did not seem to think fidelity was an essential ingredient of being a husband.

And that one glimpse she'd had, of what her life without him would be like, had been too bleak to contemplate.

As she waited for the maid to answer her summons, she went to the little ormolu clock that sat on the mantel. It showed almost eleven o'clock. Not too late for a woman who was about to become Lady Matthison to be ringing for some breakfast! That was what fine ladies did. Lounged in bed half the day, taking their meals on a tray.

She had a sudden vision of the former Lady Matthison doing exactly that. Wallowing in self-pity! She pressed her lips together, disgusted with herself for even contemplating going down that road. She would be nothing like her predecessor!

She marched herself to the dressing room and poured the last of the water from the jug into the basin. The night before, she had, out of long years of habit, emptied the wash water into the enamel bucket under the stand, for the maid to remove this morning.

She expected Mrs Paulding would frown on her saving her staff so much work. The thought rather cheered her as she finished her brisk wash, and pulled her wrap back round her just as she heard a knock on the outer door to her chamber.

His lordship and her brother, the girl informed her when she asked, had breakfasted earlier, and then gone out riding together.

'Of course they have,' Cora replied with a tight smile. Healing the breach that had grown between them would be extremely important to him. Kit had never had many friends, and none so close as Robbie. When she had disappeared, he had lost what he held most dear. Oh, she did not flatter herself that it was her, so much! But his best friend, and his reputation. All gone, at a stroke. He would regain it all by marrying her.

She had it within her power, to grant him his heart's desire. Of course she would not deny him that!

She trailed over to the window, gazing out over the park where they had gone riding, just as they had done each day when she had last been here. How left out she had felt.

How much more would she hurt from now on, knowing she would have his name, but not his heart? But she would get used to it. It would not be anywhere near as painful as leaving Kingsmede, perhaps never to see him again.

She ate her scrambled eggs, and drank her tea slowly, wondering how she would fill her days as Lady Matthison. If the place had been as dilapidated as it had been seven years ago, she would have enjoyed setting it all to rights.

But Lord Matthison had done it all on his own.

Feeling restless and disgruntled, she decided to take a tour of the house, and see what other improvements he had made, apart from the ones she had already noticed. She did not ring for the housekeeper, whose task it should have been to escort her new mistress over her domain. She had enough on her mind already, without having to deal with her open hostility.

It was not long before she found herself in the portrait gallery, gazing up at the canvas that Kit's grandparents had commissioned on the occasion of his parents' betrothal.

The former Lady Matthison had been pretty as a girl. She was shown sitting on an armchair out on the front lawn, with the façade of Kingsmede angled behind her to reveal a stylised version of the surrounding lands spread out beyond. She looked very young, and very happy as she smiled down at the enormous ruby ring that adorned her finger. Kit's father lounged languidly against the bole of a tree looking down at her. Cora had never met the man, but she could just see that bored young fop turning into the rackety gamester Kit had described.

Twenty years of being married to him had reduced the happy, smiling girl in the portrait into the fretful woman who had been desperate for her only son to marry an heiress.

But she would not end up like her! Kit had promised, in the coach on the way here, that they would never suffer from the financial constrictions that had driven a wedge between his own parents. And that he would not neglect her, or make her unhappy.

And whatever happened, she would never, ever treat

any child of hers the way those two had treated poor Kit. They had been so wrapped up in their own problems, they had completely neglected him. And turned their backs on him when he had most needed their support.

Her breath hitched in her throat. Last night, all she had been able to think about had been seeing Kit with that half-naked woman. She had not spared one thought for what he had been through, in the seven years since she had lost her memory.

He had suffered a great deal. Whatever that incident in the hut had been about, it did not alter the fact that he had never stopped wanting Cora. Missing her so much that he had even invented a ghost to haunt him. He had been half out of his mind when she had met up with him again. She could not forget the look of anguish in his eyes when he had grabbed her in the Flash of Lightning, and asked why she had run away from him.

She felt quite indignant on his behalf. Surely somebody could have stood by him, no matter what he'd done? But nobody had. Not Robbie. Not his parents…

She pressed her hands to her mouth to stifle a sob. Not her, either. She had been as self-absorbed as his parents. She had been so focused on her own problems last night, she had turned her back on him. Left him all night to wonder if she was going to leave him all over again, which was his greatest fear.

'Oh, Kit!' she moaned.

Being unfaithful was not such a heinous crime that he deserved to suffer complete ostracism for seven years. Especially not when she took into consideration the fact that he had been coerced into proposing to her.

She felt thoroughly ashamed of herself for joining the ranks of people who had let him down.

She went to the window, and looked over towards the woods where her love for him had undergone its greatest trial. If she had not met with that accident, would she have had the courage to have fought for his love? To have marched up to him, and demanded an explanation? To insist he give up that woman if he wanted to marry her…oh, dear, she feared not! She had been so sure by that time that she was unworthy of his hand, that…

She remembered the way he had held her hand, all the while he had been introducing her to his mother. And the defiance in his voice. And his insistence that Lady Matthison hand over the betrothal ring that had been in his family for generations.

Her heart began to beat very fast. She had been quite wrong to let others persuade her he did not love her at all. She only had to consider the wreck he had been when she met him again, and the way he had subsequently treated her, to know he cared for her to some degree. More than his father seemed to have cared for his mother.

If she really loved him, would she not prove it by standing by him, no matter what he did or how he felt? And she did love him. As Cora, she had fallen in love with the sombre, cultured boy who had offered to make her a lady. As Mary, her heart had gone out to the hardened, bitter gambler who had sworn he would always take care of her.

And now…she loved him still. Through all the changes that suffering had wrought on him, he was still her Kit. The only man for her, no matter what he had done or who she was.

She had to find him, and tell him! She whirled round to make her way downstairs, only to almost jump out of her skin to find the butler standing right behind her.

'Excuse me, Miss Montague,' he said. 'You have a visitor. Miss Farrell,' the butler continued, 'walked over as usual this morning to visit Mrs Paulding, and when she heard of your return, asked if she might have the privilege of being the first of your neighbours to welcome you back.'

'Did she, indeed?' Cora supposed she had to admire the woman's sheer nerve. She had temporarily pushed the Frances Farrell issue to the back of her mind, while she had wrestled with the more important question of how she was going to cope with marrying Kit.

'I did say you had been unwell last night, and that his lordship had said you were not to be disturbed this morning.'

Had he? Oh, see! He did care for her! It might not be the all-consuming love she felt for him, but…

'But Mrs Paulding told her you were up and had breakfasted, and Miss Farrell was most insistent that I enquire as to whether you are receiving.'

She had the perfect excuse to avoid dealing with Frances.

But had she not decided to grit her teeth and get on with her new life? No hiding from reality by blotting out painful memories, or fuzzing her perception with alcohol, nor, she stood a little straighter, hiding in her room like the last Lady Matthison. Or using butlers to avoid unpleasant scenes.

'Thank you. That was thoughtful of you, but I shall see her.'

Frances had all but destroyed Cora, by making her believe she was not a fit bride for Kit Brereton.

But since then, she had spent seven years working for a living. She had learned to stand on her own two feet. She had established a position for herself, in that workroom above Madame Pichot's shop.

It struck her that once separated from her domineering male relatives, and with no preconceptions about how she ought to behave, she had been set free to become herself.

She had finally learned who she really was.

And now, armed with the knowledge of Cora's social position, bolstered by Mary's hard-won sense of self-worth, she was more than ready to go downstairs and tell Frances Farrell that she no longer had the power to scare her!

'Miss Farrell is in the morning room,' said the butler. 'Do you wish me to escort you down?'

'No, thank you. I know the way. Tell her I shall be down presently.'

The butler glided away, while Cora turned back to the painting and regarded Kit's mother one last time.

The ring she was wearing in the portrait was unmistakably the one Kit had slipped on to her finger in spite of his mother's protests. The same one she had seen Frances trying on, during the nights she had lain, drenched with fever, imprisoned in the attics at the vicarage.

Suddenly she was glad Kit and Robbie had gone out. This was something she had to deal with for herself. She had not had the courage or the self-confidence to fight for Kit's love last time she had been here. She had ended up cowering under the blankets while Frances flaunted her victory.

But the ring belonged to Lord Matthison's betrothed! She whirled round and marched down the corridor, fists clenched at her sides.

And it was up to her to insist that the thieving witch gave it back!

Chapter Twelve

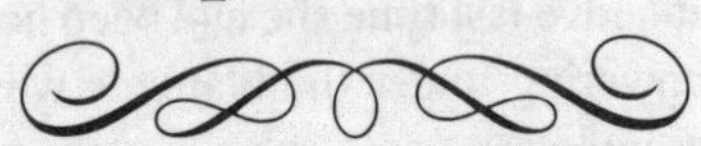

Frances Farrell was sitting on what Cora had once, long ago, thought of as Lady Matthison's sofa. Lady Matthison *had* sometimes come downstairs, when Frances had come to call, and received her there in state. 'Such an obliging girl,' she would say to Mrs Paulding, in Cora's hearing. And then it would be, 'Frances dear, I know you won't mind me asking…so fatiguing for me…' and they would put their heads together and discuss people and places she had never heard of. And then Frances would go off on whatever errand Lady Matthison had given her. Once or twice, on her way out, seeing Cora's crestfallen expression, Frances had paused and patted her hand and promised that one day, perhaps once she had settled in a little better, she could go with her and meet the tenants she was visiting on behalf of the lady of the manor. And Lady Matthison would sniff, and turn on her heel, and float back up the stairs trailing shawls and scarves behind her.

Cora blinked away the slights heaped upon her in the past, and advanced on Frances Farrell with her shoulders squared.

Frances looked up at her and smiled. The open, friendly smile she had once upon a time employed to such devastating effect.

'Would you care for some tea?' she asked pleasantly.

In front of Lady Matthison's sofa was a low table that held cups, saucers, a sugar bowl and a plate of freshly baked biscuits. All the paraphernalia associated with the ritual of receiving morning callers.

Cora halted in her tracks as Frances lifted the teapot.

It all looked so civilised, so normal.

Except that *she* was presiding over the teapot as though *she* were the hostess and Cora was the one who was visiting!

'How dare you stroll in here, and sit on that sofa—' Cora jabbed her forefinger at the floral-patterned upholstery of the bow-legged, claw-footed *chaise longue* on which Lady Matthison had loved to recline '—and offer me tea, as though…as though butter wouldn't melt in your mouth!'

'Oh, dear,' said Frances, putting down the teapot and eyeing Cora with disdain. 'I see your manners have not improved since last we met. A lady who aspires to become mistress of Kingsmede,' she went on witheringly, 'really should know how to receive morning callers.'

At one time Cora had stood in awe of Miss Farrell's vast store of knowledge about the running of Kingsmede, gleaned not only from her kinship with Mrs

Paulding, but also her relationship with Lady Matthison. Frances had always been dropping 'hints' about how the future mistress of Kingsmede ought to behave. And Cora had drunk it all in, assuming Frances was trying to help her. But now she knew that all those hints had been dripped into her ears like so much poison, causing what little self-esteem she'd had to shrivel until she felt she was not even worthy to visit the place, never mind marry the man who would one day inherit it!

'That tone won't work on me any more,' said Cora defiantly. 'Because I know what you are now. I have remembered what you did. You should be in prison, not wandering about freely—' she sucked in a deep breath, her sense of outrage growing by the second '—offering people tea!'

Frances rose gracefully to her feet, her greater height making it all the easier to look down her nose at Cora. 'Perhaps we should take a stroll in the gardens,' she said, going over to the French windows that led out on to the terrace. 'So that the stridency of your voice may not reach the ears of the servants. We would not want them thinking his lordship has brought home a fishwife, now would we?'

With a supercilious smile, Frances unbolted the doors, and went outside. For a moment, Cora stood stock still in the middle of the floor, stunned by the way Frances was treating the place as if it were her own. And, most annoyingly of all, forcing Cora to trot along behind her, like some kind of supplicant if she wished to continue with the conversation.

Which of course she did.

'You mean you don't want to risk anyone overhearing what I have to say to you,' she retorted, plunging through the French doors in pursuit.

Frances had gone down the terrace steps, and was crossing the velvet-smooth lawn towards one of the rose borders.

'I trusted you!' Cora panted, catching up with Frances, who was examining the bushes with a critical eye.

'You made me believe you were my friend. But all the time, you were looking for ways to hurt me!'

'Not at all,' Frances replied mildly. 'I only wanted you to go back where you had come from. I had hoped,' she said with a doleful shake of her head, 'that seeing him with his paramour would have made you realise there was nothing for you here. My purpose was not to hurt you, but to open your eyes. You do remember,' she said with apparent concern, 'seeing him with that woman? You did just say your memory has returned.'

'Of course I remember seeing him with her, but…'

Frances frowned quizzically. 'Then why have you come back? Have you not learned what he is like yet? Or are you still claiming to be infatuated with him, so that you can pretend to be blind to his faults?'

The dart struck home. Was that not exactly what she had just been doing? Deciding to turn a blind eye to his infidelities, because she could not bear to contemplate living without him?

'You…you are twisting everything!' she cried.

'Besides, it is not his faults I came out here to discuss with you…'

'Good. Then we may discuss yours.'

'Mine?' gasped Cora, as Frances frowned, then stooped to snap a withered bloom from its stalk.

'You have no education, no fortune—' she tossed the spent bloom into the hedge at the back of the border with a grimace '—and no connections. You have never been a suitable partner for his lordship. And now—' she shook her head reprovingly '—I cannot think what has made you believe you can push your way back into his life.'

'It is not like that! It was his decision to bring me here. Besides, what right have you to say I am not suitable?'

'I only say what everyone thinks.' Frances turned away abruptly, her skirts releasing a cloud of fragrance into the air as they brushed against one of the low-growing lavender bushes.

'Nobody approved of his choice. Especially not his parents! None of his tenants would ever have accepted you, either. For we all knew how you and that brother of yours trapped him into making a proposal of marriage. Robbie,' she said, smiling maliciously over her shoulder, 'told me all about it.'

So that was where Mrs Paulding had got the story of the fight by the boat-house from. She felt slightly sick. Robbie had confided in Frances about how he had made Kit propose to her. How could he?

She watched Frances progress along the border,

stopping to sniff at a full-blown rose here, snapping off a spent one there… Frances, who had tricked her into believing she was friendly, when all the time she had been looking for ways to get rid of her. She had duped Robbie too. He had thought the world of her. He had spent a great deal of time going over to the vicarage. At one point, she had wondered if the two of them would make a match of it. She shuddered at the thought.

'You used that knowledge to try to get rid of me,' she said, and then, because Frances had nearly reached the end of the rose border, hitched up her skirts and trotted after her. 'What right had you to interfere?'

'Well, somebody had to do something about it. Poor Lady Matthison was prostrate with distress. And Christopher was far too much of a gentleman to tell you to your face that he could not stand the sight of you.'

The shaft went wide. For she knew now that Kit did indeed want her. He could not keep his hands off her! Oh, he might not feel the romantic love she had dreamed about inspiring when she had been a girl. But he certainly desired her, in a very basic way. Why, he enjoyed taking her to bed so much that he had stopped the carriage on the way here, and spent an entire afternoon naked in her arms, when he could just as easily have pressed on and arrived at Kingsmede in time for supper.

'Frances…' Cora stepped up to her and looked her straight in the eye. 'You and I both know that is a lie. Christopher wants to marry me.' For whatever reason. 'He told me he organised search parties—'

'Only to satisfy your brother!'

'No, Frances, that is not true. You have to stop this right now! He wanted to find me. You know he did.' It seemed so obvious now, she did not know why she had not seen it before. 'That was why you deliberately kept me hidden away up in the vicarage attic!'

'I was tending your injuries,' Frances argued, her eyes darting away. 'You were too ill to move.'

'You moved me from your hallway when I collapsed on your doorstep!' Cora scoffed. 'It would have been far less trouble to carry me into your parlour, and send word to Kingsmede that you had found me, than it was to heave me up all those stairs! And if you were really concerned about how ill I was, why did you never send for a doctor? No, you cannot use that excuse on me. Even back then, though I had a high fever, and had no idea who I was, or how I came to be there, I was fully aware that you hated me. You hated me so much, you sent me to Oakham Hall. You knew you were handing me over to a…a rapist, didn't you!'

Frances looked a little contrite. 'Yes, I did regret the necessity of taking that step. But by that time, it had become clear to me that little, short of death, would halt your ambitions. When the horse threw you, and I saw you lying there all covered with leaves, your head and limbs at such peculiar angles—' she tilted her head to one side, a reminiscent smile playing about her lips '—like a little broken doll.' Her eyes snapped back to Cora. 'I thought, for a few, blissful hours, that it had all been taken out of my hands. That death had provided the ultimate answer to the problems you posed. Even if the fall had not quite killed you, I was sure that lying on the ground in all that rain would have finished you off. Instead, you crawled to my door. It was quite a shock to see you standing there wringing wet, and with blood running down your face, asking me for help. You are like—' her face spasmed with disgust '—a pernicious weed, that will keep springing back up. You had to be rooted out for good!'

'You saw me fall? And did nothing to help?' No, it was worse than that. She screwed up her face as she tried to remember the actual words Frances had used when telling her about Kit's tryst in the woodcutter's hut. It was all terribly hazy…but unless Frances had put the idea in her head, she could not see why she would have gone to the stables and saddled a horse that was far too spirited for a novice to ride, when she could as easily have walked to the hut, as Kit had done.

'Frances!' she gasped. 'You tried to kill me!'

'Don't be silly,' Frances retorted. 'I merely concealed your whereabouts while considering what to do with you.'

Cora blinked in temporary confusion, until she realised that Frances was thinking about her stay in the vicarage, rather than the 'accident' in the forest.

'Your head injury had left you confused, which gave me a little time to come up with a solution to the problem you posed. For a few days, you became so ill that I began to hope you might just die and put us all out of our misery. But no…' She sighed. 'You began to recover. I feared it might only be a matter of time before you remembered who you were, and would start demanding you return to Kingsmede. So I went to visit the housekeeper at Oakham Hall. She was always in need of staff. The turnover there was very high.'

'And you told her I was an orphan, dependant on the parish…'

'In need of light work because you had been ill,' Frances nodded. 'A brilliant plan, I thought.'

'You deliberately put me in the way of Lord Sandiford, expecting him to…?'

Frances nodded sombrely. 'I dare say it must have been terribly unpleasant for you. But you had to learn your lesson. Your sin was overweening ambition. You wanted a lord. Well,' she tittered, 'I gave you to a lord who would humble you! So the punishment fit the crime. It was a very neat solution. A man of Christopher's standing would never marry a woman who had been sullied. Particularly not by a man of Lord Sandiford's reputation. So that even when your memory returned, and you found your way back to Kingsmede, I knew you would no longer pose a threat.'

'I cannot believe you are admitting to all this so calmly.' Cora felt as though she was in a waking nightmare. 'To talk of wishing me dead, of conniving at my utter ruin…are you not ashamed? Your father is a vicar, for heaven's sake!'

'Why should I be ashamed? I only did what was best for everyone concerned.'

'You are unbelievable! No decent person would have acted as you did…'

'You are such a simpleton,' Frances sneered as she unlatched the gate that led through to the orchard. 'History is full of good Christian folk girding up their loins, and acting decisively to save those around them from a greater evil. Just think of all those men of the cloth who condemned heretics to burn at the stake,' she said triumphantly, striding into the trees, her skirts flattening a trail through the long grass. 'It cannot have been easy to send a woman to die such a horrible death. And yet they did it. Because they knew it was the right thing to do, to purge the church from a greater evil.'

'I am not evil!' Cora gasped as she followed in Frances's wake. 'And nobody thinks it right to burn people at the stake any more. Frances, you have taken leave of your senses!'

Frances stopped so suddenly Cora almost ran into the back of her.

'No! I am the only one who sees things clearly. You are not fit to be Lord Matthison's wife! Not then, and especially not now! Not after spending seven years hiding away in shame, earning your living as a dressmaker and no doubt keeping low company.' She bent down, and hissed into Cora's face, 'Did you bear Lord Sandiford a child, Miss Montague? I have often wondered if he managed to make you pregnant before you escaped, like so many of the other girls who took employment at Oakham Hall. I could get no news of you once you had left. But then, of course, they are well used to covering up Lord Sandiford's peccadilloes.'

Cora reeled back. 'No! He did not manage to rape me.' She lifted her chin proudly. 'I fought him off.'

Frances raised a disbelieving eyebrow.

'Ah, so *that* is the tale you have told Christopher. That is how you persuaded him to take you back.' She shook her head and clucked her tongue in reproof. 'You really are shameless in your determination to ensnare him, are you not? And he, being the gentleman he is, will not question the word of his dearest friend's sister.' Her pale eyes turned flint hard. 'But I am warning you now, nobody else will believe you, once they hear you worked at Oakham Hall. Nobody will receive you. You will be a social pariah!'

'And you will make sure they know, won't you, Frances?' Cora retorted, the past becoming clearer as Frances spelled out what her future would be like. When she had first arrived at Kingsmede, as a shy young girl, the staff had been somewhat surprised that master Christopher had brought back a fiancée. Surprised, and warily watchful, but not hostile. That attitude had only developed gradually. As Frances, she now saw, had worked behind the scenes to paint a picture of her as a greedy, scheming seductress.

'Well,' said Frances with a calculating look. 'It all depends on you. I take no delight in spreading gossip, you know,' she said piously. 'I would much rather not have to speak about such a sordid incident. If you were to just break off this ridiculous engagement, and go back to where you came from, there would be no need for any more unpleasantness. And, my dear—' she placed her hand on Cora's forearm, and looked intently into her eyes '—if you have any real affection for him, you must surely see that the best thing you can do for him is to release him from the intolerable burden of this unequal alliance. Sometimes it is necessary to sacrifice our personal happiness, for the good of those we love.'

Cora swayed. If Frances had come to her last time she had been here, and delivered that little speech, with such sincerity that she had managed to bring tears to her eyes, Cora might have done exactly as she suggested. Frances might have won!

But she had not. No, Frances had sent her out on a horse she could scarcely ride, hoping to break her heart, if not her bones. And then locked her away, denying her the medical treatment she had so badly needed. She had lain in that attic, shaking with fear and fever while Frances sat at the foot of her bed, turning her hand this way and that so that the ruby ring she wore on her finger gleamed and pulsed in the candlelight. With a gloating expression on her face.

Angrily, Cora flung Frances's hand from her arm.

'You want him for yourself, don't you!' She did not know why she had not seen it before. But every time Frances mentioned Christopher's name, her eyes shone. Her whole face softened. 'That is why you have worked so hard to get rid of me. All that talk about working for the greater good is so much sanctimonious claptrap!'

Frances's mouth thinned with disapproval. She took a breath to refute Cora's accusations, but this time Cora was not prepared to listen.

'Don't bother to come up with any more of your clever little stories to try to hoax me! You took his ring from my finger, and you wore it. I saw the expression on your face as you sat there, night after night, hoping I would die.'

Cora's legs were shaking. She had never had the courage to stand up to anyone before, and she was not sure where she was getting the strength to do it now. It was just unthinkable to leave without saying what she had specifically come here to say.

'Frances, you must return the ring you stole. If you do not, I will have to tell Lord Matthison that you have it.'

'I did not steal it!' Frances looked outraged. 'I was keeping it safe. I have kept it safe for years. Lady Matthison asked me to hide it when her husband would have sold it off to pay his gaming debts.'

'And then she asked you to bring it back, so that Kit could give it to me,' Cora deduced.

'She did not want you to have it!' Frances spat. 'She wept when she told me how Christopher was throwing it away on an unworthy woman.'

'But it is Christopher's right to throw it away, if that is what he wants to do. It is not for you to decide who should wear it.'

'It will not be you!' Frances hissed, total hatred blazing from her eyes.

'Nor you!' Cora retorted without thinking.

'Why should it not be me?' Frances seized her upper arms and shook her. 'You hooked him, and you are only a parson's daughter!' She flung Cora from her with such force she stumbled, and would have fallen if the lower branch of a pear tree had not struck her in the small of her back. She clutched wildly at the trunk of the tree, steadying herself while Frances continued to rant.

'He has known me all his life. I was his friend before he even met Robbie! Lady Matthison looked on me as a daughter. I know his land, his people, in a way you never could, and never will. You have no idea what it means to be mistress of Kingsmede!'

The wild desperation in her eyes tugged a strand of sympathy from Cora. For some time she had known there was something not quite right about Frances. Now she saw that the woman had been so hopelessly entangled in the coils of unrequited love for such a long time that it had affected her ability to reason.

'Have I not been waiting patiently for him all this time? Helping him refurbish Kingsmede?' Frances gesticulated towards the house. 'Showing him what a comfort I could be,' she finished, tears welling in her pale eyes, 'when he was sad?'

What was sad, was that Frances had convinced herself that what she was saying was true. But it wasn't. Oh, she might have had a hand in redecorating the house. But Lord Matthison had never once mentioned Frances, not in any context, let alone as a friend who brought him comfort. When he described the years she had been missing, he had spoken of loneliness, pointlessness and hellish darkness.

Frances half-turned away, fumbling with the strings

of her reticule. After the amount of tears Cora had shed over the past few days, she had provided herself with several clean handkerchiefs when she had dressed that morning. Feeling heartily sorry for Frances's heartache, she pulled one from her sleeve, and went to offer it to her.

But Frances had already found what she had been searching for in her reticule. And it was not a handkerchief.

It was a little knife.

For a few seconds Cora stood there, holding out her handkerchief, while the dappled sunlight glinted on the lethal-looking little blade as the wind ruffled the overhanging branches.

And then Frances came at her.

Cora instinctively flung up her arm to protect her face as Frances slashed out viciously. She felt a sharp sting, and then a spreading warmth as blood streamed from a wound that had been intended to disfigure her.

'Frances!' Cora gasped in appalled disbelief. There remained no trace of the genteel, pious façade that Frances employed to deceive people as to her true nature. She was no longer bothering to conceal the murderous hatred that had simmered inside her for years. Her eyes burned with a kind of devilish excitement as she swung the lethal little blade in a wide arc, almost as though she was taunting Cora.

Cora took a hasty step back, her heart pounding so hard it felt as though it was trying to punch its way out of her chest.

Frances took a step forwards, keeping the distance

between them equal. 'If I can get rid of you,' she said, with a chilling smile, 'he will turn to me!'

Cora's heart sank. They were too far from the house for anyone to hear if she cried out for help. And she would not get far if she tried to make a run for it. She had barely been able to keep up with Frances when she broke into a brisk walk!

But she had, once, seen the landlord of a tavern disarm a customer who had come at him with a knife. He had done it by seizing his attacker's arm as he lunged, deflecting the knife's trajectory. He'd then slammed his fist into the other man's face, and the pair had gone down in a welter of mud and blood and beer. She didn't know how effective punching Frances might be. In any case, she rather thought, given the woman's superior height and strength, she would need to use both hands to simply block any blow Frances might strike.

But she had to at least try to disarm her.

No sooner had the vague plan for self-defence begun to form in Cora's mind, than Frances stopped toying with her, and came at her with a wild cry.

The first part of Cora's plan went surprisingly well. She managed to grab her knife hand and deflect the blade away from her face. The impetus of Frances's attack carried Cora backwards, and they both fell to the ground, with Frances on top, the weight of her body slamming the breath from Cora's lungs. And the knife went flying.

But Cora only experienced a fleeting moment of

relief, because Frances promptly fastened both her hands about Cora's neck, and began to squeeze.

Cora scrabbled at Frances's fingers, trying to prise them from her neck. She was already winded from the fall, and she feared that if she couldn't take a breath soon, it would be all up with her. But she could not break her stranglehold.

Desperately, she tried to pitch her attacker off, but Frances was bigger than her, stronger than her, and was pressing all her weight down on Cora's windpipe. Cora's strength was fading swiftly. In one last effort to save herself, she reached up, trying to claw at her attacker's face. Frances reared back, laughing in open mockery. Her arms were longer than Cora's. She was having no difficulty in squeezing the life from her victim, while Cora could not even mark her face.

Blackness was creeping in round the periphery of her vision. Stars began exploding in front of her eyes. Dimly, from beyond the sound of a murderess's demonic laughter, she thought she could perceive Kit's voice, calling her name.

And then suddenly, just when it seemed all hope was lost, someone loomed up behind Frances, and another pair of hands was trying to break her grip. Frances fought to keep up the pressure on her throat to the last, her nails clawing at Cora's neck even as she was dragged bodily away.

And then Kit's face swam into view.

And she could definitely hear him calling her name, above the noise Frances was making as she was dragged away, kicking and screaming the kind of curses no vicar's daughter should have known.

She felt Kit haul her into his arms, urging her to breathe. But it still felt as though Frances had her by the throat. No matter how desperately she tried, she could not seem to draw any air past the constriction she could still feel there.

The darkness was creeping between them now. But as his voice began to fade, she felt a wave of immense gratitude that she had lasted long enough to die in his arms. The last sound she would hear on this earth would not be the demonic laughter of a woman who hated her, but his voice, so beloved, begging her not to leave him.

Chapter Thirteen

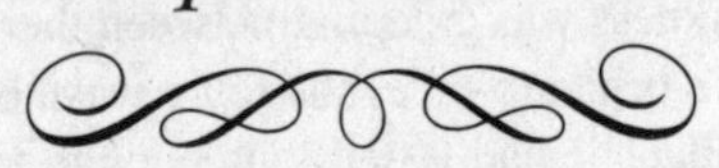

'Cora, don't be dead. Oh, dear God, please don't let her die!'

It was too dark, down in the void where she drifted, to see anything, but she could hear his voice, calling to her.

'Come back to me, Cora. I swear I won't force you to marry me if you can't bear the thought of it, only don't die. I couldn't stand it!'

'Kit…' He sounded so upset, she wanted to comfort him, but nothing emerged from her throat but an agonised croak. Oh, it hurt to try to speak. In fact, it hurt to breathe. She wished she did not have to bother. It would be so much easier to sink back down into the velvety soft darkness…

'Oh, thank God! Thank God!' she heard him say. 'She tried to speak. She's waking up! Come back to me, Cora, and I will give you anything you ask. Only don't leave me alone!'

No, she did not want to leave him alone. And so she breathed. And reached out for him.

And a room materialised around her.

The morning room. And she…she bit back a groan…in spite of determining she would never do so again, she had wound up lying on Lady Matthison's sofa!

'You will give me anything?' she rasped. 'Truly?'

He was kneeling on the floor beside her, his eyes glistening with what she suspected were unshed tears.

'You heard that?' His face went white. But then a look of resolution came over him. 'Whatever you ask of me, I will give it. Just tell me what you want!'

'I want you to burn this sofa,' she whispered, discovering that whispering caused her less pain that proper speech.

His eyes widened in surprise, but making a swift recovery, he said, 'If that is what you want…'

'And a drink…' Her hand fluttered to her throat, which felt bruised inside and out. Though there was not an inch of her that did not hurt to some extent. Her back, her legs, and especially her arms. Her right arm also felt strangely stiff and awkward. Raising it slightly, she saw that someone had torn the sleeve off her dress, and applied a bandage to her forearm where Frances had cut her.

'Do not try to talk any more,' he said, darting away and coming back with a tumbler of what looked and smelled like brandy. He slipped one arm under her shoulders, and raised her head while he held the glass to her lips.

'I know you don't like spirits,' he said, as she opened

her mouth to voice a protest, 'but this is one of those times when nothing else will do.'

Ruthlessly he tipped the liquid into her mouth. She spluttered a little as it burnt its way down, but presently she welcomed the reviving warmth it sent flowing through her veins.

She welcomed the feel of his arm round her shoulders, too. And the depth of concern she read in his eyes, and the persistent way he had kept on calling to her. He had not let her go.

She breathed in deeply through her nose, savouring the spicy scent of his soap, and his clean linen, and his warm skin. She tilted her head so that she could rest it on his shoulder, and sighed out her gratitude. She was alive. And for quite some time it was enough just to lie there, feeling him close as she breathed in and out.

But eventually she knew she would have to find out what had happened.

'Where is Frances?'

Lord Matthison's shoulder tensed under her cheek. 'Locked up,' he said grimly. 'She has gone completely mad! Even after Robbie dragged her off you, she kept trying to break free and get at you. In the end, I had to pick you up and run with you to the house, or I don't know what she might have done.' His arm tightened protectively round her shoulder. 'It took both footmen and the butler to subdue her. She did not calm down completely until the doctor who came to tend your injuries, gave her a sleeping draught. And even asleep…'

'Not in the dark!' she gasped. It was horrible to hear

of another woman suffering the same indignities that had been heaped on her. But then she recalled Frances's pious tone as she had declared that the punishment should fit the crime…

No! No, she did not want *anyone* to go through what she had done.

'Don't lock her up in the dark, alone. Frances is sick,' she whispered. 'She needs care, not punishment.'

Lord Matthison nodded gravely. 'Her aunt is with her for now. They are up in one of the guest rooms, which has a good stout lock on the door. But I will find a place where she can get the help she needs. Where they will treat her kindly.'

She relaxed immediately. But then she felt him shake his head. 'I am so sorry I left you unprotected. I brought you back to Kingsmede, promising to protect you from your enemies. Instead I exposed you to the most dangerous of them all.'

'You did not know what she was like,' Cora murmured.

'Not when I brought you here,' he said earnestly. 'But after last night…' He shifted his position, looking so guilty that she reached out and took his hand. He grasped it, as though she had flung him a lifeline.

'Robbie and I sat up for hours last night, going over it all, and gradually piecing together what happened to you. It was Robbie who worked out that the woman who kept you up in her attic was Miss Farrell. I did not recognise her from the description you gave, in fact I argued that it could not have been her. But he was adamant we at least check out his theory. Because he had seen that other side of Miss Farrell, during that last summer when he had begun courting her in earnest. He discovered she had eyes for nobody but me.' He cleared his throat self-consciously. 'He never told me about her infatuation. He did not have the time. It was shortly before you disappeared, and then everything fell apart between us…' He pressed a kiss to the hand he had been crushing between his fingers.

'Last night he told me that your description of a hard-faced, hard-eyed woman tallied exactly with the opinion he had formed of Miss Farrell just before he returned to Scotland. Her behaviour towards him was…unforgivable,' he grated. 'She offered him no sympathy, no condolences on his loss. Just told him it was all for the best. The best!'

Lord Matthison ground his teeth. She felt his jaw working against her forehead. She looped her injured arm about his waist, and hugged him.

He snatched in a ragged breath. Then another. Then, with a strangled moan, he flung both arms round her, and hung on to her tightly.

It seemed to take him an effort to continue talking, but eventually he went on, 'This morning, we went over to the vicarage, and once we saw her leaving, we… This will sound reprehensible, Cora, but we broke in. Well, not exactly broke in. The back door was open. Sneaked in, is what we did. And ransacked the attics. And we found it.'

He drew the arm that had been round her waist away, and dipped into his pocket. When he withdrew it, he was holding the ring.

The ruby ring.

'It was concealed in a secret drawer of an old bureau, under a mound of moth-eaten curtains, just as you described it.' He turned it slightly, so that it caught the light, making it gleam and throb as though it had a pulse of its own.

Cora stared at it in sick fascination as he continued, 'When we got back to the house, and heard that Frances had come to visit you, we came straight in here to confront her with what we had found. But by then, you were entering the orchard. I could not understand why you had gone so far from the house, but Robbie, bless him, knew at once she was up to no good. He ran out after you. And caught up with you just in time. I was only a second or two behind him. But it was as well he got to you first.' He tilted up her chin, and ran the backs of his fingers gently over the scratches she could feel scoring the skin of her throat. 'That woman has the strength of ten men. I never want to have to see a sight like that, ever again.' And he lowered his head, and touched his lips gently to the livid wounds.

The sensation sent a shiver of longing through her. She felt his lips curve briefly into a smile against her neck.

'Does that response mean what I hope it means?' he said, reaching down for her hand, and positioned the blood-red ring over her third finger.

'No!' Cora snatched her hand away.

'Don't…don't you want to marry me?' His voice was as hoarse as her own when he went on, 'Can you at least explain why? I deserve to know that much, don't I?' He withdrew his arms and sat back on his heels so that he could see her face. His own eyes were bleak, his mouth a taut line bracketed by two deep grooves.

'I have always wanted to marry you,' she whispered, determined he should not suffer even one more second of pain on her account. If only Robbie had not seen them kissing!

'And even though I learned that it was not your choice to begin with, if you really, truly want to marry me now…'

'Not my choice?' He reared back. 'What are you talking about?'

'I know that Robbie forced you to propose to me. After he saw us kissing in the boat…'

'He did no such thing!'

'You don't need to try to cover it up, Kit,' she said wearily. 'I don't care about that any more.'

'Just you listen to me, dammit!' he growled. 'It is true Robbie confronted me about us kissing out on the loch. He accused me of toying with you, the minute his back was turned. Said I had betrayed his trust, and I would never be welcome in any home of his again. How he could have thought…' He laughed bitterly. 'Well, his opinion of me was so poor that not long after he accused me of murdering you!'

His face took on what she thought of as his devilish mask.

'He would have thrown me out of his house right then, only I refused to go. Not until I had the chance to at least find out if you were willing to have me. That was when he went berserk. And said he would never consent to a penniless degenerate like me marrying his little sister. I had to fight him for the right to let you make up your own mind, Cora.'

'You fought him for the right…' Her mind was in a whirl. 'Does that mean…?' but she lacked the courage to ask what she really wanted to know. She turned her head away, shutting her eyes against the foolish hope she could not bear to have snatched from her.

'What else could it have meant? I was in love with you. Desperately in love.'

Her eyes flew open. She stared at him in wonder, still hardly daring to believe she had heard him correctly.

'I think I had been in love with you for years. It was not only Robbie I came to Auchentay to see. I looked forward to seeing the changes in you, as you grew from an enchanting girl, into a lovely young woman.'

'But you never said…'

'Your father guarded you too closely for me to get anywhere near you. And you were so shy.' He stroked the curve of her cheek with the back of his forefinger. 'I feared that if I went blundering in, telling you…' He thrust his fingers through his hair, his cheeks flushing a dull red. 'Well, what would I have spoken to you of, at that age? A boy's thoughts are of touching, and kissing, not love and marriage! And you were so prim and proper…

'Only the way you looked at me sometimes kept my hopes alive. And the little things you did for me.' He knelt up, and took her hands between his own. 'I will never forget opening my trunk when I got back to school, and finding you had tucked a couple of new shirts in amongst my ragged collection of clothing. And recalling how many nights, during my visit, you had sat sewing, with a little smile playing about your lips.' He bowed his head and kissed her fingers one by one.

'I put my heart into every stitch,' she admitted, raising her free hand to stroke his hair.

'When your parents died,' he went on, 'and Robbie was making all those plans for your future…there was some aunt or other he said he was going to send you to…well—' he looked up at her as though pleading for understanding '—I knew very well that you were far too young to be thinking of marriage, but I could not bear the thought I might never see you again. I felt as though it was my last chance. I know it was wrong, the way I went about binding you to me, but I did at least ask your permission before I kissed you,' he pointed out. 'I know things got out of control pretty quickly…hell, I'm not surprised Robbie was furious with me. I threw you down in the bottom of that boat and practically ravished you!'

Cora blinked at him, wondering how two people could have such divergent memories of the same event.

'And then, when you kept raising objections to my proposal… I…kissed you into submission. That afternoon, in the boat…you came alive in my arms. You had been repressed for so long, that when I began to rouse you, it was like letting the genie out of the bottle. We both discovered what a sensual person you are. And I shamelessly used that discovery against you. Because you are highly moral, too. I did not believe you could accept feeling that degree of passion, without linking it to a deep emotional commitment. So I stoked up the passion until you fancied yourself in love with me. Don't deny it,' he said, when she would have interrupted. 'Subsequent events have shown me that it was never more than lust that I could rouse in you. But, oh, how I longed to believe you meant all those things you said to me…'

'I did mean them,' she husked. 'I do! I love you so much.'

His answering smile was sardonic. 'But you won't marry me.' He glanced at the ruby ring he still held in his hand, and the determined way she was keeping her left hand well out of its reach.

'Do you love me, Kit?' she asked him earnestly. 'Do you really want to marry me?'

'I do not know how you can even ask me that,' he replied bleakly.

'Because I saw you with that other woman!'

He looked completely baffled.

'Other woman?'

'In the hut. In the forest. That last day!'

He shook his head slowly. 'There was no other woman. There has never been another woman for me, Cora.'

She felt his denial like a blow. 'Why bother to lie about it now?' she hissed angrily. 'I saw you with my own eyes. She had hardly any clothes on. And you kissed her!'

'In a hut…' he echoed, mystified. And then his expression cleared. 'Maggie.' He shut his eyes, and bowed his head. When he opened them, they were flat, and dead looking. 'I had forgotten all about that, in the light of everything else that happened that day…' He leaped to his feet. 'You seem determined not to believe a word I say!' He stalked across to the window, where he stood with his back to her.

Cora struggled to sit up, every muscle in her body protesting. 'Kit,' she croaked. Then, forcing as much volume from her battered vocal cords as she could, 'Kit, please! I need to know why you lied to me. You told me you were going to Bamford, when really you were going to meet that woman. What was I supposed to think?'

'Oh, obviously—' he spun round and looked at her bitterly '—that I was being unfaithful.'

She sank back, exhausted. But with her eyes fixed on his silhouette, outlined against the bright sunshine that poured into the room, she grated, 'Kit, you had never once told me you loved me. I thought Robbie had forced you to propose to me. And then Frances told me you loved that other woman. It was…awful…' She covered her face in her hands as the tears began to flow.

But then she felt the cushions dip as he sat next to her.

'Frances again, damn her!' he grated, and pulled her into his arms. 'She was lying, Cora. About everything.

She knew I was never in love with Maggie. Maggie was just…one of the reasons Robbie thought I was not fit to go near you. And you saw her, for goodness' sake. You must have seen she was a good bit older than me.'

'I was not looking at her face,' she mumbled into his neckcloth.

'Ah, yes, the enthusiasm of her greeting took me by surprise, I must confess. But did you not see that a kiss was all that passed between us?'

Cora shook her head. 'The kiss was all it took to make me lose my breakfast.'

His arms tightened convulsively about her. 'And then you galloped off in that storm, and Bobby threw you. My God, I can see it all now. You were too upset to think straight.'

'It felt as though my heart was breaking,' she admitted.

'You did not mean to run away for ever,' he said, a tremor of hope in his voice. 'You galloped away from that hut, all upset because you thought I had played you false,' he mused, as though to himself. 'You were never all that good a rider. Because of the storm, and your state, you lost control of Bobby, and fell. When you came to, you did not know who you were, did you? It had all been wiped away. What did you do, make your way to the nearest house?'

'I saw a light,' she whispered.

'The vicarage. Frances opened the door…the vicar was here most of that night, trying to bring us consolation…but I have never felt any, until now. Cora, you don't know what it means to finally know you did not mean to leave me.' He hugged her tight. 'You didn't, did you?'

She shook her head. 'I think I would have come back here eventually, when I had calmed down, and told you I could not bear to share you with another woman, and begged you to give her up.'

'I *was* giving her up,' he broke in. 'That was why I sent for her! Maggie could not read or write. So I had to meet her, one last time, to tell her I was getting married. I did not want her to hear it from anyone else, and think I did not care about her feelings. She did not deserve that. Besides, I needed to make sure there were no...obligations I needed to meet.'

'She was—' Cora sniffed '—just your mistress?'

'Not even that. She was a very generous woman, willing to share her favours with a growing lad. I am sorry you had to find out about my baser instincts the way you did. Would it do any good to explain that it meant nothing? That all young men experiment to some degree...'

'You met her to end it,' she sighed. And then she re-examined the scene that had all but destroyed her, because Frances had primed her to see Kit meeting the woman he loved. All she had actually seen was Kit, entering a tumbledown hut, and a woman, who had been in the act of stripping off her blouse, flinging herself into his arms. He had smiled, she had seen that much. But she had not stayed to see any more.

She had not trusted him. She had told him she loved him, but she had believed the very worst of him. Guilty tears sprang to her eyes. But she had been so insecure! She had never had much self-confidence, and what little she had, Frances had whittled away with her cutting little remarks.

'I'm so sorry,' she wept. 'All these wasted years…'

'It was not your fault. It was Frances Farrell at the back of it all, driving us apart! When I think of what she put you through…hiding you away when you were ill, then sending you off to Oakham Hall—' his face grew thunderous '—I could wring her blasted neck!'

Inadvertently, Cora's hand flew to her own throat. He looked stricken.

'I should not have said that! I'm sorry! So sorry. Hell, Cora, I cannot seem to do or say anything right with you! No wonder you don't want to marry me. Darling—' he grasped her hands in his, his expression pleading '—I am not a violent man. I have never struck a woman in anger. I am not like your father.'

When he saw her frown, he reminded her, 'You told me that your father beat your mother to death. I can understand why you find it hard to trust men, but I am nothing like him! I might speak intemperately, but—'

She reached up and laid her hands to his mouth, stopping the torrent of words. 'I have always known you are a far better person than him. But even he was not as bad as I imagined. He did not kill my mother. Not exactly.' She sighed. 'That scene I recalled, when I thought I was Mary, was the very last time he hit her. The time he went too far. Until then, whenever he lost his temper, she tried to pretend it had not happened. She would wear clothes that concealed her bruises. She was always determined to uphold his reputation in public. But that last time seemed to break her spirit. She went in on herself, and ceased carrying out her parish duties no matter how much he ranted and roared at her. And then, come winter, she took a cold, and it went to her lungs. She just gave up on life. And he knew it was his fault.' Her face went hard. 'But in his guilt, as in all else, he was out of control. Those last few months…' She shivered, and hung her head. 'When he died, all I felt was relief.'

'No wonder you were so afraid of men, while you were Mary. All you had ever known was violence… and—' his voice hitched '—betrayal. But couldn't you learn to love me again? Or at least—'

'I do love you,' she interjected. 'With all my heart.'

'Then…' He proffered the ring again.

'Kit,' she said with a frown, 'you will think I'm being really silly, but I don't want you to put that ring on my finger again.'

'Why not? If you love me? You were willing to be my mistress…when you thought you were Mary.' He speared his fingers through his hair again. 'Now you know who you are. It all started to go wrong when your memory came back.' His face darkened. 'I wish to God I had never brought you back here!'

'Kit, please just listen to me! I do want to marry you. So much. Last night I realised I would marry you even if you took a dozen mistresses. I cannot bear the thought of living without you!'

'Cora,' he grated, 'you don't know how I have longed to hear you say that.' He crushed her to him, kissing her in almost frenzied desperation. 'I have missed you so much,' he said, pulling back, and smoothing away the hair that had tumbled over her face.

'You are the only person who has ever really cared much for me. Me, not the position I could provide, or my wealth, or, latterly, my notoriety.' His dark eyes blazed with fervour. 'You loved me enough to follow me from your home land to this miserable barn of a place…it almost broke your heart when you saw me kissing another woman. Even when you forgot who *you* were, you fell in love with me all over again. You gifted me your virginity. Trusted me to take care of you when everyone else said I was some kind of demonic—' his face twisted '—murdering…'

She shook her head, and stroked his tortured face with her injured hand. 'Don't think about that any more. It is over now. We are together again.'

'What as?' he bit out. 'If you cannot bear to marry a man whose reputation is as tarnished as mine has become, if you wish to remain as my mistress…'

She shook her head again. 'I would be honoured to be your wife. But not…' She looked at the ring, glowing in his outstretched hand. 'Not with that ring. Is there…have you ever heard there was a curse on it?'

'A curse?' He looked at the ring, mystified.

Cora felt her cheeks grow warm, but she had to tell

him what was bothering her, even if he did think she was being overly fanciful.

'It seems to bring nothing but misery to those who covet it. Your father was a rotten husband to your mother. You would not have thought she would have any sentimental feelings about the ring that betrothed her to him, and yet she hung on to it, when he had sold everything else of value. She gave it to Frances to hide. Frances kept putting it on, and dreaming of becoming Lady Matthison and went completely mad…and I wore it for only seven days, and we both went through seven years of utter misery. I suppose it could all be coincidence, but…'

With a shrug, he tucked the ring into his pocket. 'The ring is of no consequence. If you do not like it, I shall buy you another. An emerald—' he smiled '—to match your eyes.'

The shadows Cora had sensed hovering in the corners dissipated. Sunlight flooded the room.

'Now,' he said, determination jutting his jaw, 'Miss Cora Montague, love of my life, will you please marry me? Now that I have dealt with the obstacles thrown up by—' he raised one hand, and began to count off on his fingers '—Robbie, and Frances, and Maggie, and Miss Winters, and Madame Pichot, and Lord Sandiford. And now that I have promised to burn the sofa, and buy you a ring that no other woman who wanted to be Lady Matthison has ever worn…' He paused, the light of challenge in his eyes. 'Come on, Cora, I know you want to. You promised me for ever.'

'I did.' She smiled, flinging her arms round his neck. 'I do.'

'Then nothing,' he growled, 'and nobody shall ever part us again.'

* * * * *

1109/04a

On sale 4th December 2009

Regency

COMPROMISED MISS

by Anne O'Brien

Despite being unconscious at the time, Lucius Hallaston of Venmore has been accused of compromising a lady! The Earl is lethally attractive, and Harriette Lydard's reputation is in tatters – now she must agree to a marriage with this disreputable, dangerous devil of a man!

Regency

THE WAYWARD GOVERNESS

by Joanna Fulford

Claire Davenport flees to Yorkshire, where enigmatic Marcus, Viscount Destermere employs her as a governess. Revenge has all but consumed Marcus until Claire enters his life. She is irresistible – but forbidden fruit. When their secrets threaten them both, Marcus realises he cannot let happiness slip through his fingers again…

Available at WHSmith, Tesco, ASDA, Eason and all good bookshops

www.millsandboon.co.uk

On sale 4th December 2009

Regency

THE EARL'S DILEMMA

by Emily May

James Hargrave, Earl of Arden, needs a marriage of convenience, and plain Kate Honeycourt has been on the shelf for years – so why does she turn him down? Yet the more he sees of Kate, the more attractive she appears. Perhaps love isn't as impossible as he'd once thought…

RUNAWAY LADY, CONQUERING LORD

by Carol Townend

Lady Emma of Fulford is a fallen woman desperate to escape the brutish father of her son. She begs honourable Sir Richard of Asculf for help – but Sir Richard is only human, and Lady Emma tempts him. Can the conquering knight be the one to tame this runaway lady for good?

THE MAGIC OF CHRISTMAS

by Carolyn Davidson/Victoria Bylin/Cheryl St John

Three festive stories with all the seasonal warmth of the West – guaranteed to keep you snug from the cold this Yuletide!

Available at WHSmith, Tesco, ASDA, Eason and all good bookshops

www.millsandboon.co.uk

2 FREE BOOKS
AND A SURPRISE GIFT

We would like to take this opportunity to thank you for reading this Mills & Boon® book by offering you the chance to take TWO more specially selected books from the Historical series absolutely FREE We're also making this offer to introduce you to the benefits of the Mills & Boon® Book Club™—

- **FREE home delivery**
- **FREE gifts and competitions**
- **FREE monthly Newsletter**
- **Exclusive Mills & Boon Book Club offers**
- **Books available before they're in the shops**

Accepting these FREE books and gift places you under no obligation to buy, you may cancel at any time, even after receiving your free books. Simply complete your details below and return the entire page to the address below. You don't even need a stamp!

YES Please send me 2 free Historical books and a surprise gift. understand that unless you hear from me, I will receive 4 superb new books every month for just £3.79 each, postage and packing free. am under no obligation to purchase any books and may cancel my subscription at any time. The free books and gift will be mine to keep in any case.

Ms/Mrs/Miss/Mr______________ Initials ____________

Surname ______________________________

Address ______________________________

____________________________ Postcode __________

Send this whole page to: Mills & Boon Book Club, Free Book Offer FREEPOST NAT 10298, Richmond, TW9 1BR

Offer valid in UK only and is not available to current Mills & Boon Book Club subscribers to this series. Overseas and Eire please write for details.. We reserve the right to refuse an application and applicants must be aged 18 years or over. Only one application per household. Terms and prices subject to change without notice. Offer expires 31st January 2010. As a result of this application, you may receive offers from Harlequin Mills & Boon and other carefully selected companies. If you would prefer not to share in this opportunity please write to The Data Manager, PO Box 676, Richmond, TW9 1WU.